Kesira Minette Offered Up the Small Baby to Its Cowering Mother.

"It is your baby, no matter who the father is," Kesira said. "You must tend him." The baby looked well enough nourished, but the pale eyes stared out at her with preternatural intelligence more expected in a child ten times this one's age. And there was no cry.

"Hell spawn!" shrieked Parvey Yera. "It is demon spawn and I want nothing to do with it. Or you!"

The sudden attack took Kesira by surprise. One moment she had studied the small baby, the next clawed fingers raked at her face. Only instinct saved Kesira. She threw up one arm and deflected the blow but lost her balance and stumbled over a low table made from a rotting log. Above her Parvey Yera straightened, a gleaming axe in her hands.

Kesira watched in mute fascination as the nicked blade began its descent, aimed directly for her skull . . .

Other Avon Books by
Robert E. Vardeman

THE QUAKING LANDS: *Book 1 in* **The Jade Demons**
THE FROZEN WAVES: *Book 2 in* **The Jade Demons**

Coming Soon

THE WHITE FIRE: *Book 4 in* **The Jade Demons**

THE JADE DEMONS #3
THE CRYSTAL CLOUDS

ROBERT E. VARDEMAN

◢ AVON
PUBLISHERS OF BARD, CAMELOT, DISCUS AND FLARE BOOKS

THE CRYSTAL CLOUDS is an original publication of Avon Books. This work has never before appeared in book form. This work is a novel. Any similarity to actual persons or events is purely coincidental.

AVON BOOKS
A division of
The Hearst Corporation
1790 Broadway
New York, New York 10019

Copyright © 1985 by Robert E. Vardeman
Published by arrangement with the author
Library of Congress Catalog Card Number: 85-90667
ISBN: 0-380-89800-4

First Avon Printing, September 1985

AVON TRADEMARK REG. U. S. PAT. OFF. AND IN
OTHER COUNTRIES, MARCA REGISTRADA, HECHO EN
U. S. A.

Printed in the U. S. A.

WFH   10   9   8   7   6   5   4   3   2   1

For those printers' devils, Dale Goble and Mike Horvat

Chapter One

As KESIRA MINETTE placed one small foot on the rotting ice, she felt it give way. Cold water and knife-sharp edges raked at her leg as the nun tumbled forward, flailing futilely for balance. Strong hands caught her and pulled her upright, but the frigid water took its toll on her already depleted strength. She had been through so much. This new danger only drove her into further despair.

She needed to add one final verse to her personal death song, though, before succumbing. So much had happened; there was such a great need to put it all into the lyrics that would sum up her life's struggles and triumphs.

Kesira glanced back over her shoulder at the Isle of Eternal Winter towering above the ice-dotted water—the jade demon Ayondela's stronghold. Ayondela's power had been thwarted, and the dancing, cold white flame powering her evil momentarily extinguished to give the land back its normal summer warmth. And in that release from the potent magical spell Kesira found herself caught in a trap.

The nun and her companions, Molimo and the brilliantly plumed *trilla* bird Zolkan, had penetrated the fastness and fought the female demon—and won. To get to the Isle they had crossed the frozen waves of the Sea of Katad.

Now that frigid expanse thawed. Ice floes slammed together all around them, forcing Kesira and Molimo to agilely leap from one treacherous perch to another. Above, Zolkan circled, squawking instructions to them, seeking

7

out the safest path, if any path across the melting sea might be considered safe.

Molimo's strong hands again pulled her upright. Kesira shivered as her immersed leg turned blue with frostbite. The man knelt and saw the deathly pallor of her legs. Gently he began kneading and massaging the flesh to restore circulation.

Another ice floe smashed into the one on which they stood. The impact almost knocked Kesira and Molimo into the deadly, freezing waters.

"Later, Molimo," she said, urging the handsome, dark-haired man to stand. Cold, black eyes bored into her softer brown ones. She might live to be a thousand and never understand what thoughts surged behind Molimo's eyes. Love? Anger? Triumph? Fear? And asking did no good. He had been trapped in a rain of deadly jade caused by two fighting demons, barely surviving it. One handicap he bore from the cataclysmic battle had been the loss of his tongue.

Kesira shivered and not from the cold. The other loss suffered by her friend bothered her even more. Molimo had scant control over his shape. One moment he stood a robust young man, intelligence shining in those dark eyes. The next he shape-changed into a green-eyed wolf with no humanity in the savage snap of strong jaw or rake of sharp claw.

"If we don't hurry, we'll be trapped out here. I never thought the summer could come so quickly after we broke Ayondela's spell," she said.

From on high came the oddly accented words, "Left! Go left. Many floes, but move quick. Quick!" Zolkan wheeled above, a spot of green against the vivid blue of the new summer sky. Warm sunlight dropped down on them like melted butter. Kesira had battled the jade demons Ayondela and Emperor Kwasian to restore that natural warmth, and now she cursed uncharacteristically, praying that the freed season hide its warm fingers for just a few more hours.

The heat from the revitalized summer sun accelerated the melting of the floes.

Another minor iceberg crashed into the one on which they stood, driving her to her knees.

"Jump," urged Zolkan. He squawked loudly, then began a singsong speech meant only for Molimo. How they communicated, Kesira did not know. A sudden jolt of jealousy passed; they excluded her. But whatever Zolkan told Molimo, the man-wolf understood and acted on it immediately. Kesira shrieked as Molimo lifted her and jumped to the next floe and the next and the next.

She started to relax by the time he'd made the jump to a third ice floe. And then his foot slipped on ice turned into slush. They fell heavily, sprawling over the blunted edges of the frozen, protruding waves on the floe.

"How much farther?" she asked, panting. Kesira tried to focus her eyes on the shore, safe land where they might rest. Sweat—or was it blood?—dripped down her forehead, blinding her. Never had the nun felt so tired.

Life in the convent had been easy for her, too easy. Prayers to her patron demon Gelya had occupied much of her time. Tending the fields and doing the chores required by those of her order had delightfully filled the rest of her day. Easy work, pleasant times, a bubble of serenity floating along in a menacing and disordered world held together only through faith in the Emperor and the rightness of Gelya's teachings.

Kesira fought back tears forming at the corners of her eyes. Her ordered life had been cast into brutal ruins by the jade demons and their insane urge to conquer all. For centuries there had been no conflict between demon and mortal. The demons were content to walk among their worshipers from time to time. Their petty indiscretions, their couplings with humans, their more-than-human failings and charities, made up the universe as it was. No human emperor challenged the demons, and in return, the demons occupied themselves with their own dealings, leaving rule of the world to mortals.

The infernal jade had changed all that. Howenthal, Eznofadil, and Lenc had partaken of the jade, augmenting their powers—and their cruelty. Their rule over other demons had grown pallid; they sought more. Their battles overflowed and involved humans. But even as the jade gave them incredible powers, it robbed them of others. No longer immortal, time pressed in on them.

Kesira, Molimo, and Zolkan had crossed the Quaking Lands to confront Howenthal, and slayed the demon with the aid of another. Kesira reached up to her left breast. Glowing warmly there, Wemilat's kiss reminded her of the ugly toad-demon's goodness. He had perished in the struggle; only his lip print remained to protect her.

Kesira closed her eyes and rested. So tired. The fight had gone on for so long. Molimo had killed Ayondela's half-mortal son and driven the female demon into the ranks of jade. And they had invaded the Isle of Eternal Winter, destroying Eznofadil. But Ayondela still lived. The curse of winter she brought to the land had been removed, but the female demon still sought revenge for her son's death.

Ayondela. Lenc. Only two jade demons remained now, but they might as well have been a legion. Kesira's body refused to stir. Every ounce of energy had been drained. She could not go on.

Sharp pain lanced into her left shoulder, and a hard, sharp beak ripped at her ear. "Move. Floes come apart. Move!" Zolkan squawked, and jerked his talons on her shoulder to force Kesira to her feet.

"Go away. So cold, so tired. Let me sleep. Sleep..."

Zolkan flew off, but the pain did not diminish. A hard slap knocked her head to one side. Kesira's eyes flashed open. Anger burned within her. None dared touch her. She reached for her stone-wood staff and failed to find it. Her hands balled into fists, ready to strike out. Molimo stood above her, watching, waiting. He swung again. Her quick hand deflected the blow and turned it against him. Catching his hand and bending it backward, using the weakness in the joint, Kesira forced the man-wolf to his knees.

For a brief instant she saw the ebony eyes flicker with green light. Fear of bringing on the transformation to wolf caused her to release her grip. Molimo rubbed his injured hand.

"I'm sorry," she said. "I didn't mean . . . you shouldn't have slapped me."

"I wanted to," Zolkan piped up, "but I have no hands. Molimo did right. Move! Get off ice! Now!" The *trilla* bird strutted about, stretching his wings and trying to preen. Ice crystals caught the bright summer sunlight and blasted it into rainbows off the bird's feathers. "Need food, need bath, and you prattle on about being tired." Zolkan snorted, then took to wing.

Kesira struggled to her feet and found the ice too weak to support her. A chasm opened between her and Molimo. The man lithely vaulted across and joined her on the smaller ice floe.

"Can we swim to shore?" she asked. Molimo imitated a man freezing to death. They were caught between disparate seasons. The summer heat melted the ice, but the sluggish seawater took longer to shed its winter cloak. They wouldn't be able to swim more than a dozen yards before the water sucked the warmth from their flesh.

"Then we jump," Kesira said. She paused for a moment, reaching deep within herself for the strength she knew resided there. Kesira almost panicked when she failed to find that reservoir. She had done so much, so much. . . .

The dull, leaden, soul-depressing sense of duty rose within her and forced her to make the next jump and the next and the next. Kesira slipped and slid on the melting ice, cutting hands and legs, tearing her gray robe to tatters, leaving behind bloody streaks on the polar white, melting the ice further with her hot tears. But she went on without thought of pausing.

She had a duty to her dead sisters to avenge their deaths by Lenc's hand. She had a duty to stop Ayondela. She had been so lucky in life that she owed all this and more. Kesira Minette would not shirk her duty to those she thought of as family, to Emperor Kwasian, to the memory of her dead patron.

Kesira struggled on until Molimo tugged at her robe. Her feet slipped and slid, finding no purchase. Her hands had long since turned numb, but they clutched and clawed and moved her onward. Molimo jerked harder, tearing her robe.

"On," she said in a weak voice, eyes closed. Only slowly did Kesira realize that she slipped not on ice but on wet sand, that her hand found solid rock instead of razor-edged ice upjuts. "We made it," she said in a voice mixing surprise and triumph.

Molimo quickly wrote in the sand.

"So close?" she asked. Molimo had indicated that Nehan-dir and others loyal to the Order of the Steel Crescent were nearby. Molimo nodded briskly, pointing toward the foothills running parallel to the Sea of Katad. In those winding, twisting canyons entire armies could hide without being seen. Kesira sighed. The agony never stopped for her.

They had dodged Nehan-dir and his mercenaries to reach the sea, had followed the soldiers of the Steel Crescent across the frozen waves, and had for a second time killed that order's patron.

"Worshiping only strength is not doing Nehan-dir much good," she said to Molimo.

"Nehan-dir angers now," came Zolkan's squawks. "Every time he gets new patron, you kill him. Both Eznofadil and Howenthal are dead."

"Three patrons lost," mused Kesira. "How sad." She had lost only Gelya, but her belief in his teachings remained unshaken. Nehan-dir and his followers sought out the demon offering the most and did not truly believe in anything more than the intoxication of power. It was hardly her fault that they had chosen so poorly on all occasions, because they sought patrons for all the wrong reasons. The Order of the Steel Crescent's first patron, Tolek the Spare, had traded them for money to pay off gambling debts with another demon. Kesira could sympathize with the hurt and rage of Nehan-dir and the others over that, but selling their swords to the jade demons amounted to a crime against humanity that no previous sorrow could ameliorate.

"Is Nehan-dir nearby?" she asked.

Molimo shook his head. Zolkan cocked his crested head to one side, as if thinking on it, then agreed that no imminent danger threatened.

"Let's return to Parvey Yera's hut, then," Kesira said.

"Why?" Molimo etched into the wet sand.

"Her husband died by Ayondela's hand. We owe it to the woman to tell her. Raellard Yera was our ally."

"We must avoid Nehan-dir," wrote Molimo.

"We have our duty. Family ties are of the utmost importance, even more than saving our own lives," Kesira pointed out. "Raellard might have been only a dirt farmer, but he died nobly and in our service. We owe his memory this much."

"To south. Go south. Ayondela is there. Do battle with her," urged Zolkan. "Let this be Yera's monument." Kesira ignored the *trilla* bird. He'd never liked Yera, not that she blamed Zolkan. Yera had been unable to grow his crops due to the magicks-generated winter laid on the land by Ayondela, and the man had turned to hunting. The sight of a green-plumed bird had almost been too much for a hungry farmer to bear. In some parts of the country *trilla* bird meat counted as a delicacy.

"We go to Parvey."

"Leave her," Molimo wrote. "She and her son are trouble."

"They've probably starved to death by now," said Kesira. "But do as you choose. I know where my duty lies." On shaky legs she started off for the steep slopes leading to the top of a hill. Once there, the nun decided that she might meditate and say her daily devotionals, then find the path back to the Pharna River and from there upriver to the ravine leading to the Yera cabin.

Kesira smiled but tried not to show any further emotion

when she heard Molimo stomping along behind her and felt the warm downdrafts caused by Zolkan's beating wings above. They, too, knew where their duty lay. All it took was a little goading on her part from time to time to remind them. By determined effort they ought to be able to reach Parvey Yera in three days.

It took five.

Molimo hung back and shook his head. Kesira looked at the pathetic hut and knew what she had to do. The coward's way out would be to do as Molimo hinted: leave without once confronting the woman inside the log cabin. And, even as Kesira knew she couldn't walk away, she wanted to acquiesce and let Molimo convince her.

He pulled out the writing tablet that he had somehow managed to keep with him throughout their ordeals and hurriedly scratched his message.

Kesira read it and shook her head. "We've come this far. We can't simply turn and walk away. We owe it to Yera, if not to the woman."

"She's crazy," Molimo wrote.

"Yes." Kesira knew the man was absolutely-right. The few hours she'd spent with Parvey Yera before had convinced her that the woman had become demented, by hardship or a vagrant touch of the demons or something else. Whatever the cause, the effect proved the same. "But if she is, this is all the more reason to aid her."

"No aid. She *likes* to eat birds," complained Zolkan. "I see it in her beady eyes. Cannibal. She is cannibal!"

"She's not a cannibal, Zolkan. Even if she does like *trilla* bird meat. You'd be the cannibal if you ate your own kind's flesh." She felt the bird shudder and tense his talons. The pain lanced deep into her shoulder; her robe no longer provided any cushioning. The only consolation to having her gray robe in tatters lay in the warmth of the wind slipping through the rents. Where it had previously admitted vicious winter breezes, she now felt the languid softness of summer airs.

"Don't like her," the bird said, sulking. "Molimo doesn't, either."

Kesira took a deep breath and composed herself. She had never been the one to shirk onerous duties and wasn't about to begin now. On that road lay personal humiliation and the death of courage. Gelya had taught that inner triumph led to outer victory. Strong inside, strong in all things.

"Steel Crescent follows," said Zolkan.

"They've been on our trail ever since we washed up on the beach," Kesira said softly. "While they might find us if we linger overlong, I don't intend to be here more than a few hours."

"Ayondela is to the south. At Lorum Bay."

Kesira jerked her head around and stared at the *trilla* bird. "How do you know that? You haven't left my sight since we escaped the Isle of Eternal Winter."

Zolkan started to take wing rather than answer. Kesira grabbed him by the neck and held him back. Powerful wings beat at her face. She ignored them and dangled the bird by his neck.

"I'll give it a good crank unless you tell me. How do you know where Ayondela went?"

A hand on her shoulder made Kesira loosen her grip. Zolkan sputtered and flopped to the ground. The bird batted about, got to his feet, and then launched himself with powerful wing action. Molimo held up his slate.

"So *you* told him, eh?" Kesira said skeptically. "And how is it that you came by this interesting tidbit of information? You've not been out of my sight for an instant, either."

Molimo wrote quickly, but Kesira studied the man's face. Her heart gave an extra beat. So handsome, so strong. What a pity he had been caught in the battle between Lenc and Merrisen. She believed the jade illness that afflicted Molimo had been produced by the demon Merrisen's body shattering into millions of shards. Eznofadil had perished that way—and what horror resided in the tiny fragments of a truly evil demon's body?

Kesira forced her thoughts to other paths. It would take so little for her to love Molimo, and she dared not do so. His shape-changing was only a part of it. She had nursed him back to health and felt sorry for his tongueless condition. That had to be it, she told herself. Pity. She pitied the young man. He was a friend and nothing more, and could be nothing more until the jade demons were put to route.

And even then . . .

Molimo held up the tablet. On it he had written, "Ayondela and Lenc must join forces. Lenc still uses her for his own ends. He is not strong enough to rule without her—not yet."

"You're saying that with Eznofadil and Howenthal gone, Lenc will continue to play on Ayondela's hatred and sorrow over Rouvin's death?" Molimo nodded. "So? So how do you know she and Lenc are to the south? You said you told Zolkan."

"A guess," Molimo wrote. The expression on his face remained impassive, but Kesira had the innate feeling that he lied. The man-wolf had obtained the information in ways other than logic. This was but another mystery about him that would be cleared up one day. But not now.

"We will examine your guess more closely. After I have spoken with Parvey."

Molimo started to restrain her, but the cold look she shot him stayed his hand. He shrugged and settled down onto a stump outside the hut. Whatever she did, Kesira knew, she wasn't likely to convince Molimo to join her inside.

Nor did she want his company. What she had to do was better done alone. How can anyone tell a woman that her husband and the father of her child had perished?

"Parvey?" she called out. "Are you inside?"

A sound more like the scurrying of rats than the movements of a human echoed from inside. Kesira cautiously pushed aside the door. It had been pulled off its hinges and never repaired. That told Kesira more about the condition of the woman inside than anything else. The nun slipped past the door and peered into the dim, smoke-filled haze within the tiny cabin. Her eyes adjusted to the dark and allowed her to make out the huddled figure near the back of the hut.

"Parvey, do you remember me? Kesira Minette. I was here before, with Raellard."

"Raellard?" came the cracked voice. "My husband?"

"I have an additional sorrow for you." Kesira's voice came out in a choked whisper, barely audible. She did not want to be the one to tell the poor woman of her husband's demise, yet there was no other to do the sad task.

"Raellard's dead," came the emotionless voice before Kesira could speak. "I knew it. The whoreson's gone and died on me, leaving me with the demon spawn."

"Parvey!" Kesira said sharply. "Raellard died in a valiant effort to rid the world of Ayondela's curse. As you can see, the winter is lifting. Raellard helped accomplish that. He was a brave man." Kesira winced, thinking of how Raellard had died under Ayondela's tortures. No one deserved such a fate. No one.

"He left me. Me and that hideous creature." The emaciated woman held out a bony hand with a finger looking more like a talon. She pointed at the small bundle in the rear of the hut. The child stirred, pudgy hand gripping the threadbare blanket swaddling it. The entire time Kesira had been inside the cabin, the baby had not uttered a sound.

"That is your son, Parvey. He is your flesh—yours and Raellard's."

"Not Raellard's! Not his. No, no," the woman cackled. "Not his. Another's."

Kesira swallowed hard, her mouth filled with cotton. Raellard had mentioned that he thought the baby had been fathered by someone else. Kesira had passed it off as paranoia generated by famine. Could both this crazed woman and her husband share the same delusion? Or was it delusion at all?

"He was gone too much. Worked too many hours. And for what? Nothing!"

"Yera, your husband was a good man who knew his duty. He did all he could to feed you. It is the jade demons' curse that drove him off the land and afield to hunt." Kesira remembered the pitiful few items Raellard had returned with. Tubers, a rabbit—the wolf he had slain on the doorstep. Kesira saw no evidence of the wolf skin or anything more than had been in the cabin the last time she had visited here.

"It is your baby, no matter who the father is," Kesira said. "You must tend him." The baby looked well enough nourished, but the pale eyes stared out at her with preternatural intelligence more expected in a child ten times this one's age. And there was no cry.

"Hell spawn!" shrieked Parvey Yera. "It is demon spawn, and I want nothing to do with it. Or you!"

The sudden attack took Kesira by surprise. One moment she had studied the small baby, the next clawed fingers raked at her face. Only instinct saved Kesira. She threw up one arm and deflected the blow but lost her balance and stumbled over a low table made from a rotting log. Above her Parvey Yera straightened, a gleaming ax in her hands.

Kesira watched in mute fascination as the nicked blade began its descent, aimed directly for her skull.

Chapter Two

ALL KESIRA MINETTE saw was the crazed woman holding the ax. The edge of the weapon took on intense meaning for her, every nick and flaw magnified a million times over. In spite of this, in spite of the danger, Kesira found herself frozen and unable to avoid the blow.

"Die, demon lover, die!" shrieked Parvey Yera. Muscles tightened and the heavy blade descended.

Blood fountained over Kesira, blinding her. She let out a tiny gasp when she realized it was not her own. The nun wiped away the gore and heard the chewing, gnawing, wetly ripping sounds. Her stomach rolled over and threatened to lose what little it contained. Kesira held down her gorge and forced herself to a sitting position.

"Molimo, stop!" she cried. It was too late by far. The man-wolf had transformed totally to wolf and now fed on Parvey's scrawny throat. Blazing green eyes swung on Kesira, studied her, appraised her for a better meal than that offered by the undernourished woman now dead on the dirt floor. Even as Molimo's wildness surged, Kesira felt inner calm returning.

This peace communicated to the wolf more fully than mere words. The feral light faded in Molimo's eyes, and powerful muscles rippled under the gray fur before beginning the shape-change back to human. Molimo huddled on the floor near his victim, gasping for breath. Kesira went to him and put her arm around his bare shoulders,

pulling him close. Blood soaked into her robe from his
lips and chest; she took no note.

"It's all right, Molimo. You saved my life. She had
been driven crazy by her ordeals. You saved me. It's all
right." She rocked him to and fro as if he were a small
child.

As the thought occurred to her Kesira turned, still hugging Molimo's naked form. The baby lay in the corner of
the hut, pale eyes taking in everything. Not once had the
baby cried out.

"Sit quietly for a while," she told Molimo. "Don't get
upset over this. You saved me." Kesira didn't want him
reverting to wolf form. Every transformation, she felt,
committed him that much more to permanence as an animal. Seeing that Molimo rested, the nun picked up the
infant. Wise, old eyes peered at her, perfectly focused. A
tiny smile crossed healthy pink lips, then the baby stuck
one thumb into his mouth and closed his eyes. In seconds
he slept contentedly.

"What are you to do with that?" came Zolkan's grating
words. "Leave it!"

"How can I leave him?" asked Kesira. Yet she agreed
with Zolkan's implied question of being able to care for
the infant. He hardly ate the fare of a seasoned traveler—
Kesira herself had been living on little more than tough
jerked meat and the occasional root or tuber these past
five days' journey from the coast. Dodging Nehan-dir's
soldiers had added to the necessity of hurried meals and
forced marches. How could a newborn possibly survive
such hardship?

Thoughts of giving up her pursuit of Ayondela and Lenc
flitted across the fringes of Kesira's mind. Battling the
jade demons might eventually prove impossible. She had
considerable luck so far, destroying two of them—but the
cost! Tears welled at the corners of her eyes as she stared
down at the sleeping infant in her arms. This little one's
mother and father had died because of Ayondela's wintery
curse. And others? Their names were legion, those who

were even noted in passing. Even greater numbers had died with no one to mourn their deaths.

"Gelya," the woman said softly. "Why did they have to slay you also? You could guide me now."

Zolkan squawked loudly for her attention. "It will die, no matter what we do," the *trilla* bird declared.

"You might be right. But we must try."

"Needs mother's milk," insisted Zolkan. "Nowhere to get it. Do it a favor by killing it."

To Kesira's surprise Molimo reacted strongly. A croak came from his sundered mouth, and he slammed his fist into the palm of his other hand. Hurriedly Molimo left and returned, pulling on his clothing and scribbling away on his tablet. Kesira looked over the man's shoulder as he wrote.

"The boy goes with us," Molimo wrote with bold, forceful strokes.

"You are right," said Kesira, "but without milk he cannot live very long."

"There is a way." Molimo's words seemed to burn with a phosphorescent fire. Kesira blinked and the effect died.

"What way? I can't supply it." Kesira frowned when Molimo bobbed his head up and down. She smiled gently and shook her head. "My friend, there are some things you do not understand." Not for the first time, Kesira had the feeling that Molimo's education in wordly matters had been neglected. On some topics he showed incredible astuteness, but on others the abysmal ignorance made her want to laugh. Even as a nun locked away most of her life in a convent, she had experienced more of life than Molimo.

Or perhaps his mind had become addled through hardship and the awful wounds inflicted on him by the jade rain. More than his tongue might have been lost.

Again Molimo shook his head. With gentle fingers so different from the wolf's claws he reached out and pulled open her gray robe. The fabric had reached the limits of its endurance and tore, in spite of the light touch. Molimo exposed her left breast where Wemilat the Ugly had kissed her. The lip print pulsed warmly, pinkness spreading from the imprint throughout her breast.

"I don't understand," she said.

Molimo turned the baby so that she held it in her left arm, her nipple close to the infant's mouth. Those hauntingly old eyes opened, and a tiny hand reached out. Kesira sighed softly when she felt the lips working against her flesh.

"So nice," she said, more to herself. Louder, to Molimo, she said, "The baby will be disappointed."

Molimo shook his head vehemently. And Kesira understood why. Stirrings deep within her breast caused her to clutch the infant more closely to her body. Ineffable sensations built inside her, bringing a peace and contentment she had seldom found even in her deepest meditations.

Milk flowed from the breast kissed by Wemilat's lips.

"How did you know, Molimo?" she asked.

"Must leave. Nehan-dir will find us," protested Zolkan. The *trilla* bird vented a loud caw, then fell into the singsong speech directed at Molimo. Kesira listened for several minutes. Whatever went on between the two, both understood, and they came to a conclusion.

"Well?" asked Kesira.

"We might elude Nehan-dir if we cross mountains to Lorum Bay."

"Lorum Bay? You mentioned that before. How do you— or Molimo—know Ayondela is there?"

"Lorum Bay is on southernmost rim of Sea of Katad. We must hurry to leave behind Nehan-dir."

Kesira frowned. Zolkan had not answered her question, and she sensed that the *trilla* bird wasn't likely to, either. When he wanted, he could become very evasive. The infant had gone back to sleep after a quiet belch or two, and not even Zolkan's flapping seemed destined to keep him awake.

"Staying clear of the mercenaries is important," Kesira said, "but we have no plan once we find Ayondela. I had

hoped to persuade her that Rouvin's death was accidental,
that she should oppose Lenc. But there is little chance for
either now. Ayondela is too firmly addicted to the power
given her by the jade."

"We have killed Howenthal and Rouvin; we can kill
Ayondela and Lenc," wrote Molimo.

"You make it sound so simple." Kesira rocked the baby
gently. "We must find a home for him before continuing
on against the demons. Do you suppose there'll be somewhere in Lorum Bay that will take him in?"

With the advent of the jade demons life had become
cheap. Entire cities had perished and more would follow.
Why should anyone want to burden himself with a newborn
when personal survival was so difficult? Kesira had seen
how her order's mission in Chounabel had fallen into ruin.
The sisters had forsaken Gelya's teachings and succumbed
to the city's carnal lure. Kesira touched the dirty yellow
sash circling her waist—the symbol of the Sister of the
Mission.

Of all those who had once followed Gelya, only she
remained true. The virtue of prosperity was temperance,
which Gelya taught. But never had her patron mentioned
that the virtue of adversity is fortitude, a much more heroic
value. She had endured so much, and so much more lay
ahead if she were to avenge the demon Lenc's cruelties.

"The Steel Crescent mercenaries still seek us," wrote
Molimo.

"I know," she said quietly, not wanting to disturb the
infant. "I wonder what his name is? Raellard said that
Parvey hadn't named him. I wonder if she did, while we
were on the Isle?"

Molimo shrugged. Kesira looked at the man curiously.
His dark hair had become matted with blood from the slain
woman, but more than this held her attention. Around the
baby Molimo seemed uneasy, as if such a small one could
threaten him.

"Are you afraid of what you might do to the child?"

she asked him. "That you will shape-change and harm him?"

Molimo shook his head. Zolkan fluttered down and perched on the man's shoulder, beady black eyes fixed on her. The *trilla* bird squawked and said, "How can we travel with it holding us back? Nehan-dir will kill us all!"

"Then we *all* die together," Kesira said firmly.

"Madness," complained Zolkan. "And no time even to properly bathe. Awful weather, cruel humans wanting to eat *trilla* birds, and I am forced to stay dirty."

"You forgot to mention hungry," added Kesira, smiling at Zolkan.

"That too. Very hungry. No fit food anywhere. And Steel Crescent chases us. Nehan-dir will have my feathers for headdress!"

Kesira put the baby down into his threadbare blanket and tucked the corners in around him. While Ayondela's curse had been lifted from the land, touches of wintry cold remained to stalk unwittingly exposed soft flesh. Even as she made certain that the baby was warm, Kesira felt cold tendrils of air whipping at her rags. The gray robe of her order no longer provided any protection at all.

She undid the knotted blue cord proclaiming her a sister and then took off the gold sash, laying them aside.

"Parvey no longer needs covering," she said. "Poor though it is, her clothes look like Empress Aglenella's compared to mine." She rummaged through small boxes and pulled out what might be most useful. Kesira almost dropped the wolfskin skirt Parvey Yera had fashioned from the beast killed by Raellard. The fur, the coloring and texture, the size all were so close to that which Molimo became.

"Hurry," said Zolkan. "I would fly. The air cleanses my feathers."

"You just don't like being shut up in this tiny hut," said Kesira. But she didn't blame the bird. Staying here longer than necessary wore on her nerves. Too many unpleasant things had occurred for her to enjoy this place. Parvey's cooling body only accentuated the problems that had been born here.

Kesira's eyes darted to the sleeping infant. He smiled slightly in sleep, hands balled into tiny fists. No sound other than gentle breathing came to her sharp ears. Would he ever cry? Was the baby capable of such emotion, after all that had happened to his parents?

Kesira stripped off her robe and discarded it.

"Molimo, you don't have to go," she called out as the man turned to leave. "We have no secrets from one another. And this is hardly the first time you've seen me unclothed." Still, her nude body affected him. Molimo flushed and averted his eyes. Kesira almost enjoyed the uneasiness she caused in him. The nun wasn't being cruel, but her own emotions about him were brought into sharper focus.

If he had turned and taken her in his arms, Kesira Minette would not have resisted.

"Must go," Molimo scribbled on his tablet. He darted out the door before she could stop him.

Sighing, the woman dressed in Parvey's discarded clothing. The wolfskin skirt swung easily around her waist, and a fine embroidered cotton blouse slid sensuously against her skin. Parvey had done fine needlework—the shirt Raellard had worn attested to that. Thinking of him, Kesira dug further and found a worn pair of calf-high boots that had belonged to the man. By stuffing pieces of her robe into the toes Kesira could wear the boots with minimal discomfort.

"Almost ready," she said. She picked up the knotted blue cord and fastened it around her waist, then added the gold sash. These were little enough reminders of her upbringing, the teachings of Gelya, the trials she had been through, and the ones still in her future. As long as she held onto the wisdom passed on to her by Gelya, she had a chance. Lose sight of that and only failure awaited her.

Kesira sighed and sat down on the rotted stump and stared at the slain body of Parvey Yera. So many good people had died. Kesira felt cold anger building within her. She did not blame Molimo for this death; full guilt lay on Ayondela and Lenc. The jade demons' curse had frozen the land and stolen away summer crops. Raellard had died, Parvey had died, her entire mission had perished. And what of the cities? Kesira saw no way for them to have endured the bleakness of a winter lasting twice as long as usual. They depended heavily on farm produce, and the farms had failed.

"Your son will see better days without the jade demons," she promised Parvey.

A scratching sound at the door caught her attention. Molimo hesitantly entered, a look of relief on his face when he saw her fully clothed. He thrust out his tablet for her to read.

"Zolkan flies far to get such information," she said after scanning it. The *trilla* bird had sighted the outriders of the Steel Crescent near the Pharna River, a full day's travel distant. They had time to rest, eat, and still be away before Nehan-dir's soldiers found their spoor.

Molimo held up a small rabbit he had clubbed. He pointed outside to indicate that he had a cooking fire started and that Kesira should join him. She checked the baby, then left the hut. The cool air outside hit her like a hammer blow, but she rejoiced in it after the musty cabin interior.

While Molimo fixed the simple meal Kesira fingered the battered box containing the bone rune sticks that were her due as a sister of the Mission of Gelya. She had thrown the rune sticks several times and had been uncannily accurate in her predictions. It was as if the demons aided her—those demons still opposing the power of the jade.

Molimo indicated that she should do another casting. With hardly a glance at the box Kesira upended it and flicked her wrist to send the rune sticks out in a fan-shaped pattern. They fell into the dust, many touching and one atop another.

The man-wolf lifted one eyebrow questioningly. Kesira hardly noticed him. Her eyes darted over the rune sticks, picking out meaning from the arcane scramble.

"Ayondela *is* to the south," she said in a low voice. "You might be right that we will find her at Lorum Bay. There is mention of water and ships and . . . and a peninsula in our future. Danger. I don't understand that. Storms and jade-spawned treachery."

Molimo gnawed on one of the rabbit's haunches, breaking open the femur and sucking out the marrow. His dark eyes fixed on Kesira rather than on the rune sticks she read.

"Inside my head," the woman said in a voice almost too low to be audible, "stirrings, as if someone speaks to me." Her fingers lightly traced over the carved sticks. "Ayondela is our enemy and we must destroy her. And Lenc. He uses her as a cat's-paw. He . . . he . . . oh, accursed sticks!"

Tears of frustration ran down her cheeks. The meaning came to her—almost. Kesira sensed more lurking in this casting of the runes and knew that she'd failed in her interpretation of it. All she got was information she already had: *of course* Ayondela was her enemy; Lenc *had* to be the one who destroyed Gelya and her mission.

"It's so murky, so unclear. Like chaos." Kesira stopped and swallowed hard. "It is as if the Time of Chaos is at hand." Her brown eyes lifted to lock with Molimo's darker ones. The man-wolf paled slightly and covered his discomfort by handing over the remainder of the roast rabbit.

"It is not an easy thing to consider," she said, taking the meat. "First there was void and dirt and air and water and fire, then animals, then humans, and then from the coupling of animals and humans came the demons."

Molimo stared into the crackling fire, pushed in a few more pungent twigs, and jerked away when a spark landed on his skin. Kesira saw that he did not want to consider that they might be poised on the brink of a new age.

Animals and humans mated to give birth to the demons, those creatures with accentuated traits. Stronger, longer-lived, more intelligent—and more venal and meddlesome and stupid also. Humans ruled themselves while the demons watched with haughty, virtually immortal, disdain.

Until the Time of Chaos, the passing of the demons. The mating of humans with demons to produce gods. Where the best and worst of humanity rested within the demons, the new gods would possess only the finest traits. So proclaimed the myth. But the birthing of the gods was supposed to be attended by upheaval and destruction and calamity for humans. The demons would not easily relinquish their position in the cosmos.

"Dark soon," said Zolkan. The *trilla* bird flapped hard, braked to a halt, and landed on Kesira's shoulder. She winced as his claws cut into her shoulder. She vowed to make a small pad for the bird before she left. Otherwise he would savage her shoulder to the point of incapacity.

"The mercenaries are still arrayed along the river?" she asked.

"We must be gone before dawn," said Zolkan. "Nehandir is no fool—and he is angry. He will kill you this time."

Kesira said nothing. She went into the hut and took up the infant, cradling him in her arm. "My little one," she cooed. "What should I name you? Even an orphan deserves a name."

Then Kesira swallowed hard. Her parents had been killed by brigands. Without Sister Fenelia and the order to take her in, Kesira would have perished. She looked down into the baby's pale eyes. The debt she owed to her sisters would be repaid by taking care of this infant. Kesira could do no less: it was her duty.

"Leave it," said Zolkan. "We must go quickly. It will hinder us."

"He is coming with us. I'll have to fashion a sling of some sort to carry him." Kesira heaved a sigh. "And I wish I had my stone-wood staff. It helps make the miles go by easier."

Molimo extinguished the fire and pointed to the lee side of the hut. Like her, he had no wish to spend the night within the cabin. They unrolled their thin blankets and lay down. Kesira soon heard Molimo's slow, regular breathing. He rested easily.

For her, sleep proved more elusive. The stars popped out, one by one, and wheeled about to form their cold, crystalline constellations set in the velvety blackness of night. The baby in her arms, Kesira eventually drifted off to a troubled sleep, doubts assailing her.

"Far behind us. We outrace them," squawked Zolkan. The bird perched on the pad Kesira had fashioned for him on her left shoulder.

"I wonder," Kesira said. "This seems too easy."

Molimo frowned and motioned for her to explain. The way for the past week had been anything but easy. At every turn they had to avoid Nehan-dir's soldiers. The weather warmed, melting the ice and snow but turning the ground into a quagmire that made walking a continual sucking, clutching struggle. And even with Zolkan's aerial reconnaissance, the path over the mountains and back to the Sea of Katad had not been easy. Before, they had followed the River Pharna to the sea. That path had been closed to them with the posting of Steel Crescent sentries along the way.

The hills turned into mountains, and even the passes required substantial outpourings of energy to traverse. With the infant strapped to her breast Kesira kept up with Molimo well enough, but if the man hadn't cut her a new staff of Gelya's sacred stone-wood, she would have faltered and lagged far behind.

"Nehan-dir must know where we're heading. Why do his soldiers hang back? On horse they could ride us down in a day. I feel that they are herding us."

"To sea?" protested Zolkan. "Our escape lies there. Why would Nehan-dir want us to escape?"

"His troops might come up the coast to meet us," wrote Molimo, awkwardly scribbling while they continued their brisk pace. "They would catch us between two patrols."

"Hardly needed," scoffed Zolkan. "Are we so dangerous to them?"

Kesira had to laugh. "We must be. Haven't we killed
two of the jade demons? Aren't we responsible for lifting
the curse of winter from the land?" She sobered, thinking
of the ordeal endured on the Isle of Eternal Winter. She
had used magicks far beyond her understanding when she
had interrupted the burning of the cold white flame powering Ayondela's curse. For the briefest of instants Kesira
had altered the flow of energy, and that had broken the
spell.

"He seeks our blood because we slaughtered his patrons, nothing more," said Zolkan. But the *trilla* bird's
words came slowly, indicating that he didn't really believe
it. They all knew Nehan-dir still sought a patron of
strength—and that the most likely replacement for Howenthal and Eznofadil would be Lenc.

Molimo grabbed Kesira by the shoulder and shook. He
pointed along the ridge. Past a jumble of rocks she saw
the chalky white cliff face and the heaving green waves
of the Sea of Katad.

"We've made it," she said with a sigh of relief. Before,
she had looked over that vast expanse and seen nothing
but waves frozen in midroll, paralyzed in their unceasing
assault on the sandy beaches. Now the waves came
smoothly, breaking with ear-numbing force and filling the
air with white froth and a sharp, salty tang.

"Down there. To right. Soldiers. Many soldiers. Nehan-
dir's!"

Kesira didn't need Zolkan's identification to know who
those armed mercenaries followed. One carried a long,
thin green banner emblazoned with a crescent moon. She
had seen similar designs burned into the vulnerable flesh
of those loyal to the Order of the Steel Crescent.

"Wait," she said. She cinched up the straps holding the
baby. A fat little hand reached up and gripped the edge of
the cloth. Those eyes stared at her, too wise, too knowing.
Not once did the infant emit even the tiniest of cries. She

laid her hand atop the boy's head, more to reassure herself than to soothe the imperturbable baby.

"If we reach the beach unnoticed, we might find a fisherman to take us south to Lorum Bay," wrote Molimo, sketching quickly in soft dirt at their feet.

"We can only try. Zolkan, keep us informed of their movement. And try not to be too obvious about your spying."

The *trilla* bird harumphed and then became airborne. Strong green wings carried him outward on updrafts, rising and spiraling away from them. Kesira and Molimo began their descent, following a path down the face of the limestone cliff. By the time they reached the beach, both were winded.

It as then that Zolkan swooped down with the bad news.

"Nehan-dir himself rides this way. Flee! You have less than five minutes!"

Kesira frantically looked up the beach, imagining the mercenaries rounding an outjutting rock, banner flying, steel weapons gleaming in the morning sunlight. To go in that direction was suicidal. Just considering the climb back up the cliff face made her shake with weakness. No amount of urging would get them far enough away; but the only alternative was surrender.

"Up, once more up," she said. Molimo pointed. High above, on the brink where they had stood only an hour before, she spotted the sharp, hard points of metal weapons reflecting down to them. "They'll catch us between the jaws of their infernal war machine," she said.

Molimo started off down the beach, the only way open to them. Less than a hundred yards of trudging through the soft sand convinced Kesira that they were doomed. Her stamina fled, and she felt the thunder of hooves through the very ground.

When the loud cry rose from up the beach, she knew Nehan-dir had spotted them.

"To left," came Zolkan's squawking command. "A sandbar. You must go out to sea!"

Kesira almost balked. To walk out on the sandbar, out past the protecting curve of this small inlet, only stranded them. She glanced down at the baby. A tiny smile darted across his lips, and the eyes told her that she could not simply give up.

"If it means an added minute of life, let's make the most of it," she said. Kesira Minette sloshed through the shallow water and found the sandbar firm underfoot. Toward the watery horizon they walked, to find a place to make their final stand.

Chapter Three

"HOW FAR DOES IT GO?" cried Kesira. She looked back over her shoulder, fearful that Nehan-dir and his troopers had reached the juncture of sandbar and beach. The mercenary leader seemed in no hurry to cut off their escape. His company rode with painful slowness, covering little more terrain with every passing moment than Kesira and Molimo did on foot.

Molimo motioned for her to keep running. The water splashed up and into her calf-high boots, wetting the hem of her wolfskin skirt. But even in this panicky retreat Kesira found a touch of beauty. The seawater dotted Molimo's hair, and the sun sent its rays through the droplets in a spectrum of color. It was as if Molimo had been elevated to Emperor and wore a crown of liquid jewels.

The man stopped suddenly. Kesira crashed into him, arching her back so that her shoulders collided with his, protecting her small ward. The baby stirred restlessly, eyes accusing.

"There, there," she said. "It'll be all right. I promise." Even as she spoke Kesira knew how futile it was to give any hope. Her only consolation was that the infant was too young to understand more than her soothing tones. The nun only hoped that her words soothed; the panic rising within her made her want to scream in anguish.

To Molimo she said, "Why are you stopping?"

He dropped to his knees, the sea rising and falling

restlessly around his thighs. They had reached the end of the sandbar. To go farther meant swimming for their lives.

Kesira turned and faced back toward the beach, her hand turning cold on her stone-wood staff.

"I'm glad you made this for me. Only the wood sacred to Gelya makes a good staff." The short time she'd used this staff, she had broken the butt end and peeled back splinters on the sides. One solid blow from a steel sword would break it. Still, Kesira had nothing better to use to defend herself, and Gelya forbade the use of edged steel weapons.

Molimo rested his hand on her shoulder, then dropped it to the infant.

"I'd forgotten," she said, ashamed of her lapse. "Help me sling the baby onto my back." But Molimo didn't help her. He swung her around and pointed out to sea, a curious croaking sound coming from his throat. And high above, hardly more than a green spot in the azure sky, Zolkan spiraled and vented his singsong words for Molimo.

Kesira squinted into the sun, trying to make out what attracted her friends' attention. Then she saw it. A small fishing boat, hardly more than an overgrown rowboat, hove into view.

"Zolkan!" she cried. "Get help. Get them to rescue us!"

Kesira was momentarily blinded as the green speck crossed the face of the sun. The churning of water as Nehan-dir's riders followed them along the bar spun her back around.

"We are lost," she said in despair. Remove hope, and only fear remained. Kesira reached down inside herself, calling on the training she had received throughout her life. Settling her emotions, finding strengths, conquering weaknesses, she prepared for the battle. Not easily would the Order of the Steel Crescent take her. They would find that her patron's teachings burned brightly within her breast. She might be the last, but her memory would endure after this day.

The banner came ever nearer. Beside the bearer rode a

man dressed in steel-plate armor. Even at this distance Kesira recognized the spiderworks of scarring on Nehan-dir's face. The man hung a helmet from a cord on his saddle, then gestured for the banner bearer to hold position. Nehan-dir came closer until his horse nervously pawed at the fetlocks-deep water only a dozen paces distant.

"You have led us a merry chase," he said without pre-amble. "Do you now prepare to die?"

"I do not fear death," she answered truthfully. "Kill me if you will. I only ask that the life of this baby be spared."

Kesira had not been able to re-sling the infant. He still nestled peacefully against her breast.

"Where did you come across this foundling?" the war-rior asked.

"His parents are both dead. One was tortured to death by Ayondela."

"Ah, yes, the dirt farmer. He died well enough. No disgrace in his passing. This is the sprig from his tree, eh?"

"You will spare the boy?"

"Of course not," snapped Nehan-dir. "After what he did to insure Eznofadil's death? After all you have done to disgrace my order?"

Kesira saw the flush rising to Nehan-dir's face, turning the webbing of pink scars a brighter hue than the rest of his flesh. He drew forth his sword and held it high, then brought it down, tip pointing directly at Kesira. The man holding the banner lowered his staff until the fabric trailed in the water. The pounding of that horse's hooves as he charged forward to impale them on the spear tip drowned out even the surf's restless action against the distant shore.

Molimo shoved Kesira aside at the last possible instant. With a move too swift for her to follow, the man-wolf twisted aside and allowed the spear to pass by harmlessly. Strong hands gripped the shaft and bent it groundward to bury it in the soft sand. The rider catapulted from the saddle and landed with a huge splash.

"Fool!" raged Nehan-dir.

The mercenary leader charged. Kesira felt herself sinking into a curious fugue state, with everything around her
moving slowly. Try as she would, though, this increased
awareness did not turn into increased speed on her part.
She moved as if dipped in treacle.

The energy is within you. Use it, came soft, distant
words from deep within her mind. Kesira's calm momentarily broke at the mental intrusion—from where?—but
she recovered and found that the words acted as a key to
parts of her hitherto untapped psyche.

She perceived with great precision that her senses had
sped up—and she moved at a rate equal to them.

Nehan-dir's horse charged by her. Kesira spun lithely
and thrust out her staff, catching the horse between the
front legs. The scissoring of those legs as the horse ran
proved to be its undoing. Fragile bones snapped against
wood, and the horse nose-dived into the water, struggling
in pain and panic. It kicked and threw Nehan-dir free,
before slipping into deeper water. Its devastated front legs
doomed it to swift, noisy drowning.

Kesira's senses slowed. She straightened, holding only
fragments of her staff. Nehan-dir flailed around in the
shallow water along the sandbar, the heavy plate armor
weighing him down.

"Like a turtle on its back," she said. A booted foot
pushed the mercenary after his horse. Yelping and grabbing
futilely for her leg, Nehan-dir slid off the side of the
sandbar toward deeper water. The soldier saw the danger
and stopped trying to grapple with Kesira and began fumbling at the leather straps holding on his carapacelike armor.

"Molimo," the woman said softly, "help the man along."

Molimo's sword rose and fell in a bright arc. The ringing impact of sword tip against armored chest produced
fat blue sparks that leapt outward to expire in the sea with
a loud hiss.

"Stop—don't—damn your eyes, let me get to my feet

so I can die like a man!" Nehan-dir spun around, but Molimo's sword followed his every movement.

"Finish him, Molimo," ordered Kesira. "The others have seen and are coming. I want him dead before they arrive. I refuse to give him the pleasure of witnessing our death."

The Steel Crescent mercenaries had dismounted and taken off their own heavy armor before advancing along the submerged sandbar. As Kesira watched Molimo went to finish off Nehan-dir.

"You damned other-beast," raged Nehan-dir, struggling with the leather straps on his armor as he slipped deeper and deeper into the water. Waves lapped around him, making the small man sputter. Molimo's sword slashed out— and missed when the mercenary slid into the water, his head vanishing under the churning surface.

Kesira glanced over her shoulder. Molimo poised, knee-deep in the water, waiting for the soldier's head to reappear so he could lop it off. The woman sighed. Such was to be their fate when the others of the Steel Crescent reached them. She placed one gentling hand on the baby's cheek. Those haunting eyes looked up at her, as if saying, "I understand. You did what you could. No one can ask more."

Kesira clenched the shattered remnants of her staff and set her feet wider apart. Where the strength and speed she'd found before had come from, Kesira had no inkling. But it had aided her once. It could be summoned again.

A loud squawk captured her attention. Flying in tight circles overhead, Zolkan sailed down wordlessly. The sound of water lapping against a boat hull caught her attention. Kesira turned to see a small skiff less than a dozen yards away. The sailor at the oars rowed furiously, cursing as he came. Zolkan swooped down to land heavily on her shoulder. Kesira hardly noticed the weight this time.

"They aid us. Good people. Eat fish, not birds."

"The fishermen in the boat?" Kesira squinted into the

sun and saw the larger fishing boat bobbing some distance away.

"Good people. Good. Get in boat. Help sailor row. Hurry, hurry!"

"You're always in too much of a rush, Zolkan," she chided. But Kesira's own haste to get to the skiff was almost unseemly. Her own death would come one day; it hardly mattered anymore when that day was. But the baby's life stretched in front of him. Kesira felt she owed him as much as she could deliver.

"Molimo, come," Zolkan cawed.

The man-wolf was obviously torn between waiting for Nehan-dir to surface, so that he could finish off the mercenary, and joining Kesira in the skiff. When his dark eyes fixed on the dozen warriors pounding through the water toward him, he abandoned all hope of seeing Nehan-dir's head separated from his torso. Molimo sloughed through the water, then swam the last few yards. Kesira and Zolkan both struggled to pull the heavily muscled young man into the boat.

"Can't expect me to do all the rowing, now can yer?" complained the sailor. "Take an oar and row as if yer life depended on it." The sailor cast a jaundiced eye on the soldiers just now arriving at the tip of the sandbar. His expression indicated that he counted them out as any real opposition. All he wanted to do was return to the fishing boat and ply his trade.

Molimo dropped onto the seat beside the sailor and gripped the oar. Four smooth pulls took them far beyond the range of the Steel Crescent. None appeared eager to leave even the tenuous contact with land and swim after the fleeing nun and her friends.

Zolkan perched on the stern of the boat and shouted obscenities at the soldiers.

"Yer friend here, he's got quite a filthy mouth on him," observed the sailor.

"Shut up and row, you pile of pigeon shit. They still might come after us," said Zolkan.

Even as the *trilla* bird spoke a hand gripped the rotted wood side and tried to capsize the skiff. The sailor yelped and flailed about, and Molimo was thrown to one side, off-balance. Only Kesira reacted. Again, from deep within, she found the odd speed within slowness to respond with superhuman quickness. The remaining piece of her stone-wood staff amounted to little more than a stake. Kesira lifted it and brought it down directly into Nehan-dir's hand.

Nehan-dir shrieked and kicked, further rocking the boat. His other hand swung a dagger, but with his right hand injured he couldn't maintain his grip. He slipped off and thrashed about in the water, trying to pull out the wood spike and stay afloat at the same time.

"Bitch! You will suffer for a thousand days! I'll see that Lenc uses you for—"

Nehan-dir sputtered as Zolkan swooped low and clawed at his face. Only by submerging did the Steel Crescent's leader succeed in avoiding new facial scars.

"Fish-faced enemy of decency," grumbled Zolkan, re-alighting on the stern of the boat. By this time both the sailor and Molimo had recovered. They bent their backs and rowed, making the small skiff glide across the water with impressive speed.

Only when they touched against the hull of the larger fishing boat did Kesira relax. The soldiers still stood at the end of the sandbar shouting curses and promising death and torture. She watched as two of them rescued their leader and led Nehan-dir off to be bandaged.

"Come on up, milady. You look the worse for wear, you do." The captain of the small boat thrust out a gnarled hand for Kesira. Gratefully she let the man lift her the few feet to the boat's heaving deck. "Breezing up a mite, she is. Have to get 'er turned into the wind or ship some water."

The man was short, hardly taller than Kesira herself, but what he lacked in height he more than made up for in bulk. A heavy sea jacket strained at the seams to hold in the muscle, and his bandy legs showed long years at sea. His rolling gait exactly matched the boat's motion so that

Kesira felt she danced around while the captain and his ship stayed perfectly stationary. It made her increasingly queasy.

"Still, it's a good thing to be on the sea again, storm or no. That blasted winter kept the entire Sea of Katad froze over, it did. Never seen its like. And I ast my old da about it, I did. He never saw the like, neither."

"Thank you for rescuing us like this." Kesira perched against the rail and swallowed hard. The boat's surging motion made her seasick.

"Think nothing of it. When your bird landed and spoke with us, we knew what had to be done. A pleasure to do it, mark my words."

"Yer letting that damn feathered menace run the *Foul,* if yer ast me," grumbled the sailor who had rowed them to the boat.

"No one's asking you, bilge." The snap of authority entered the captain's words. Perhaps he commanded only a small fishing boat, but he was captain and brooked no rebellion in his ragtag ranks.

Zolkan landed beside Kesira and asked, "Met captain yet?"

"Of course," she said, wondering at the bird's lapse. The *Foul*'s captain stood not five feet away.

"Not *him,*" Zolkan said disdainfully. "Captain. Him." One vivid green wing extended and pointed toward a cross bracing where another *trilla* bird sat, surveying the world as if he owned it.

Kesira smiled a little at the sight of the other bird. This explained what the sailor meant when he took the captain to task for letting the "damn feathered menace" run the boat.

"Name's Yinzan," said Zolkan. "Not a bad sort but aggressive. Very opinionated."

"You mean, this Yinzan doesn't always agree with you," said Kesira. She had to laugh now.

The other *trilla* bird fluttered down to perch beside Zolkan. Beak to beak, particolored crests furling and unfurling, they chattered away in shrill notes, ignoring Kesira. She heaved herself to her feet and lurched off to find the captain. He worked to get the sails furled against the wind's increasing force.

"Captain, is there a place where I might get out of the spray?"

"The wee one's needin' his lunch, is that it?" asked the weathered man. He peered down at the infant, then frowned, as if looking into a charnel pit. "Down there. Take my cabin, such as it is."

Kesira wondered at his reaction, then shrugged it off. She sat on the edge of the hard bunk and brought the baby out, holding him up so she could get a good look at him. "What is it about you that strikes everyone as so strange?"

The infant didn't cry or even gurgle. The pale eyes stared fixedly.

"Zolkan doesn't want anything to do with you, but that is only normal. *Trilla* birds aren't noted for liking anything that takes away from their adulation. As for Molimo, he seems almost frightened of you, yet protective enough. What secrets do you hold in that tiny little body?" Kesira bounced the boy up and down in synchronization with the rolling of the boat.

No answers came. Kesira fed the infant, sighing as she felt the hungry mouth begin its meal.

Later she slept on the hard bunk, more from exhaustion than from normal need. The tossing and wallowing motion of the fishing boat awoke her near sunset. Kesira rocked the baby but he still slept, even as she put him into the sling around her shoulders. Wobbling, the nun made her way to the deck, now washed constantly by the heaving green water from the Sea of Katad.

"Stay below," shouted the captain. "The *Foul* is a staunch boat, but this miserable, demon cursed weather . . ." The rest of his words were swallowed by the high wind singing through the masts.

Kesira needed no urging to return to the relative safety below decks. She found Yinzan and Zolkan still engrossed in complex bird arguments. Molimo held on to a brace in the boat's hull and looked more than a little sick. Kesira dropped down beside him, hand resting on his shoulder.

"Try not to fight it so," she said. "The motion is violent, but you get used to it. I almost have." Even as she spoke Kesira knew that she lied. Her stomach tensed into a small fist, then tried to rush up her esophagus and erupt from her mouth. It didn't do her any good when Molimo laughed at her discomfort. The odd croaking noise had to be a laugh, she thought.

Together they sat and rode out the storm, each lost in deep thought. The two *trilla* birds conversed loudly and unintelligibly. From the expression on Molimo's face she doubted that he understood what passed between the birds, either. Kesira's mind wandered away: from the baby, from Molimo, from Zolkan and the boat, and back to the fight on the sandbar. She had *heard* a voice inside her head, and that voice had triggered her speed and power. It was her body, her muscle, her reaction, but the voice had released it when the nun had thought herself totally drained.

What had it been?

Kesira looked up at Molimo, but the man-wolf sat with eyes squeezed shut and lips pulled into a thin line. She couldn't help but feel proud of him. He had worked hard to keep control of the transformation, and had, for the most part, succeeded. The few times he had slipped and let out the animal, he had killed—and saved her life.

"Yinzan says boat founders."

"What?" Kesira's attention snapped to Zolkan. "What are you saying?"

"*Foul* is doomed ship. Prepare to sink."

"What about you?" Kesira demanded. "Can you fly in this weather? The wind? The rain?"

"Captain works us toward shore. No problem for *trilla* birds," Zolkan assured her. "But you and Molimo must prepare."

"Does the crew know?"

"Only four of them. They know. They are sailors and

no fools. Storms left from Ayondela's curse, Yinzan thinks. Smart bird, that Yinzan. Runs *Foul* and keeps captain in line."

Kesira shook Molimo awake, if he had been sleeping at all, and quickly repeated all Zolkan had said. The man heaved himself up on unsteady legs, checked Kesira and the baby, then led the way to the deck. Below, Kesira had doubted the bird's appraisal. When she saw the broken spars and the way the decking pulled up to expose the slowly filling cargo holds, she believed.

"Captain!" she shouted into the gale-force wind. "Should we take to the skiff?"

The man either didn't hear or he ignored her. He continued pulling at the rudder, muscles bulging and his own curses shoved back down his throat by the wind.

"What are we going to do?" she called to Zolkan. The *trilla* bird stood in the doorway with Yinzan. The two conferred. Zolkan took to wing and landed ponderously on Kesira's shoulder so that his beak pressed hard and wet against her ear.

"To skiff. Try to stay afloat for another hour. Storm nears peak as demons battle."

"What? Demons fighting?"

The *trilla* bird stared at her with one beady black eye, as if she were demented. "What else do you think causes such storm winds? Demons everywhere—and their spawn litter ocean depths. Beware sea, Kesira. Beware!"

Kesira and Molimo lurched toward the skiff just as the *Foul* split in half. Curtains of cold green water rose up on either side, waiting to swallow them without a trace.

Chapter Four

THE *FOUL* BROKE APART with a deafening roar. One half of the fishing boat twisted crazily and floated away, caught on high waves. The other half started straight for the bottom of the Sea of Katad—Kesima and Molimo clinging to its railing.

"The skiff!" the woman cried. She felt Molimo's strong hand gripping her skirt, pulling her along. Her own arms cradled the baby nestled against her breast. Together the three managed to get to the tiny skiff bouncing like a cork on the stormy sea. Sputtering, swimming, flailing, Kesira fought her way through the water, keeping on her back to prevent the infant from drowning. Molimo pulled her into the small boat.

She examined the infant. While awake and aware the boy did not cry out. Kesira wondered if the baby bore Molimo's affliction, but she remembered the feel of the tiny tongue, and this wouldn't affect crying. In a way, the infant's fortitude shamed her. She reacted more strongly to all that happened than to the baby—and babies were supposed to cry whenever something angered them or they grew fearful or scared.

Molimo just sat in the boat, slumped forward.

"Shouldn't we row?" Kesira called over the roaring winds. The cutting edges of the storm raked at her cheeks and brought tears to her eyes. While summer had reasserted itself after Ayondela's curse had been lifted, the water only slowly warmed. She felt every droplet of salty spray that hit her as a cold, wet fist. Kesira flinched and dodged the blows, but it did her no good. She kept her arms wrapped tightly around the baby, protecting him the best she could.

Molimo pointed: no oars. During the storm they had been washed away. Kesira wiped the water from her eyes and looked for them. The sight of what remained from the *Foul* convinced her that they were lucky to be alive.

"We must look for survivors," she said. Then it struck her; they had no choice in the matter. The wind and wave action carried them like a fallen leaf in a millrace. Without oars they were at the mercy of the elements. If they happened on one of the fishermen, fine. But they had no way to actively seek out those who might still be alive.

Kesira watched in mute horror as the part of the *Foul* that had stayed afloat broke into smaller pieces under a twenty-foot-high wave's crushing fall. In minutes no trace of the fishing boat could be found in the heaving ocean.

"See anyone?" she shouted.

Molimo shook his head.

Kesira settled down in the tiny boat, praying that the waves wouldn't inundate them, that the storm would die down, that they'd sight land soon. Most of all she prayed that the baby would survive. Kesira carried a heavy burden with the child. Not only had she seen the boy's parents killed, but also she had been directly responsible for their deaths.

Even deeper, she had a debt to repay. Sister Fenelia had taken her in when she had scarcely eight summers to her credit. Kesira had to see the boy placed in a good home where his upbringing would follow the moral teachings of Gelya. As the boat bucked and jerked in the storm she wondered how she would accomplish such a noble goal. Her mission had died with Lenc's attack on the nunnery.

The sight of Lenc's cold, white flame burning hungrily on Gelya's altar had become indelibly etched on her consciousness. No matter how long she lived, how quickly she died, that memory would fester within her.

"Oh, Gelya, you were too good," she said, sobbing. "The power of the jade made Lenc the stronger, and your integrity didn't allow you to truly fight him."

Arms circled her. She blinked away the salty mat forming over her eyes and saw Molimo. She snuggled closer, his strength flowing into her. If she died, she would do so knowing that her life had not been lived totally in vain. She had friends, she had performed duties for Emperor and her order the best she knew how. Never had Kesira Minette disgraced their name or her own.

Molimo holding her, and she holding the baby, they went to sleep.

Hot sunlight poured over her, drying her skin and caking on itchy salt. Kesira stirred. A voice demanded, "Will you pay their freight or not?"

"Zolkan?"

"Who else?" the *trilla* bird said, obviously irritated. "Yinzan will negotiate, but you must assure them of good seas. Superstitious lot, those sailors."

Kesira struggled to sit up in the unsteady boat. They had taken a considerable amount of water. Even with Molimo's constant bailing they sat ankle-deep. She supposed some of the boat's seams had opened during the storm. It amounted to nothing less than a miracle that a huge wave hadn't engulfed them and sent them to the bottom of the sea—like the *Foul*.

"They will haul you into port if you promise them clear sailing."

"I can't do that. Even when my order existed, we didn't converse directly with our patron. How am I supposed to say whether there'll be another storm?"

Molimo dug in his pack and pulled out his tablet. A quick move of his stylus produced, "Promise them. We sink."

"But what if there *is* another storm?"

"No storm," assured Zolkan. "Yinzan and I both see nothing but clear skies all way to horizon."

Kesira looked at the bird skeptically, then stood and put cupped hands to her mouth. "Hello!" she shouted. "Will you grant us passage to Lorum Bay?"

"The bird's relayed our terms. Will there be fair weather or nay?" came the reply. A short, gray-haired man clung to the side rail. Nothing differentiated him from the other sailors except for the snap of command in his voice.

"I am a sister of the Mission of Gelya," Kesira called back. "The power to cast the rune sticks is vested in me. There will be no adverse weather for . . ."

"Tell him two weeks," said Zolkan.

". . . for a fortnight."

"A full fortnight?" the captain shouted back.

"One day less," said Kesira, deciding that this sounded better than simply agreeing. The authority in her voice as she told the lie impressed even her—and it carried with the fisherman.

"Catch the line. We are bound for Lorum Bay. But there is one more matter to decide."

Molimo pulled the battered skiff along a line toward the fishing vessel and tethered it to a dangling, rusted metal ring. Even as one of the sailors helped Kesira onto the main deck, the skiff started to sink. Molimo had to tread water before shinnying up the rope lowered for him. With a careless whack a sailor used his long knife to sever the rope binding the skiff to the ring. Tiny bubbles rose to mark the watery grave that might have been theirs.

"Never seen wood sink," muttered the captain. "Strange times, strange beasts out here in the sea."

"What was the other condition?" asked Kesira, settling the baby in her arms as she glanced around.

"Might be more'n you're willing to trade," the man said. "But you got little enough choice. Might heave you back into the drink if you don't agree."

"This matter is one you feel strongly about?"

"Aye, that I do. I want the *trilla* bird."

"Zolkan!" she said in surprise. "I can't barter him away. Even if it means swimming for shore."

"Shore's a long ways off. A good three leagues."

"He is not mine to give. He—"

"Agree," came Zolkan's broken squawk. "Captain does not mean me. He talks of Yinzan. Yinzan wants to be aboard another boat, now that *Foul* is sunk."

Kesira let out a gusty sigh of relief. The other *trilla* bird's motives were unclear to her, but he had obviously found himself a post aboard the fishing boats that made him indispensable.

"Certainly," she said to the captain. "Yinzan will be happy to continue on with you, and I give you my blessings on this also." Zolkan launched himself into the air and flapped hard to gain altitude. In a few seconds he joined a second green spot aloft. They circled one another for a full minute before a loud caw sounded and both Zolkan and Yinzan fluttered down from the sky, zigzagging around one another, forming a chain pattern of emerald-green feathers as they came. Zolkan landed on the deck railing and began to preen. The other *trilla* bird perched on the captain's shoulder, peering curiously at Kesira, as if she had taken on the appearance of some odd deep-sea creature washed ashore.

"How long till we reach Lorum Bay?" she asked. "I think my friends and I need a good rest."

The captain squinted and rubbed a stubbled chin. "We struck a good bargain, so we'll head directly for the port. Three days. Less, if the winds favor us." He hesitated, then asked, "That your boychild?"

Kesira stiffened; his tone was all wrong. "Yes," she answered. "He is in my care."

"Lost my own son." The captain hesitated, then moved closer, staring down at the infant. Bold, pale eyes peered up at the weather-beaten sailor. "Shame he's not an orphan. Give you good money in exchange for him. Raise him as my own."

Molimo stood behind the captain and slowly shook his head, but Kesira didn't require the prompting.

"We have family in Lorum Bay we haven't seen in some time." The captain seemed to know that Kesira was lying but did not pursue the matter. He turned and began bellowing out orders to get the boat moving.

With Molimo close by her side Kesira said, "Strange. He was more interested in the baby than he ought to have been. I didn't believe him when he said he'd lost a son, either."

Molimo hastily wrote, "We are better off away from this boat."

Kesira agreed. And she got nothing when she questioned Zolkan. Neither he nor Yinzan had any explanation for the captain's roundabout request to adopt the infant. And, through it all, the baby watched silently, never emitting even a whimper.

"They look as if they are coming out to meet us," Kesira said uneasily. Four longboats filled with armed men slid through the calm waters of Lorum Bay's smelly harbor.

"Routine, nothing more," said the captain. "The harbormaster's an old friend of mine. He and his drinking cronies a'times come to personally greet me."

The man moved away to tend to lashing down some small boxes on deck. Kesira turned to Molimo and said, "The captain's lying. I don't know why, but those soldiers come for us."

Molimo hurried below decks to get their sparse belongings. He returned carrying the infant, as if the child might break at any moment. Kesira laughed and took the baby, slinging him in front. She stretched and settled the straps, then motioned for Zolkan to join them. The *trilla* bird dropped to the railing in front of the nun and nervously sidestepped back and forth.

"What do you make of the captain's visitors?" she asked the bird.

Zolkan turned his head around fully and cast a biased

eye on those rowing out to the fishing boat. "Yinzan knows nothing of them," the bird said. "I am inclined to believe him. Captain is nothing more than pigeon shit—Yinzan will soon enough change that. But these?" Zolkan let out a mournful squawk.

"You don't trust the captain? Does Yinzan?"

"All humans untrustworthy," said Zolkan. "Yinzan can remake captain. But these do not look peaceful."

Molimo tugged at her arm and motioned for her to join him on the far side of the deck, out of sight of the long-boats. Strangled noises came from Molimo's throat, indicating his extreme agitation. He pointed to the water. Bits of garbage and other harbor debris slapped against the side of the fishing boat.

"I don't understand," Kesira said. "What do you want me to see?"

On the wood railing Molimo outlined "Off!"

Without even tensing he jumped flat-footed over the railing and into the water. He surfaced and motioned for Kesira to follow. She looked over her shoulder and saw that the captain's attention focused on those in the approaching boats. The man yelled his greetings and lowered a rope ladder. Kesira slipped over the railing and kicked free, falling into the water.

She surfaced and floated on her back to allow the baby to breathe. The infant smiled at her, seeming to enjoy the unexpected bath.

"What now?" she asked. Molimo pointed toward a rocky breakwater, then began swimming with powerful, slow strokes. Kesira found herself hard-pressed to keep up with even this slow pace because of her need to hold the baby's head above water. But they had reached the largest of the boulders and were pulling themselves up when the cry rose from the fishing boat. Armed men stormed about, screaming and cursing, brandishing their swords and having at the sailors.

Snippets drifted across to where Kesira and Molimo crouched.

". . . lied to me!" The soldier lifted a heavy-bladed sword and brought it down with a meaty *thunk!* Kesira winced as red exploded from the captain's neck. The sailor half turned, to tumble over the railing and into the bay.

"Are we the cause of that?" she wondered aloud.

Zolkan alighted on a nearby rock and stretched one cramped wing. He carefully tucked it back before saying, "Yinzan apologizes for this. Shit for brains thought this treacherous captain good man. He sold us to soldiers."

"But how?" asked Kesira, confused. "We just dropped anchor an hour ago."

Zolkan snorted and shook his head at her stupidity. "Semaphore. Flagman relayed message to shore."

"Are those mercenaries?"

"Not Steel Crescent," said Zolkan. "Others. Many seek us now."

"Wonderful," Kesira said, sinking down to the ground. "Two jade demons seek to kill us, the entire Order of the Steel Crescent hunts us like rabbits, and now a new player comes into the game. And we don't even know who it is or why they want us!"

A tiny hand clutched at her blouse. Kesira looked down into the baby's pale eyes. No matter who sought them, it was suppertime. Irritated, Kesira allowed the infant to feed.

"Yinzan wants nothing more to do with us," explained Zolkan. "Bird thinks we are jinxed." The bird landed heavily on the street after an hour's reconnaissance of the village. He yawned and clacked his beak, then settled down as if to roost.

"He might be right," grumbled Kesira. "Nothing has gone our way since we came ashore." All day had been spent tramping along the cobblestone streets of Lorum Bay looking for—what? The woman couldn't say, but she figured that she'd know it when she saw it. A friendly face, a tiny mission to Gelya or another sympathetic patron, even a chance meeting in the street.

All of Lorum Bay walked as if it had been sentenced to die within the month. No one smiled. Children hunkered fearfully in doorways, not laughing or playing or begging. The street vendors listlessly pointed to their wares instead of actively hawking them. What few entertainers lined the byways sang off-key or juggled poorly. If Kesira hadn't known better, she would have thought that everyone in Lorum Bay had died and only their bodies inhabited the streets and alleys.

Never before had she seen a town without soul.

Even the thieves refused to ply their trade.

"Well, Zolkan, you're the one who insisted that Ayondela could be found in Lorum Bay. Where is she?" asked Kesira, not certain that she really wanted to find the female demon.

"Many talk secretively of clouds," said Zolkan. "Do not understand it. Foolish humans know nothing of clouds, of soaring through them, of feeling icy tingles along your feathers. Wondrous sensations." The bird waddled back and forth, doing a little dance. "They wet the wings so that—"

"Never mind, Zolkan," Kesira said, forestalling further discussion of how it felt to soar. "Did you happen across any information about those soldiers who met the boat?"

"Not of Ayondela's service," he said. "Nor of Steel Crescent."

Kesira gently rocked the baby as she thought. Finally she said, "There's no evidence Ayondela is here. Let's leave the village and see if we can't find more information in the foothills. Lonesome farmers tend to accumulate gossip from any traveler. These tight-mouthed city folk aren't any help at all."

A nearby man gasped and then let out a wordless cry of alarm. He levered himself to his feet and raced down the street, his boots click-clack-clicking as he ran. Others hearing the outcry hurried indoors, slamming shutters and barring their entryways.

"What did he see?" Kesira asked. Neither Zolkan nor

Molimo seemed to know. She had to trust their more acute senses.

"Fog drifting down street, nothing more," said the bird.

A wolf's howl cut the stillness. Kesira spun. Molimo had transformed into his wolf form and surged forward, fangs snapping at the foggy tendrils reaching out with mist-damp intent.

If Molimo's first cry had been one of challenge, the second, when he entered the fog, turned to pain and fear. The sleek gray wolf bolted from the fog, covered with a myriad of tiny cuts. Kesira tried to grab him as he ran past and failed. Her arms came away covered with the other-beast's blood.

"What happened?" she asked.

"Stay back," cautioned Zolkan. "Fog deadly."

"Why? How?"

"Leave *now*." Zolkan took to wing, not waiting to see whether Kesira followed his advice. She stepped toward the silent fog, frowning at the texture. In the Yearn Mountains, where she had been raised, fog banks were common. She remembered fun-filled days as a child romping in them, she and the other sisters laughing and hiding, letting the floating clouds veil them as they acted out passion plays.

A tiny hand tugged at her blouse. "I'm not going to enter," she told the infant. "I saw what happened to Molimo." But Kesira held out a hand as the vaporous wisps drifted closer.

She screamed as wet droplets lacerated her flesh. She jerked away, almost stumbling. In confusion Kesira stared at her injured hand. It looked as if some demented demon had taken razors to it. Long, thin streaks of blood sprang up and dripped to the paving.

"Enough of this," she said, backpedaling from the mist. The woman turned and found only locked doors. And at the other end of the street came a new bank of fog, moving with a relentless pace toward her.

Kesira yelped as the other blanket of fog stroked over

her arm. Cuts only a fraction of an inch deep appeared wherever the mist touched her.

She didn't have to be told that she'd discovered yet another magical weapon of the jade demons.

"Ayondela!" Kesira called. "This will not stop me. You will not triumph. *You will not!*"

Like the jaws of a vise, the clouds of floating death closed on her.

Chapter Five

THE MIST TOOK ON an ominous life of its own, gray tendrils turning into grasping hands that followed Kesira's every move. She dodged; the vapor flowed to block her escape. She clutched the baby to her chest as she sought a path away from the deadly, cutting fog.

Kesira saw no escape.

All the doors had been securely fastened, and not even a curious eye peered through cracks or knotholes in the shutters.

"Help me!" she called out. No response. Kesira yelped in sudden pain as a thin tendril of the mist wrapped around her ankle. Where it touched, bright red blood sprang from new wounds. Another thready line of gray dampness sank from above, lightly brushing her cheek. This time Kesira experienced no pain, but the blood trickling down her face told her that she would soon perish unless she found shelter.

"What's wrong with you?" she called. "I will *die* if you don't let me inside!"

Kesira kicked on door after door. Behind one, she heard angry voices: a woman wanting her let in, a man protesting. Kesira had to hurry along because of the encroaching fog. She found fewer and fewer doors to knock on, fewer shutters to try to open with her fumbling fingers. The mist circled her now, moving closer and closer with every light puff of breeze off the harbor.

"No," she said in horror. "Not this way." Kesira had

survived battles with two jade demons. Dying in a magical mist mocked her earlier successes.

"The little one," came a broken, gravelly voice. "Is he all right? This is important!"

Kesira whipped around. Pressed into a niche in the stone wall stood an old man with long, flowing white locks; rheumy eyes; a nose the size of a potato, complete with sprouts; and a face that seemed kindly, concerned.

"The boy is unharmed—so far. There's nothing I can do to get away from the fog. What is it?"

"A curse," the old man said. He gusted a deep sigh of resignation. "If I could make it vanish, I would. But, alas, this is beyond my feeble abilities."

"Then there's no hope for us," Kesira said. Already her mind turned inward and sank quickly to the depths where her darkest nightmares lurked. She sought them now, facing them squarely so that death would not be feared.

"Wait!" the old man said. He hobbled forward, making an impatient gesture with his hand when a wispy column of fog swirled around him. The fog slid away from him, refusing to touch his flesh, just as oil and water refuse to mix. "You must come with me."

Without waiting for an answer the old man forged ahead, ignoring the fog. Kesira hesitated. A small wake of safety formed behind him as he went. Kesira knew she would have no better chance than this. She plunged into the deadly fog, cringing as occasional moist fingers probed for her flesh. While she sustained a few bloody streaks, the fog seemed unable to do more serious damage as long as she pressed close to the old man.

"Who are you?" she asked. "How is it that you know about the baby? How do you keep the fog at bay?"

"I watched you earlier with the boychild dangling around your neck. It must be a fearsomely tiring way to go through life, burdened thus."

"It's comfortable enough. More so than holding the baby in my arms."

"Ah, so it is, so it is." The white-haired man turned

and made a quick ninety-degree turn that confused Kesira. She had tried to keep a mental image of their path through the fog, but now she saw only gray swirls and the cobblestones beneath her feet. She pressed even closer to her guide.

"How do you keep the mist away from us?"

"The mists," he said, never slowing his pace or looking at her, "are magical. You knew as much. Lenc sends them to cow the good people of Lorum Bay."

"Effective," Kesira said bitterly.

"Aye, effective. Lenc is quite astute in knowing another's weakness. Remember that. He sniffs out weakness the way a hunting dog follows a spoor."

Kesira frowned. The old man spoke too intimately of Lenc to be a simple citizen of this coastal village.

"You are quite correct," he said, answering her unspoken thoughts. "I know Lenc. Ayondela also. Actually it is she who sends these cursed mists. Poor Ayondela, gone astray. The death of her son unsettled her fragile mind."

"Who are you?"

"Which demon, is that your question?" The old man laughed delightedly as they emerged from the fog and into the wan sunlight that was trying to instill some joy to Lorum Bay's fear-cloaked streets.

"I have met several," Kesira said, carefully choosing her words. "Some have been very nice."

"Gelya? No, you never met your patron, did you? Pity. He was an exceptional one, Gelya was. One of the few who bothered with dropping down among you mortals to impart some small gems of wisdom."

The old man—the demon—pushed open a rickety door and bowed low, indicating that Kesira should enter first. She protected the infant with her arms and bent body, then went inside. The dimness brought her up short. She imagined that she had walked into a black velvet curtain, but when her eyes adapted to the low light, she saw a nicely appointed, if somewhat Spartan, dwelling. On a low table stood a ceramic water pitcher and several glasses.

"Those are special," said the demon, following her in and closing the door. "Crystal from the Emperor's very own supplier. You mortals do some things very well and making leaded crystal is one. I envy you this art."

"You've tried it?" Kesira asked in surprise.

"Of course I have. Isn't creation of beauty one of Gelya's teachings? It is certainly worthy of anyone's time, whether they be mortal or demon. My crystal, however, never quite attained such clarity or tone." He thumped a finger against the rim of one glass. The pure, clear note seized Kesira and shook her gently, evoking pleasant memories, inciting a riot of tastes on her tongue, softly stroking her cheeks, summoning memories of first love. A single tear ran from the corner of her eye.

"That's the prettiest sound I've ever heard," she said, wiping away the tear. "It . . . does things to me."

"The maker of the glass is imbued with a gift unlike any other mortal's," said the old man. He settled down into a chair. Kesira couldn't tell if the sounds she heard now were from joints creaking or the wood protesting its slight burden.

"And your gift," the demon continued, "is even more amazing to one such as I."

"What? But you're a demon," Kesira blurted.

"A minor one, a very small one in the pantheon of the great." The demon stroked over his bare chin, then ran long, bony fingers through his white hair. "If I had any true power, I'd not be long in this body. Every movement is a trial for me." He straightened his legs. The popping sounds confirmed what Kesira had guessed at before. Joints too arthritic for fluid motion plagued him.

"I don't even know your name. I am—"

"Kesira Minette," he interrupted. "I have followed your path with some interest since you came to my attention on Ayondela's Isle of Eternal Winter." He poured water from the pitcher into one of the crystal glasses. "I am Cayabbib."

Kesira took the water gratefully. It had been too long

since she had eaten or drunk. But as thirsty as she was, she found it impossible to swallow more than a single mouthful; and even stranger, this one swallow sated both her thirst and hunger.

"Don't feel guilty that you have never heard the name. Cayabbib is hardly rolling off everyone's tongue these days."

"What's your interest in me?" she asked, putting down the glass with great reluctance. Kesira wanted to sample the strange brew further, even though it had slaked her thirst and hunger. She remembered all too vividly the times when she and Molimo had suffered from starvation. A single pint of this elixir would have carried them over nicely.

"You remember Toyaga?" the demon asked. He shifted around and moved to a more comfortable chair. He settled with obvious relief. Again sounded the crackling of his joints. "He summoned me for a small chat while running from Ayondela and Eznofadil. This was before your friend Zolkan convinced him to return and battle the jade power."

"So?"

"I am a minor demon, worshiped by some, ignored by the rest. Here in Lorum Bay rose a tiny group of followers loyal to me. I visited them on rare occasions, but it satisfied them. Unlike Gelya, I placed no stringent teachings upon my disciples. Perhaps I was too lenient. They seemed to prefer it that way, and I was only too happy to oblige."

"Why bother at all? Many—most—demons never sought worshipers or proselytes."

"My dear one, I felt a duty to humankind. Foolish, yes, time has shown that. I did too little, contributed too little time to the effort. Gelya created a positive force in this world. You are proof of that. But I?" The old man snorted in self-deprecation. "I had nothing to offer and gave of it stintingly."

"Why did you save me from the fog?" Kesira perched uneasily on the corner of the low table, trying to decide whether she really faced a demon or a demented old man lost in the wandering corridors of senility. The only tangible fact that remained was the way the mist had parted for him, and this might be some simple trick anyone could learn.

"You have a destiny far outshining anything I can offer this poor world. Do you think Ayondela and Lenc have stopped visiting their terror on humanity because you broke Ayondela's spell?"

"I didn't really break it. The white flame faltered. I . . . I had nothing to do with that."

Cayabbib shook his head sadly. "You do not believe that. You are intelligent and fearless. Your courage broke the flow of evil feeding the Lenc's flame. And thus was broken the spell. On my most potent day I could never have accomplished a fraction of that awesome deed. You did it. You and your friends."

"You must possess some power. You know so much about me."

"Even this, my dear, requires no great skill. I listen. The Steel Crescent seeks you. The Emperor's guard seeks you."

"What?" Kesira shot to her feet. The baby stirred, both tiny fists gripping the edge of the sling and shaking angrily at the upset. "What has Emperor Kwasian to do with me?"

"There are nodes of power, lines of flow, spots where nothing occurs—and other areas where all the magical worldlines coalesce. Inside you there is such a spot. You lack the power of jade, but there is something more, something different from the jade that Lenc fears."

"And what Lenc fears, others seek, is that what you're saying?" Kesira sat down again. "I don't believe your ravings."

Cayabbib smiled benignly. "I can do nothing to make you believe. That is beyond my power. Everything is, these days. As the power of the jade demons mounts mine declines.

"Listen," Cayabbib continued earnestly. "You have immense ability in casting the runes. Do you know its source?"

"From within. Gelya taught that we are able because we think that we are able."

"Sounds like Gelya's double talk," muttered Cayabbib. "Your ability is not shared. You of an entire world can accurately read the rune sticks. But the power is not yet refined and your control is spotty."

Kesira said nothing. She knew this better than Cayabbib ever could. The feel of the five bone sticks slipping from her fingers to fall was one thing, the interpretation of their positions another matter altogether. Sensations rose within her as she gazed at the lay of the bones, and the feelings hinted at vast wildernesses of meaning only vaguely comprehensible to her. But truth rested in those throws of the rune sticks.

Once, she had sensed another's presence guiding her.

"Merrisen," said the demon in a voice almost too low to hear.

"He died," she said, tiring of this. "He perished in battle with Lenc."

"A demon's body can die while his spirit lives on. Merrisen might have chosen this path to confuse his enemies. The power of jade is too great, even for one such as Merrisen."

"You speak in riddles. I must go find my friends." Kesira cradled the baby in her arms and went to the door. She saw the light mist forcing its way inside through tiny cracks and knotholes.

"Open the door and the fog will slice you to bloody rags," Cayabbib said. "I can part the fog, but that is the limit of my power. Ayondela seeks your death. The fog is her way of doing it. The crystal clouds do her bidding."

The infant bubbled and spat at the door. Only drool ran down his chin. Kesira absentmindedly wiped it away, her attention on the mist sliding into the room.

"You're saying I'm trapped here?"

"Ayondela wants you. Lenc wants more." The old demon took on a more substantial air, as if he had made a decision and knew it meant his death.

"You want something from me. What is it?"

"Poor Kesira Minette, your burden will be more than I could bear. But you will triumph—as long as you do not doubt yourself. Fear kills small parts of your mind, but doubt will play the traitor and make you lose the good that might be won by action."

"You're starting to sound like Gelya." Kesira had to smile, but Cayabbib's expression chilled her. He meant all he said.

"You need powers not yet within you," Cayabbib declared.

"And how am I supposed to get these powers? By..." Kesira's words trailed off. She remembered how she had filled Wemilat the Ugly with the strength to fight Howenthal—and how some of that good demon's power had been transferred to her because of the lovemaking.

"It is your decision. I can promise you nothing. I can say this, however. Unless you accept the feeble skills I can give to you, Lenc will rule the world. This I know with absolute certainty."

Kesira stared at Cayabbib. She was a sister of the Mission of Gelya. More than the gold sash and the knotted blue cord around her waist proved that. While Gelya's death meant less to her than his life and teachings—and how she venerated those—Kesira carried the seeds of revenge within her bosom. Gelya had not approved of revenge.

Sister Dana, her best friend. Dead by Lenc's hand, burned by his cold, white flame. Sister Fenelia, a surrogate mother to her. Dead. And all the others that had become her family.

Kesira owed fealty to the Emperor, but most of all she owed an obligation to her slain sisters. Honor required that. Deep down she felt that carrying out her duty would benefit the world. The power of the jade would be crushed.

"The Time of Chaos is near," Cayabbib said in a low, quaking voice. "I have no will to survive it—or even see it arrive. The Time after will be yours, my dear. Seize this chance while I am still able to offer you what I can."

"You said Merrisen still lived. He opposed Lenc and the others. Can he aid me?"

The expression on Cayabbib's face was unreadable. "He is—or was—a force for good. You must discover much before you can tap powers as great as his."

"But he lives?"

"That is not for me to say. With the energies I can pass to you perhaps you will know." Cayabbib slumped. "Or perhaps not. I can't say. Even as we speak my abilities fade into darkness, and I slip silently behind them."

Kesira looked down at the baby. Those all-knowing eyes stared up at her. She wished the baby could speak, could tell her what thoughts ran through the tiny mind. What she sought was an answer.

That had to come from her own soul.

Kesira slowly pulled the sling straps off her shoulders and placed the baby in a padded chair. Cayabbib watched as she began to disrobe.

When they were finished, Kesira sat up in the soft bed and stared at the demon's husk beside her. All his energy had passed into her in a single rush of ecstasy—and dread.

For a long while Kesira simply sat and stared at the fallen demon. She had known him only a few minutes. This short span had not allowed her to come to like or dislike him, but she felt a certain sorrow for his plight. To be powerless and still see wrongs being committed tore a feeling person apart inside.

Kesira knew. She had witnessed the death and destruction wrought by the jade demons and had been able to do so little.

For another demon to see it and be unable to stop them, it had to be even worse.

For Cayabbib, Kesira held no emotion. For the future, she exulted. She now *knew* more than before. Skin shining whitely in the dim light, Kesira rose from the bed and fumbled through her clothing. She took out the box containing the five rune sticks. A single swift cast sent them tumbling onto the tabletop.

Gone were the horrors associated with the reaching and finding of arcane answers. No longer did Kesira feel danger at every step. She read the runes with an accuracy that seemed more than human to her. And it was. She had absorbed Cayabbib's essence and now used it.

Brown eyes lifted from the runic pattern to the bundle lying silently in the chair. Pale eyes stared unblinkingly back at her.

"The runes are positive on two points," she said to the baby. The infant's head bobbed slightly, as if agreeing with her. "Ayondela's death is within my power." Kesira swallowed hard. "And you are the key to her death lock."

The baby smiled and clenched one fist, waving it.

Silently Kesira dressed and slung the baby into his usual position. Molimo and Zolkan wandered about in Lorum Bay's streets. She had to find them. Hesitant at first, then with mounting confidence, Kesira went to the door and flung it open. Gray hammers of mist surged forward to envelop her—and failed.

As Cayabbib had done, Kesira now held the mist away. The magicks employed were small, but she had gained use of the simple trick. Unhindered, she strode out into the fog and down the street seeking her friends.

Mists parted and fell away. The pale sun shone down upon her with tentative rays made lukewarm by the harshness of the sea breeze. Kesira looked behind her and saw the fog whipping away in the face of such adversity. She canted her face to the sky and let the cold wind carry her short brown hair back from her head. For the first time in weeks Kesira experienced a serenity born from strength rather than tiredness. Cayabbib had perished; she had gained.

"One by one," she said to the baby, "the good patrons are used up and discarded. Why does it fall to me to witness this sadness?" Left unspoken was her equally eloquent plea to be free of the jade demons.

"Come, my little one, let's go find Molimo. He must be in desperate need by now. The fog cut him badly, and there's no predicting what devilment he might have found in his wolf form." While her words were light, heaviness lay within Kesira's heart. Molimo's condition boded only ill. If any of Lorum Bay's fine citizens saw the transformation, they'd kill Molimo without hesitation. The other-beasts produced by the power of illicit jade roved the plains and mountains, some changed permanently, and others were doomed to half existences like Molimo's. Never had Kesira found another who sympathized with the other-beasts or who tried to aid them in escaping their affliction.

Kesira swallowed hard. She denied it aloud, but her spirit spoke with a truthfulness that pained her. She loved Molimo, transformations to wolf or not.

"Is it pity?" she muttered. "Do I pity him the lack of tongue and the shape-changing? Or do I love him for his loyalty, bravery, the nobility hidden within his soul?"

The baby gripped her blouse and tugged gently. She smiled and stroked over the virtually hairless head. The baby turned and nestled closer to her breast, a contented smile on his face.

"Finding Molimo is important," she said, "but we must give you a name." She heaved a sigh. "We must find you a home."

Pale eyes shot open and stared at her with unflinching directness.

"The rune sticks," Kesira muttered. "How can a mere babe in arms be the weapon against Ayondela?"

The rattle of weapons startled her. Kesira looked up. Fear clutched at her throat, constricting it, making her giddy. The soldiers, marching along the street crossing perpendicularly to the one in which she stood, were all too familiar.

They followed the banner of the Steel Crescent.

Trying not to appear to hurry, Kesira walked to the storefront and peered into the tiny window, as if she were only a young matron out seeking a new dress. She used the glass as a mirror. The reflections of one mercenary after another marching along showed that Nehan-dir had mustered his full complement. Sounds of metal clashing against metal echoed down the deserted street. Wood creaked and splintered, and a woman shrieked in pain. Deeper voiced protests rose, only to be silenced with a quick dagger slash.

The Order of the Steel Crescent plied their trade in Lorum Bay. They killed and looted and raped.

Kesira's anger boiled, but the nun restrained herself from seeking open confrontation. Against armed soldiers she stood no chance at all. She turned and walked away, seeking Molimo or Zolkan. So intent was she on eluding the soldiers behind her and finding her friends that Kesira walked into someone.

"Sorry," she said, not paying any attention to the short man.

"Why? You have saved me much hunting. I was prepared to burn this village to the ground to find you." Kesira gazed in horror at the pink cobwebbing of scars on Nehan-dir's face. The diminutive mercenary's smile spread crookedly until his thin, cruel lips pulled back in a sneer.

Kesira turned to run, but fingers like steel bands closed on her arm and spun her around, slamming her hard into a stone wall.

"Don't run. There's so much we have to talk about," Nehan-dir said. His evil laugh mingled with the sounds of death created by his soldiers. Kesira stood motionless in his grip, too frightened to respond.

Chapter Six

"YOU HAVE DISGRACED ME for the last time," Nehan-dir said in a voice colder than a demon's curse. The man's scars began to pulse with the intensity of his emotion. Kesira tried to pull free, but the mercenary gripped down even harder, bruising her upper arm.

"I have no reason to attack you," Kesira said. "My fight is with Ayondela and Lenc "

"I serve Lenc."

"Don't," she pleaded. "Not all patrons are like Tolek the Spare."

"Never mention his name," Nehan-dir snarled. Lips pulled back and yellowed teeth revealed, the soldier looked more like a beast than a human. Kesira sensed the wrath bubbling up from the injury caused by the profligate demon. Tolek had traded all his worshipers to another demon in exchange for a small island and cancellation of his gambling debts. When those still loyal to Tolek discovered the trade, they had abandoned their patron and sought only those demons holding real power. Thus was born the Order of the Steel Crescent.

"Will there be any place for you in a world ruled by Lenc?" asked Kesira. "He is a cruel master now. What will happen when total power rests in the palm of his jade-green hand?"

"Even a demon cannot be in all places at once. He will require human captains to rule in his stead." Nehan-dir obviously considered himself a candidate for this exalted rank. "We of the Steel Crescent do our jobs well. We will be rewarded."

"As Tolek rewarded you?" Even as Kesira said the words, she knew she'd made a mistake. Nehan-dir doubled his fist and struck her squarely on the jaw. Only his other hand, still gripping her arm, prevented her from falling to the pavement. Nehan-dir jerked the nun erect and slammed her against the stone wall.

The buzzing in her head deafened her and turned her stomach. "Can't stand," Kesira muttered. She winced as pain shot into her jaw from even those few words.

"Killing you will be such a pleasure. I admired your stand against Ayondela on the Isle. True courage is seldom seen outside my order. But you go beyond courage to foolhardiness." Nehan-dir spun her around. All Kesira could think of was protecting the baby. Both arms cradled the child slung at her breast as she lost balance and went tumbling into the middle of the street.

As short as Nehan-dir was, he towered above her. Merciless eyes bored into her. "The only question is whether to kill you immediately or to allow my troops some small amusement with your body before you join your sisters."

Kesira hunched over to keep the infant from harm as Nehan-dir raised his fist to land another blow.

Zolkan launched himself into the air, flapped hard to hold position, then plummeted to land on the wolf's back.

Molimo twisted agilely and snapped at the *trilla* bird. Zolkan used both wing and talon to leap up and avoid the snapping fangs. With a movement even more dextrous, the bird dropped forward and sank his claws into Molimo's neck. Powerful pinions creaked and snapped as Zolkan lifted Molimo off his front paws by force of wing. A twist, a lunge, and Zolkan exposed the wolf's soft underside.

"Rip out your throat," promised Zolkan. "Calm yourself. Now. Do it *now!*"

The thrashing subsided as the gray wolf gave in to the inevitable. Zolkan's claws relaxed when he felt fur changing to human skin, steely tendons shortening and becoming heavier human muscle. Zolkan hopped off the supine figure and watched the last stage of transformation back to human with an air of resignation.

It could be so difficult keeping Molimo in a usable form.

"All right?" the bird asked.

No, spoke Molimo, his answer ringing inside the bird's skull. *I tried to keep from changing when the mists rolled down the street. I failed. I tried and failed!*

"Ayondela's magicks are potent," said Zolkan. "Never have I seen a spell like this one."

Molimo snorted and shook his head. *Of all beings I ought to be able to confront her magicks.*

"As you confronted Lenc's?"

Molimo shoved himself to a sitting position and glanced around. The street was still deserted, even though it was just an hour past midday. The cutting fog had driven the citizens of Lorum Bay indoors to stay. For that Molimo gave a quick but fervent thanks. When the transformation had seized him, he had slipped free of his clothing. Upon returning, he couldn't remember where his clothes were.

"Half a mile back in that direction," said Zolkan, lifting one wing and pointing. His heavy beak clacked several times. "Forget clothing. Get new."

Kesira?

"Concentrate," ordered Zolkan.

Molimo pulled up his knees and circled them with his arms. Naked in the street, he let his mind drift like a leaf on a softly flowing brook. His entire body stiffened when his questions found answers.

Cayabbib is dead, he told Zolkan.

"Cayabbib?"

A minor demon, hardly of Ayondela's stature. He . . . gave of himself to aid Kesira.

"She has partaken of his energy, as she did with Wemilat?" The *trilla* bird's voice carried a tone of disdain with it. "Human mating rituals are silly enough. Demon and human make even sillier pairing."

Molimo got to his feet and looked around for a few seconds. His dark eyes fixed on one small house set apart from the others. His hard fist pounded on the door. From inside came the tremulous voice, "What do you want?"

Molimo emitted a croaking noise that produced even more fear on the other side of the door. Zolkan fluttered to rest on the man's shoulder. The *trilla* bird let out a loud squawk of indignation. "Let us in! How dare you keep His Imperial Majesty waiting!"

The door almost shot open. The mousy man inside stared with saucer-round eyes. "Y-you're not the Emperor."

By then Molimo had pushed into the house and left Zolkan to explain.

"Stop that," protested the owner of the house. "You can't steal my belongings. Stop!"

"Be of good cheer, kind sir. Know you and His Puissant Majesty in most delicate mission."

"But he's not the Emperor." The words came with less conviction. "Is he?"

"Would you admit to having seen His Majesty naked?" Zolkan asked. "When this is capital crime?"

"I . . . why, no."

Molimo found a cloak, breeches too small but adequate, and a long tunic of soft, staple cotton. He donned what he could and hid the poor fit with the cloak.

"Your name, good sir, your name," demanded Zolkan. "How else can His Imperial Majesty properly reward you?"

"T'gobe," the man got out. "Oldfar T'gobe."

"Your Majesty," Zolkan said, landing on Molimo's shoulder. "Your beneficence ought to grant this good citizen at least a small duchy. At least."

"A duchy?" T'gobe bowed deeply as Molimo whirled past. The man was awed by such a dignitary blessing his humble abode with the Imperial presence.

You should go into politics," Molimo told the *trilla* bird. *That poor soul believed you.*

"What is not to believe? Are you not of nobility?"

Hardly.

"Gelya said belief is triumph of hope over reality."

Gelya prattled on too much for my taste. Molimo's long legs began pumping faster, his strides longer in his haste to find Kesira. Cayabbib's death assured Kesira of additional powers, but Molimo was at a loss to say exactly what those powers might be. He feared that the woman might feel invincible and attempt to confront Ayondela directly.

Cayabbib had never possessed powers adequate for more than trivial matters. Kesira might find herself in deadly trouble if she believed otherwise.

"Ahead," cawed Zolkan. "Soldiers."

Molimo frowned. These were not troops of the Steel Crescent.

"Emperor's guard," said the *trilla* bird.

This is why you were able to dupe the man so easily. He saw the Emperor's soldiers in town and believed it possible Kwasian himself commanded them.

Zolkan shrugged, sending a small flurry of green- and blue-tipped feathers to the ground. "Sometimes luck is better than skill."

"You there, halt!" called out an officer marching beside the squad. Gold braid gleamed in the strengthening midday sunlight. Several gaudy campaign ribbons on the officer's chest attested to a remarkable career—this was no palace dandy sent on a whimsical scavenger hunt.

Are there other soldiers nearby?

Zolkan took to the air, spiraling upward. The singsong speech he used when communicating directly with Molimo showered down: troops everywhere.

"You're not a local," the officer stated. "Who are you?"

Molimo pointed to his sundered mouth. The officer's attitude didn't change. Captain Protaro had seen worse during his military career. He only had three fingers on either hand, the others lost to battle and gangrene. The Sarabella campaign had reduced his regiment to seventy-three. By the time reinforcements came at Reun, the barbarians had slain all but four of his men. Not one was left whole, in body or mind. Oh, yes, he had seen worse than a clipped-out tongue.

"You can write. Who are you?" Protaro impatiently motioned for a tall, husky soldier and a companion to join them. The smaller soldier held out a pad with a stylus while the larger fingered his sword, obviously awaiting the command to slay.

"A poor peasant escaping the unnatural winter," Molimo wrote.

Protaro knocked him to the ground with an openhanded blow. "None of that. Who are you?"

Molimo shrugged. Protaro kicked him hard in the ribs.

Zolkan landed heavily on a rail and watched. The Guard captain studied the *trilla* bird, connecting his presence with Molimo.

"These might be the ones we seek," Protaro said to his clerk. "Has a more detailed description arrived?"

Zolkan began the singsong speech with Molimo, saying, "Can they truly identify us?"

Yes. Lalasa aids the Emperor. Just because she opposes Lenc does not mean she looks favorably on us. Her goals are not necessarily ours. Take to wing.

Some subtle muscle twitch warned Protaro. The Guard captain dived forward, fingers reaching for Zolkan. The *trilla* bird snapped at the hand and missed or he might have removed another or Protaro's fingers. By the time the captain recovered, Zolkan had jumped and become airborne. Heavy flaps took him beyond reach of the Emperor's Guard.

"Seize this one," Protaro commanded, indicating Molimo. "He must be the one Kwasian seeks."

The soldiers circled Molimo but did not consider him dangerous. He looked more like a clown in his ill-fitting clothing than a dangerous man. Joking and laughing, the guardsmen reached for him. Molimo kicked, spun, grabbed, and came away with one corporal's sword.

The corporal stood for an instant, stunned at being disarmed. Then he did the only honorable thing. He threw himself forward, oblivious to Molimo's thrust. The corporal's body wrenched the sword from Molimo's hand, even as it robbed the young soldier of his life.

"To left," squawked Zolkan from his aerial post. "You can escape them. And hurry! Kesira is captive of Nehan-dir."

Molimo damned himself for being so feeble. Once powerful, he was now trapped in weak flesh. Time healed him but slowly—too slowly.

He sprinted away from the soldiers, to their surprise; they had expected him to attempt to regain the fallen weapon. But Molimo had evaluated his chances and discarded any idea of rolling the corporal over and jerking free the sword from its bloody sheath.

The corporal had redeemed himself in the eyes of his comrades. Losing his weapon disgraced him; subsequent actions proved his devotion to the Emperor. None of this helped Molimo, however. Without sword he had little chance to fight off either the Emperor's Guard or stop Nehan-dir.

"Ahead," came the singsong direction from Zolkan. "Steel Crescent mercenaries ahead."

Molimo slowed his pace to allow Captain Protaro and his men to catch up. Even though he courted death, he had to keep the Guardsmen close. As he ran for where Nehan-dir held Kesira, Molimo began the spell given him by the demon Toyaga.

The world about me . . .

Molimo dodged a well-swung sword. A lock of his raven-dark hair leapt from his head as the backswing almost decapitated him. Protaro yelled that he should be captured, not slaughtered.

There are no eyes.

The second line of the spell rattled in his head, as if

parts had come loose. Power welled as he tapped the magicks known by the demons. "See her?" asked Zolkan. "Hurry! Oh, hurry! Nehan-dir will kill her!"

Freedom of the air and sky,
I fade into nothingness.

The spell finished, the power surging, Molimo was no longer visible. Not invisible, but non-noticeable. Protaro and his men found it difficult to focus on Molimo when Nehan-dir and a dozen other Steel Crescent mercenaries lined the street.

"The woman," snapped Captain Protaro. "She is the one. Stop those mercenaries. Attack!"

Molimo slipped across the street and under a low overhang to watch as the Emperor's Guard rushed forward in a broken line to meet the scattered followers of the Steel Crescent. To his surprise both sides proved equal in battle. Protaro and Nehan-dir squared off, the sounds of steel ringing against steel as they dueled. Well matched, they fought with silent competence.

Zolkan dropped into the middle of the fray and landed on Kesira's shoulder. Molimo heard the *trilla* bird say to her, "Escape now. Hurry! No time to dawdle."

The demonic spell began to fade as Molimo's strength waned. He motioned to her to join him, but the battle still separated them. Molimo agonized over aiding the woman.

Zolkan, he sent the silent message, *is she able to flee unaided?*

"Yes," came the immediate reply. "She was not harmed."

Molimo fumed. He saw the dark purple bruise forming on her chin where Nehan-dir had struck her. But the injury was minor compared to her fate if she stayed in the street.

Get her away when I create a diversion.

Zolkan thrust his beak close to Kesira's ear. When Molimo saw her nod, he acted. He ran from cover and dived, body level with the street. He smashed hard into two of the fighters. Both went down in a struggling pile. Molimo rolled on top of them, forced them back into a heap, then scooped up one's sword. A quick slash severed a hamstring muscle and produced a geyser of slippery blood.

Molimo darted here and there through the fray, not caring which side he attacked. Confusion was his ally. His fighting style left much to be desired, but Molimo accomplished his goal.

Zolkan called out, "All clear. Flee!"

The man-wolf gasped as a Guardsman's sword opened a shallow gash on his chest. Molimo fought to control his shape. Pain often triggered the other-beast change. He had to remain in possession of his human faculties if he wanted to escape and rejoin Kesira.

Dizziness passed and, with it, the urge to transform into wolf. Molimo lunged, parried, twisted free. His deft riposte robbed a Steel Crescent mercenary of life.

And then Molimo was alone in an alley. Sounds of battle dwindled as he staggered along. Panting, he halted and carefully checked the wound on his chest. Even though it was shallow and hardly more than a scratch, it produced a continuous trickle of blood that wouldn't clot. Molimo ripped off his stolen shirt and crudely tied it tightly around his chest as he exhaled. This restrained his breathing but kept constant compression on the wound.

Zolkan? went out his summons. *Where is Kesira?*

He received no answer. Cursing, Molimo doubled back to find the woman and the *trilla* bird.

"Down street. Hurry. Now!" urged Zolkan. The trilla bird almost fell from the woman's shoulder as she lurched to her feet and began running.

Zolkan craned his head around and saw Nehan-dir kick the feet out from under the Guard captain. And Zolkan never paused when he flung himself forward to intercept the blow intended for Kesira's head. The *trilla* bird met the flat of Nehan-dir's blade squarely. It sent Zolkan tumbling through the air, unconscious. He landed in a clump of lore weed, barely distinguishable from the bright green spines.

Kesira thought her friend had simply taken off in protest to her uneven gait. She fought to right herself, to get back the ground-devouring stride she normally used. Carrying the infant around her neck threw her off-balance, but Kesira kept moving.

In less than a minute she had thoroughly confused herself. Down alleys, through littered streets, past the deserted central market, she stumbled and ran, more unconscious than aware. When she stopped, she had the feeling she was near the harbor. Odd sounds drifted on the breeze, sounds she associated with wooden ships and saltwater-soaked hemp rope mooring them to piers.

Kesira rubbed her temples and eased some of the tension. The baby stared up at her, eyes accusing.

"Hungry?" she asked. "Not now. You'll have to wait until there's time. I've got to find Molimo." Kesira frowned. "And Zolkan. He took off in a way different than he usually does." She rubbed the spot on her left shoulder where the bird perched. Tiny spots of blood soaked through her blouse, showing how precipitous Zolkan's launch had been.

She sought shelter from probing eyes, then settled down to compose her thoughts. As she did so she let the baby suckle.

"Those were the Emperor's Guard fighting Nehan-dir," she decided aloud. "Molimo led them to me, but he fought both sides." Kesira frowned. Trying to sift through so much confusion left her with a new headache that threatened her composure. Meditation techniques eased the tension and brought forth a clearer mind. By the time she had regained her composure, the baby had finished his meal.

"You never cry, do you? So strange, after all you've seen in your young life," she said, soothing herself as well as the baby. "And you deserve a name."

Kesira felt a new bleakness in her soul. The baby did not belong with her. Duty forced her to battle the jade demons; this was no place for an infant. Only the powers she'd received from Wemilat's kiss on her breast allowed her to nurse the baby. He wasn't hers, and she ought not become too attached to him. Along with this, Kesira re-alized she had not given a name to the boy because, had she done so, parting with him would have been impossible.

"If only a mission remained. You would have flourished under Gelya's gentle hand," she told the boy.

"There is a place for the infant," came a deep voice. Kesira started to rise but found a sword point at her throat. Her gaze worked from the flat of the blade along the blood gutter, to hilt, to deformed hand holding the sword. "The Emperor orders your presence. Or rather, Kwasian orders the baby's. I see that the two of you are inseparable, if the youngling is to feed."

Kesira looked past Captain Protaro at the ring of Guardsmen. She had gone from being Nehan-dir's prisoner to the Emperor's in less than an hour. She wasn't certain this was any improvement in her condition.

Chapter Seven

"THERE'S NO NEED to cut my throat by inches. Either do it or take that thing away." Kesira Minette reached up and shoved Captain Protaro's sword from under her chin. The soldier's slow smile showed that he approved of her courage.

"The Emperor requests your presence."

Kesira blinked in surprise and then shook her head. She felt the muzzy clouds of fatigue circling her brain, hemming in her thoughts, dulling her senses. No matter where she turned, someone wanted her killed or imprisoned.

"What does the Emperor desire from a poor nun belonging to the Order of Gelya?"

"Nothing," replied Protaro. He motioned. His Guardsmen formed a circle around them. Kesira saw several hurrying on ahead to accomplish some unspecified task. She guessed they went to stables and mounts ready for a long journey. Emperor Kwasian's capital of Limaden lay many weeks' journey to the west. Just thinking of those tedious miles and days in the saddle tired Kesira further.

"If the Emperor wants nothing of me, then why arrest me?"

"No one has arrested you," Protaro said, too quickly for Kesira's taste. He spoke as if he had memorized this portion of his orders. "You are to be Kwasian's guest at the palace for the equinox."

Kesira's mind almost stopped functioning entirely. Only the highest nobility received invitations to the Equinox

78

Festival. Never in her wildest dreams did she imagine she'd attend—nor did she believe for an instant that the Emperor intended to honor her. Lowly nuns were not permitted into the most festive of courtly events, even on the Emperor's whim. Society demanded that everyone know everyone else's standing so that all stayed in their correct place and acted accordingly.

If Kesira had met this Guard captain on the road, they would have nodded politely but never spoken. If he had entered a shrine where she worshiped, the Guardsman would not have spoken, but she might have ventured words to him had some wrong been committed that the Emperor's Guard was responsible for punishing. The code of social interaction, even though unwritten, held strict sway over all citizens.

The lower in social standing, the freer one became. The Emperor barely spoke without his every word being ritualistically required and ordained.

Kesira violated all social conventions by asking, "What does Kwasian really want of me? Not my presence. He can have a thousand sisters of the Mission, should he feel the spiritual urge. And never would he invite one of us to the equinox."

Protaro's face set into an unreadable mask. He almost drew his sheathed sword to run her through for this affront to decency. Kesira had passed caring about breach of etiquette. She wanted nothing more than a warm bath, a soft bed, and a long sleep. If decent food accompanied it, there was little more she could ask of life.

"The Emperor desires the company of the baby." Protaro lifted his head slightly and pointed with his chin, indicating the infant strapped around Kesira's body. Tiny pale eyes fixed on Captain Protaro's ribbons and glistening gold rank braid. The baby shifted to peer up and study the officer's lined face. Such scrutiny unsettled the battle-hardened veteran.

"The Emperor did not take me into his confidence. My orders are simple. Return the infant to the Imperial Court."

Kesira fought a silent battle with herself. Ever since she could remember, it had been ingrained in her how duty was paramount in everyone's life. Without honor and duty the realm disintegrated. Each person knew the role to be filled and did it. Whether one died as a result did not matter. Duty was carried out, honor was never besmirched with cowardice or inattention to the niceties of proper behavior.

Duty to family ranked high. For Kesira this had become shifted at an early age. With parents dead during a brigand attack, her family had become those with her in the nunnery. Gelya had become her teacher, Sister Fenelia a mother, Dominie Tredlo a father, Dana and the others her siblings. Lenc's destruction of the nunnery had made her duty clear. Honor demanded revenge on the jade demon and all his allies. No matter if the task looked impossible; the attempt had to be made. Those she had considered family must be allowed to rest in peace, knowing their own flesh and blood had fought and won—or fought and died nobly.

But above familial duty lay obeisance to regional lords and Empire bureaucrats. Kesira had none. As a member of a religious order, she owed fealty to no lord.

Above a regional lord, however, sat the Emperor and his Court. To the Court Kesira had no duty, but the Emperor reigned supreme in the land. His power extended from the highest lord to the lowest peasant. Duty to Emperor carried the greatest moral responsibility, greater even than duty to family.

Kesira walked beside the Guard captain and worked through the intricate maze that detailed her duty. For the naive nun recently gone from convent, duty seemed simple: Obey the Emperor. Kesira Minette had fought and defeated two of the jade demons, had lain with two more demons, and had assumed responsibility for a boychild. In all but the strictest sense the baby was her family, and her duty to him conflicted with the Emperor's request.

Folklore held obedience to the Emperor above family duties as the sign of true courage. Kesira wondered.

The rune sticks had shown her to be the one best able to fight Ayondela and bring the jade demon crashing to defeat. Didn't her duty to the Emperor require her to do all in her power to help him maintain his throne? By wasting time in the long journey to Limaden and allowing Ayondela and Lenc to consolidate their power, she doomed Kwasian. If she felt real devotion to the Emperor and wished to uphold his position, she had to ignore his edict.

Kesira's head ached from such contorted logic. To aid the Emperor she had to disobey a direct order. Duty—to destroy the jade demons—started with resisting the Emperor's Guard, normally an offense of the severest order.

Her world and rules had turned upside down, but Kesira knew it had been this way ever since the demons partook of the jade. They were the ones responsible for disrupting the smoothly running social fabric of the Empire. If Lenc, Eznofadil, and Howenthal had not aspired to more than their due, Kesira would still be safely sequestered in her nunnery, learning Gelya's teachings, making occasional trips to Blinn for provisions, and enjoying the company of her sisters.

Kesira made her decision quickly and with no regrets. Treasonously she sought the weaknesses in Captain Protaro's squad, looking for a path to escape.

"Will the smaller mare be adequate for you?" Protaro asked. Three of his soldiers rode up, leading enough horses for Protaro and the others. "It is sturdy and has a gait not too unsettling for someone unused to riding."

"I've ridden a great deal."

This surprised the officer. "My apologies. The mare is still a fine choice."

"I would rest before we leave Lorum Bay," she said. "I only arrived off a fishing boat. The storm that tossed us prevented me from sleeping and . . ."

"There will be ample time to sleep once we are on the road," the captain said brusquely. Kesira wondered if she detected even the slightest hint of sympathy in the man's cold eyes. She doubted it. Protaro knew his duty to the

Emperor and performed it well. If he had to die accomplishing his mission, he would, without a qualm.

Fleeting admiration for Protaro passed through her mind. Why couldn't she be more like the stern officer?

"You realize that the Order of the Steel Crescent is trying to kill me?" she asked.

Protaro shrugged it off. To him Nehan-dir meant nothing more than another obstacle to be overcome. He might not even know it had been Nehan-dir he'd fought in the brief street skirmish.

"Your ribbons attest to fierce battles with the barbarians," she said. Kesira remembered Rouvin's stories of the Sarabella front and the horrendous losses there. "A friend of mine fought at Sarabella. He was a captain of cavalry. Soon after the barbarians had been driven back into the sea, he resigned. No chance for advancement."

"I understand that," Protaro said. "My chances of attaining the rank of commander are nil." He frowned, previously hidden scars popping out in the furrow across his forehead. "Who is your friend? I knew most of the survivors."

"Rouvin the Stout."

"Rouvin? I knew him. A daring captain."

"He is dead," Kesira said carefully, trying to judge Protaro's reaction. "He fought the jade demons and it cost him his life." That wasn't the precise truth but neither was it a lie.

"Lalasa will want to hear more of this from you," the officer said. "She advises the Emperor but is unable to gain proper intelligence concerning the other demons. As a result, not all our forays have ended in victory. General Dayle was sorely wounded after attacks across the Quaking Lands."

"I know," Kesira said. "I watched from within Howenthal's castle. Your general did not realize the power he faced."

"You watched?" Protaro did not believe her. Kesira shook off the indignation of being thought a liar.

"I joined forces with Wemilat the Ugly and we killed Howenthal," she said, taking no joy in the telling. "Then I invaded Ayondela's fastness and killed Eznofadil."

"You, a slayer of demons?" Protaro laughed heartily. "I was wrong. Kwasian might desire your company. You are finer with the jest than his fool. You will be the talk of the Equinox Festival with your tall tales."

Kesira glanced down to make sure the baby rested comfortably. A small smile split his face and the eyes twinkled. He seemed to understand what decision she had reached and approved. This made it easier for Kesira to evade the Guard captain.

The runes had foretold that the baby was the key to stopping Ayondela's rampage. The only way Kesira could conceive of that being possible was a trade—the infant to replace Ayondela's lost son Rouvin. If she had another son to care for, to love, to nurture, the female demon might give up the power of the jade and abandon Lenc.

To offer the baby Kesira had to avoid being taken to Limaden.

In the saddle she waited for her chance to escape. It came sooner than she expected. Kesira saw Molimo crouching near a drainpipe, sword in one hand and dagger in the other. She put her arms around the infant, then spurred her horse forward at a pace faster than the Emperor's Guard. Protaro kicked at the flanks of his horse to catch up, and as he passed Molimo's position, the man-wolf leapt.

"Aieee!" the captain shrieked as a dagger drove into his left arm and a sword raked across a muscular thigh. The Guardsman lay writhing in pain on the pavement, unable to stand because of his wounds. Molimo hit and rolled to his feet, sword and dagger flashing toward new targets.

Kesira jerked around in the saddle when she thought she heard Molimo scream *Ride!* at her. She pushed such foolishness away. Better than anyone else, she knew Molimo had no tongue. Kesira bent forward and rode with the wind, taking the streets of Lorum Bay with reckless abandon. As she rode she worked out what might happen. Retaining the horse for too long would prove her downfall. She saw no way to outrun the Emperor's Guard. Better to hide and force them to search for her. That way, the Steel Crescent and the Guardsmen might clash again.

"Pit one enemy against the other," she said aloud. The idea appealed to her.

She rode for several more minutes, then vaulted from the saddle to land heavily in the cobblestone street. Kesira stumbled a bit until she regained her balance. The mare galloped on, as she'd hoped it would. That would leave a false track for the Guardsmen while she went in the other direction.

On foot she sought out the marketplace. Fear of the slashing mist had passed, and the citizens of Lorum Bay now conducted business in tiny stalls, stores opened to the sea air, and from pushcarts dotting the market area. Few took note of her and then only as a potential customer. These merchants were used to seeing strangers passing through their port town. No cry lifted, and for that Kesira breathed a sigh of relief.

"Many fine rugs," one merchant cried. He rushed out of his store and grabbed her arm. "Come inside. Look. Aheem the Rugger is honest and sells honest merchandise. Ask anyone."

"Aheem's a cutpurse and a fraud," yelled a neighboring merchant. "Come, noble lady, come to Yeeramian's store and see *real* bargains. Even the Emperor himself walks barefoot on such rugs."

"If the Emperor bought Yeeramian's rugs, he'd *have* to walk barefoot," countered Aheem. "That bandit's shaggy rugs would cut boot leather to ribbons!"

"Not interested," Kesira said, laughing. She enjoyed the friendly byplay between the rug sellers. When the day ended, Kesira thought it quite possible that Yeeramian and Aheem got together for a few friendly mugs of ale to discuss the day's business and how to squeeze an extra coin from unwitting customers.

Kesira found herself wobbling along, dizzy and disoriented. She sat down. It had been too long since she'd had a meal. The baby had eaten well enough, but she had neglected her own food. A pushcart passed close by. Kesira hailed the food vendor.

"Flayed rats on a stick?" the vendor asked. "Special-sized ones we got this fine day. Caught 'em in the fog. Freshly dead, they are."

"Something else," Kesira said, feeling queasy at the idea of eating wharf rats.

"Got some good *trilla* bird meat."

"Fresh?" she asked, afraid of the answer. She heaved a sigh of relief when the vendor admitted that his supply had been brought in from the tropics and might be a month old.

"Aged, I call it. Good 'n' aged *trilla* bird meat."

"I have very little money. A hunk of bread and some cheese is all I can afford."

The young vendor took this in stride. For three coppers Kesira bought a large piece of dark bread and a sharp cheese "from the monastery of Gelya in the Yearn Mountains," the vendor assured her.

Kesira had no idea where the cheese had been produced. Her nunnery had not exported any cheese and wasn't likely to have started in the past few months, not with the buildings reduced to rubble and Lenc's cold white flame burning in the stone altar once sacred to Gelya.

As Kesira ate she overheard the gossip between merchants. One conversation held her full attention.

". . . never deal with demons. Bad business. How can you collect?"

"I've had no trouble," answered another. "Ayondela buys much from me and always pays."

"In the past she has. The fog will visit you one day and leave your bloody carcass for all to see. What good, then, will your profits do you?"

"You're jealous of my contracts with her. The fog is rather pretty, if you look at the sun through it. Glistens like the finest of crystal."

"There's no fool like a greedy fool," said the second. He turned and called to another merchant, inquiring of business. The one who had dealings with Ayondela turned back to his store and sat on a three-legged stool, biding his time as he waited for prospective customers.

Kesira studied the man. The merchant looked prosperous but no more so than others scattered around the market. But Kesira saw a furtiveness in the man's gaze that troubled her. She could believe that he aided Ayondela knowing fully what evil the she-demon visited on the land. This was not an honorable person: the fleshy face, the beady eyes, the weak chin, all told Kesira of the man's venality and absorbed self-interest.

She went to him.

"Ah, gracious and lovely lady, how can Esamir assist you this fine day? A brass chamber pot engraved with designs beloved of the demons? No? A woman of your breeding needs candleholders formed of the purest onyx. I have just what you need. Come inside, please, this way." Esamir rose and bowed deeply, ushering Kesira into the dim interior. Kesira's nose wrinkled at the heavy incense burning in three separate brass urns. The best she could tell, each odor differed just enough from the others to produce a totally unpleasant sensory confusion.

The effect fit Esamir well.

"Your merchandise is outstanding," she said. Kesira glanced around, back into the market, hoping to catch a glimpse of Molimo. While she doubted that the Emperor's Guard had caught him, he might have been wounded— or undergone a shape-change into his wolf form. With the general populace as nervous about other-beasts as they were, this might prove fatal for Molimo.

"There is something I can show you that will warm your heart and bring a song to your finely shaped lips."

Esamir maneuvered around so that he stood between Kesira and the exit.

"Something worthy of . . . a demon," Kesira said. Her words almost broke with emotion.

"You know of my dealings with Ayondela?"

"It is common knowledge," Kesira said. She believed this to be true. If Esamir talked openly about it outside his shop, many others might know the details also.

"What is it to you?" the flowery words had been replaced by pointed questions.

"I would talk with Ayondela. I have something that might interest her."

The merchant's eyes narrowed. He seemed to take a good look at Kesira for the first time. When Esamir noticed the baby slung at her breast, he smiled. Kesira shivered in response. This man would betray his own grandmother if it netted him a bent copper.

What he would do for a pouch of gold Kesira didn't even want to consider.

"I do have minimal contact with her," Esamir said. "Rather, she contacts me when supplies are needed."

"Supplies for what?" asked Kesira. "No, I am sorry. I have no reason to ask that of you. All I need is the opportunity to speak with Ayondela."

"She knows you?" The cunning expression flickered across Esamir's face. Kesira knew he would not make a good gambler.

Kesira nodded curtly.

"She has only recently accepted delivery of certain goods," the merchant said. "It might be weeks before she asks for more. However, there is one path to follow that will gain you an audience almost immediately."

"What is it?" Even as she spoke Kesira knew that she betrayed her eagerness. If Esamir would make a terrible gambler, she was an even worse one.

He smiled broadly. "Coastal traders venture far to the south. Ayondela, it is rumored, has abandoned her Isle of Eternal Winter in favor of another mountain peak. The

Sarn Mountains are the loftiest on this continent and Ayondela now rules from the tallest of them. She claims to be
able to see into the Emperor's bedchamber from there,
though why she bothers is a mystery." Esamir smiled and
spread his hands to show he only jested. Not even greedy
merchants maligned the Emperor.

"You have the names of traders willing to take me
south?"

"Of course, noble lady." Esamir fell silent.

"Well?" Kesira demanded. "What of the names? Who
are these venturesome sailors?"

"Everything has a price. Even information."

Kesira clutched the child closer to her body.

"If I give you the name of a trader, will you carry a
message to Ayondela for me?"

"What message?"

"Business matters. I have been seeking a courier, but
the people of Lorum Bay are afraid to leave their cozy
homes. They grow too complacent. Nobody will accept
this minor inconvenience for me."

Kesira leapt at the chance. "Gladly will I deliver a
sealed note to Ayondela if you—"

Esamir interrupted. "You must not read the contents of
the message. Some intelligence requires the utmost secrecy, even in a simple business such as mine."

"I understand. I will not open the message and will
deliver it personally to Ayondela."

"I can trust you?" Esamir asked, more of himself than
Kesira. "Yes, I feel that I can. I have not remained in
business for so many years without developing a sense of
people. You are one I can depend on in this matter."

"Yes, yes," she said impatiently.

"One moment while I get the letter. Then I will guide
you to the harbor where you can get passage south."

Esamir vanished into the back room. Kesira edged toward the exit, peering out into the sunlit market. Customers
now thronged the stalls doing last-minute shopping, all

fear of the deadly mist gone. But of Molimo she saw no trace.

"Here," Esamir said, startling her. He held out a thick packet of brown paper sealed with a sigil impressed in green wax. "Come along now and I shall take you to Leter. A knave of a man but the best sailor in all of Lorum Bay."

Just as they started to leave the store a small boy rushed from the back, yelling, "They come, master! The shipment from Chounabel has come a day early!"

Esamir cursed under his breath, then turned to Kesira. "I am sorry. My delivery demands an accounting. I cannot trust a thief such as this one." He cuffed the boy and knocked him into a pile of brass candlesticks. "He is both stupid and clumsy."

"How long will it take? To inventory the merchandise?" Kesira fretted that Protaro or Nehan-dir might find her.

"Well?" Esamir demanded of the boy.

"Four wagons, master. They bring four wagons."

Esamir gave an eloquent shrug. "Many hours, I fear. But you have the message. Go to the harbor and seek out Leter aboard the *Poxy Shrew*. Tell him of your mission and that I implore him to make great haste to the south-lands."

"Very well." Kesira relaxed as Esamir bowed deeply and hurried into the rear of the shop, the urchin close at his heels. She hadn't liked the idea of the sly merchant accompanying her. Now she could choose her own path to the harbor and hope Molimo found her soon.

Kesira sucked in a deep lungful of air and relaxed even more. The day blossomed warmly around her, and the fresh sea air invigorated her. She hurried toward the harbor, doubling back several times to make sure she was not being followed.

The harbor in view, she turned toward the nearest docks to seek out Captain Leter. She never heard the man behind her, nor did she feel the sharp impact of the club on the side of her head.

Kesira Minette slumped to the cobblestone paving, unconscious.

Chapter Eight

WATER SPLASHED on Kesira Minette's face. She snorted and sent a salty plume back into the sea. Sputtering, struggling in the damp embrace of the waves, she pulled herself erect to sit on the beach, the incoming tide lapping around her body.

For long minutes she simply sat and tried to get her world puzzled back into a coherent whole. Snippets of memory returned but not enough for Kesira to understand. The merchant. A ship. What was its name? She had been seeking Ayondela, but where was Molimo?

The pain in her skull changed from sharp stabs to a dull aching. Kesira closed her eyes and lay back, the sea washing away her misery. Slowly it all came back to her.

Kesira sat bolt upright again, clutching at the empty sling around her neck. "The baby!" she gasped. "Gone!"

She got to her feet and forced herself away from the sucking surf. A quarter-mile away ships of all descriptions bobbed and rocked gently against the docks—someone had carried her that distance and left her to drown. Or had they merely left her, not caring if she drowned or not? And who were "they"?

Quick hands searched for her pouch. It still rode at her hip, the bone box inside containing her rune sticks. Kidnapping, not robbery, had been the motive for the attack.

Kesira pushed aside the despair that rose within her. Gelya had taught that despair was a trap for fools: one could sit and bemoan her fate or one could act. Kesira

Minette acted. Returning to the spot where she had been attacked, she dropped to hands and knees and studied the cobblestones for some small clue to the identity of the kidnapper. Molimo with his animal-acute senses might have been able to understand the scuffs and nicks in the paving stones, but all Kesira could figure out was that heavy traffic passed over this spot daily.

"Pardon," came a hesitant voice. "You lookin' for somethin' in particular?"

Kesira looked up and saw a shabbily dressed man holding a small plate. A few small coins rested within it.

"I was attacked here some time ago." She peered at the sun and estimated times. "About two hours ago. They left me with a head feeling like a burst melon and no child."

"They stole your youngling?" This evoked real emotion on the beggar's part. He obviously didn't understand why any would kidnap another mouth to feed.

"Did you see anything? I don't have much." She reached into her pouch and took out the remaining four coppers and a silver centim embossed with Empress Aglenella's profile. "These are yours, if you did witness the crime."

"I'd like to be able to claim this fine reward," the beggar said, only a hint of sarcasm in his voice, "but the truth is that I saw nothin'. I work up and down the embarcadero. Sailors just in from long cruises tend to be more generous to the needy than other folks. They count it a payment to luck that they returned in one piece—or with coins jinglin' in their pouches."

"Who would kidnap an infant?"

The beggar laughed harshly. "No one. Feedin' yourself's a major concern for most people in Lorum Bay. Only the last few weeks have seen the Sea of Katad free of ice. Fishing has been poor, and no one's growin' crops yet." He restlessly rattled the paltry coins on his plate, as if in practice.

"Do you know a merchant named Esamir?"

Again came the harsh laugh. "That one? Steer clear of

him. He's bad weather, no matter what port you're hailing from."

"I know he deals with Ayondela."

"That'd be an improvement over the kind he normally has truck with. Now, I'm not one to go talkin' out of turn, but Esamir's been rumored to deal in human flesh."

"A slaver?"

The beggar's eyes widened, then he laughed. This time the sound rang out as genuine amusement. "Good lady, no! He sells people by the pound—for their flesh. He's a cannibal, he is. Expect the worst of him and you'll still be surprised at his evil ways."

Kesira had no reply. Lorum Bay had not seemed that badly damaged by Ayondela's wintery curse, but it had obviously driven some past the brink of acceptable, honorable behavior. Esamir a dealer in human meat? While Kesira had not liked the man and had believed him possible of any perfidy, this was more than mere crime against the Emperor. Cannibalism had to be a crime against society. Such a man lacked even the smallest portion of honor.

"Thank you," she said in a choked voice. She dropped the silver centim onto the beggar's plate. The man shrugged and moved on, not even thanking her. Kesira stared after him in wonder. What odd folk these were in Lorum Bay.

Or were they equally as odd throughout the Empire? Kesira had to admit that she had only recently burst upon the world outside the walls of her convent. How she longed to return to those pacific days with Sister Dana, picking the yellow wild flowers sacred to Gelya and lying in the field, hands clasped beneath her head, watching the wondrous fluffy patterns of clouds in the sky. Life had been easy before the jade had lured Lenc and the others to the ways of evil.

Kesira made her way through alleys and along shadowed lanes, avoiding the main thoroughfares of Lorum Bay. She finally discovered the service door to Esamir's shop. From the rubble in the alley, she knew that no large delivery had been made in some time, much less one totaling four entire wagonloads. He had instructed the urchin to lie.

Something niggled at her mind. Then she had it. Kesira reached inside her blouse and pulled out the packet Esamir had given her to deliver to Ayondela. She ran a ragged thumbnail under the green wax seal and popped open the pages. The pages were all blank. Holding one sheet to the sun and peering at the faint shadows cast by the watermark, Kesira decided that it held no secret message. Sister Kai had taught her much of the lore surrounding various juices and inks. Some even permitted invisible writing until the proper chemical or heat was applied, but Kesira had noted that while the message was hidden, the paper always wrinkled slightly from the ink.

No such wrinkles appeared on this sheaf of parchment. She tucked the voluminous pages away against the time when she might better study them, but she believed that this had been nothing more than a cunning ruse on Esamir's part. He had seen the baby and wanted it. The merchant's agile, devious mind had concocted a plot on the spur of the moment and had executed it perfectly.

Even if she went to the local authorities, Esamir had an alibi for the time when the attack took place. She had no doubt that he had picked a fight with another merchant or had otherwise created a ruckus to mark him in peoples' minds. One of his henchmen had performed the kidnapping—after all, he knew where Kesira was headed.

She wondered if there was even a Captain Leter and a ship called the *Poxy Shrew*. Possibly. The ring of fact in Esamir's voice had come through when speaking of them. Kesira had learned that the best lies were those interwoven with the truth. Buy an ounce of the tale, buy a pound.

She skillfully avoided the piles of debris in the alley and went to Esamir's back door. She gently tried the latch. Locked. Kesira pressed her fingers against the thin, unpainted wood and felt strong steel behind it. Esamir had well hidden the real strength behind this flimsy-looking entrance. Kesira would keep that in mind when dealing with the merchant again.

On the outside he might be a poor, simple merchant. Below that facade beat the heart of a cunning blackguard.

Kesira edged down the alley and peered around the corner toward the marketplace. The bustling crowds had thinned once more, taking time for afternoon meals. The few vendors lounged around, not pitching to those walking by.

Kesira shrieked when a heavy hand clamped on her shoulder. She jerked around as another hand shut off further outcries.

"Oh, Molimo," she said, relaxing when she saw the young man. "You startled me." Heart beating like a drum, she slumped against the cool brick wall of Esamir's store.

"Sorry," he wrote on his tablet. "Did not want you calling out to attract attention."

"What of the Guard?" she asked. "Do they still hunt for us?"

He nodded. Kesira heaved a deep sigh. Dealing with Howenthal and Eznofadil had not been this complex. And as dangerous as it had been, breaking the power of Ayondela's spell had been far easier than avoiding the Steel Crescent and Emperor's Guard on her trail.

"Someone has kidnapped the baby. I think it was the merchant inside." She tapped the brick wall. "His name's Esamir, and he claims to have dealings with Ayondela."

The accusing glare she got from Molimo chastised her. It had been foolish to approach a scoundrel like Esamir alone, and she knew it. But foolish self-reproach now accomplished nothing. They had to work to get the baby back.

"The runes say that the baby is the key to stopping Ayondela. I fear that she might harm the boy unless we are with him." Molimo vigorously nodded at that. Kesira closed her eyes and let the waves of tiredness sweep over her. "It is so strange. I read the runes with more clarity since my union with Cayabbib, but my strength wanes so quickly now. In some ways I am stronger, in others so much weaker."

Molimo's hand rested on her shoulder, reassuring her. She leaned forward and threw her arms around him, hugging him close. The weariness still plagued her, but it seemed minor now.

"Molimo, I need you so. Don't ever leave me. Please don't leave me."

He pushed her away even as she tried to hug him tighter. Kesira opened her brown eyes and saw his attention focused out in the market. She scanned the small crowd quickly, then paused when she saw a short man strutting like he owned the town.

"Nehan-dir," she said without real surprise. "Is he in league with Esamir?"

Molimo shook his head. The cocky leader of the Steel Crescent's mercenaries swung past Esamir's brasswares shop and continued on, hardly paying attention to anything inside. Whatever Nehan-dir sought—and Kesira believed it was she and Molimo—he hadn't seen it around the brass shop.

"Nehan-dir wanted the baby and so did Captain Protaro," she said. "Apparently Nehan-dir still seeks us. Unless there is a third party eager for the boy's company, it would seem Protaro has been the victor in this scavenger hunt."

"Would Esamir sell him to the Emperor's Guard?" wrote Molimo.

"I'm guessing. Why does anyone want the boy? By now he is getting hungry. I see no way they can feed him unless they find a source of mother's milk." Kesira touched her left breast, gravid with milk where Wemilat's kiss burned in the white flesh.

If anything convinced Kesira to continue the struggle against the jade demons, it was this sign. Wemilat's touch granted life. All that Lenc and Ayondela touched withered and died.

"We must be swift," Molimo wrote.

"One moment," she said, restraining him. Molimo had started out into the market area. "How did you escape from Protaro?"

Molimo stared at her, his eyes dark and lacking emotion. She swallowed hard. It was difficult when Molimo closed in on himself, shutting out both her and the world.

"You care for the captain?" he scribbled.

"Yes, of course I do," she said, a flush rising to her cheeks. "I care for all honorable men. He is the Emperor's emissary and . . . I care," she finished in a rush.

"He is injured but not mortally," wrote Molimo. "Others are dead. I escaped in the confusion."

"Good," she said, almost too softly for him to hear. A tear beaded at the corner of her eye. "Molimo, you are very special to me." He pulled away before she made eye contact. From his determined steps she knew he went to confront Esamir. Kesira trailed behind, casting furtive glances in all directions, fearful of what she'd see. Nehandir had gone; of the Emperor's Guardsmen she saw no trace. She followed the man-wolf into the brasswares store.

Already Esamir greeted Molimo, not seeing Kesira.

"Good and noble sir, how are you? Welcome to my humble shop. It is lucky for you that this very day I have on sale . . ." His voice trailed off when Molimo did not respond—or perhaps the merchant felt himself impaled by the icy gaze. When Kesira closed the door and latched it, Esamir bolted for the rear of the store.

One quick hand grabbed his tunic and lifted him into the air. His feet kicked inches above the carpeted shop floor.

"My friend is strong and quick. He also has a nasty habit of killing when someone lies to him."

Esamir's frightened stare told Kesira that he had already come to this conclusion about Molimo.

"The baby. Where is he?"

"I know nothing of this baby!" Esamir shrieked in fear as Molimo heaved him hard against the back wall of the store. The merchant smashed into the brick wall hard enough to rattle his teeth. He slumped into a pile next to a display of brass chamber pots. Molimo shoved him back down as he tried to stand.

"Molimo is very strong. Or hadn't you noticed?" Kesira said, taking a perverse joy in tormenting the merchant. She knew it was morally wrong to do so, but something deep inside pushed back all of Gelya's teachings and required this to maintain her sanity.

Molimo picked up one of the brass pots and held it between his hands. Muscles bulged as he began to squeeze. The pot flattened. Molimo took the newly wrought disk in one hand and flung it hard against a side wall. The edge of the brass dug into the brick and hung there, a testament to berserk strength.

"The baby. I want him back. Tell us or you'll not live to kidnap another child."

"This is beyond my power. I cannot say what happened. Oh!"

Molimo took Esamir's head between his hands and began to squeeze, just as he'd done with the pot. The merchant's eyes began to bulge. He beat feebly on the man's muscle-knotted belly.

"Hurry. Your tongue sticks out already. In another few seconds your head will be as flat as this."

Kesira dropped a brass serving tray in front of the struggling merchant.

"He, oh, the pain! He came to me, he bought my services."

"Who?"

Esamir let out only incoherent squeaks. Molimo lessened the pressure to allow him to speak. "The Guard Captain Protaro. He came to me. This was a duty put upon me by the Emperor himself! Kwasian demanded it of me! I had no choice."

"How much were you paid?" asked Kesira, anger rising. Bartering in babies struck her as odious, no matter how it was couched.

"F-fifty gold sovereigns."

"Some duty."

A loud rattle from the back of the store caught her attention. Kesira spun in time to fend off a mountain of a man. Arms bulging with prodigious muscles groped for her; she ducked beneath the deadly circle, kicked, and squirmed free. The dirty, blond-haired man grunted and kept after her. Kesira picked up a brass platter and flung it at him. The edge produced a thin red line in the center of his kettle belly. He came on, not noticing this slight wound.

"Kill the bitch, Wardo!" screamed Esamir.

Kesira backed away slowly. Tiredness no longer dogged her every step. She came alive in ways alien to her. Kesira felt Cayabbib's presence welling up, guiding her, giving her strength that had never before been hers.

Wardo lunged forward just as Kesira launched a roundabout kick. She landed it squarely in the pit of the man's belly. He doubled over, but the blow hardly slowed him.

"Molimo," she begged. "This is more than I can handle."

Wardo grabbed her. Kesira whirled around, caught the man's weight in just the proper spot, and hurled him over her shoulder. He landed heavily, crushing a display of wicker chairs.

"I need a staff." Longingly she eyed Molimo's sword, dangling at his waist. To draw it, to run Wardo through with it. But Kesira balked at this blasphemy. Gelya had not approved of steel weapons. She'd never received a clear answer when she'd asked Sister Fenelia and Dominie Tredlo about this prohibition, but it had been one she'd scrupulously obeyed, nonetheless. To go against it now proved more than she could do, even with the newfound strengths given her by Cayabbib.

Wardo's heavy fist smashed into the side of her head, knocking her sprawling.

"She still falls when I hit her," Wardo said, gloating. The eyes burned with small intelligence and great hatred.

Kesira had no doubt now who had committed the kidnapping. She faced him.

Wardo rushed her. Insane strength flowed through Kesira. She caught the hulking beast of a man and lifted him bodily. Swinging him around, using both his momentum and her anger-fed power, she slammed Wardo into the wall. But this did not deter him. And her own stamina drained all too quickly.

"Kill her now, Wardo! Quickly!" screamed Esamir.

A low, feral snarl pulled her attention from Wardo to Molimo. The man-wolf had become a wolf-man. Green eyes flashing, savage fangs agleam in the dim light of the shop, the gray wolf padded forward as he sized up his prey.

"No, Molimo, don't," Kesira cried.

A gray blur rocketed past her. Wardo threw up a meaty arm to protect his throat. Molimo's fangs sank deep into that arm and then began to rip and tear. Blood spurted from a severed artery. Wardo rolled over and over; Molimo followed his every move, fangs ripping, back leg claws pawing ferociously at the man's soft belly.

Wardo might have lived, had he reached the back room and bolted the door, but before he got halfway to safety, he exposed his throat for the briefest of times. Molimo's quick head jerked around, and teeth buried in the vulnerable carotid artery. Red fountains geysered over the combatants.

"The w-wolf's killed him," stuttered Esamir. "He was Lorum Bay's champion and the wolf killed him."

Kesira pulled herself together and took a deep breath. She reached out and caught Esamir's throat. Her fingers tightened.

"He doesn't like to be annoyed," she said. "You've annoyed him also." Strength flowed like a clean, pure river into Kesira's arm. She lifted. Esamir was pinned against the wall by the fragile-appearing woman's right hand. His feet kicked futilely above the floor once again.

"You have a demon's power," he gasped, the air not finding its way to his straining lungs.

"I want the baby," she said.

"I s-sold him to—I can't breathe!"

Kesira reached over and gripped a handful of fabric. Using this two-handed grip allowed her to release a bit of pressure on the merchant's throat.

"Where is Protaro keeping the baby?"

"The Guard captain will take the boy directly to Limaden and the Emperor. I am not lying!"

The way Esamir's eyes bulged and his tongue lolled told Kesira that he probably spoke the truth—or the truth as he knew it.

Kesira turned and heaved the merchant into the display of chamber pots. He seemed quite at home there.

"Do you actually deal in human flesh? For cannibalism?"

Esamir's eyes widened even more. He stuttered so badly, no coherent words formed. The fear she read in his eyes and his soul told her that the beggar near the harbor had not passed along unfounded rumors. She lost all compassion for Esamir and his gut-wrenching fears. He deserved nothing but punishment for his crimes.

Kesira didn't even try to stop Molimo as the gray wolf stalked by her, blood dripping from his muzzle. One single, loud, heart-rending shriek sounded. New blood dripped from Molimo's fangs.

Kesira sat and stroked Molimo's furry head until the transformation again seized him. Anguish showed in the man's dark eyes. Kesira's brown ones had lost any softness they once had.

"Come," she said, "we must find Protaro."

Kesira Minette never looked back at the two ravaged bodies as she stepped out into the sunlight and clear, salt-laced air of Lorum Bay's market.

Chapter Nine

THE IDEA OF BLATANT theft of such magnitude would once have appalled Kesira Minette. But not now. With cool, appraising eyes she studied the stables and evaluated their chances for making away with two of the better horses.

The chances looked good.

She motioned for Molimo to go around to the back of the barn while she confronted the owner.

Boldly she walked up to the man and asked, "Where might I find the merchant Esamir?"

The man frowned. "What would the likes of you be wantin' with scum like him?"

"He owes me a goodly amount of money. We dealt fairly and he cheated me. I've just arrived from ... the south."

"There's naught to the south, save for Ayondela's peak hidden off in the Sarn Mountains," the man said. He frowned even more. The deep furrows in his brow showed his displeasure at having to speak with someone who dealt with a female demon and a thieving merchant reputed to be selling human flesh.

Kesira saw Molimo moving silently in the back of the stable, soothing horses to keep them quiet, finding tack, choosing the best of the sorry lot. She turned her full attention back to the stable hand.

"My business is no concern of yours. However, I see that I must prove my claim. Here. Look." She reached into her blouse and found the blank sheets of paper Esamir had decoyed with her. She thrust them out for the man to examine. The man took them, as if he expected the pages to burst into flame.

"There's naught written here. What kind of game do you play with me now?"

Kesira looked perplexed as she took the pages back. "What are you saying? Of course there's something written on the sheets. Look more carefully."

As the man examined the blank pages, Molimo led two horses out of the stable. One of the animals spooked and emitted a shrill whinny. The stable hand glanced around. It took him long seconds to understand what happened.

"This knife will spit you if you move a muscle," Kesira said, thrusting the callused tips of her fingers into the man's back. "Tie him. Hurry!"

Molimo smiled as he obeyed. With the stable hand carefully tucked away in the back, the pair of horse thieves rode out. Kesira turned to Molimo and asked, "What were you grinning about back there? Did I say something funny?"

On his tablet Molimo scratched out the words, "You sounded like Zolkan. Always in a hurry."

"I did, did I?" Kesira said in mock anger. Then she, too, laughed, but the laughter died. "Where is Zolkan? I haven't seen him since the Emperor's Guard fought Nehandir's mercenaries."

Molimo frowned and made unintelligible gurgling noises. He appeared to be lost in deep thought, his eyes unfocused and his mouth slack with the effort of whatever it was he did. Finally the man-wolf shrugged and shook his head, indicating that he had no idea where the wayward *trilla* bird had gone.

"He'll have to find us," Kesira said firmly. "He takes off for days on end. I have never found where he goes or what he does, but . . ."

She stared at Molimo's guilty expression. The realization dawned on her that Molimo knew where Zolkan went when the bird vanished. It also hit her that asking for an explanation was wasted effort. The two of them shared a secret that excluded her.

"The trail," she said on a different tack. "Can you find the trail followed by Captain Protaro?"

Molimo pointed ahead, then made a snaking motion with his arm to indicate the turnings of the trail. In less than an hour Kesira found how exact that undulating description was. The trail switched back repeatedly as they climbed into the foothills—and then the foothills became full-fledged mountains.

But the woman had learned well during the past few months. While her eyes weren't as sharp as Molimo's in picking up the signs of passage, she detected bright, fresh nick marks in the rock where steel-shod hooves had recently passed, tiny leaves crushed but still damp with undried sap, the bending of twigs and branches near the path. A large party had preceded them by less than a day.

Captain Protaro and the Emperor's Guard. And a small baby who never cried.

"He must be starving," she said, her thoughts working into her words. "I'm sure Protaro would not willingly mistreat the boy, but he is a soldier. He can't know how to care for him." Kesira rode along and laughed ruefully. "We still have to call the baby 'him.' So young, and without a name."

Molimo held up the tablet for her to read.

"I know. Raellard Yera thought someone else had fathered the child, and Parvey named a demon as the father. Even if true, that's no reason not to give a name to the boy."

"Name him," Molimo wrote.

Kesira didn't answer immediately. She knew why she had neglected to baptize the boy. A name meant attachment. It would be more difficult to give him over to a foster home if "boy" became a person distinct with name. Yet this had worked against her. Now she had to find the baby, and she found it difficult to think of him as anything more than a commodity to be bartered, the rune-foretold key to breaking Ayondela away from the power of the jade.

"I am changing, Molimo," she said. "And not in ways I like. Life without honor is an abomination. So taught Gelya; so I've learned from others. But where is the honor in turning over a tiny infant to appease a demon? I consider this now without hesitation. I watched Esamir die and felt only relief that such a fiend is removed."

"He lacked honor. His actions dictated his death," wrote Molimo, his face set into a mask.

"You did well. I am not criticizing," Kesira said. "He forfeited all right to life for the things he did. But my feelings. They . . . have changed."

"Life is change."

Kesira wondered how Molimo meant that, considering his shape transformations. Would he die if he could not alter form? Or was it merely a response to progress in learning as she went through life?

"I have hardened, Molimo. That is what I fear. Inured to death, I come to despise life. It comes cheaply, as it did to Esamir. I don't want that. I won't become like that death merchant or Ayondela or Lenc or even Nehan-dir."

His hand lightly brushed over hers. She looked up. For the first time in weeks compassion shone forth from his eyes instead of the coldly emotionless stare. He squeezed lightly, then faced forward and spurred his horse to a faster pace. The trail narrowed rapidly and forced them to ride single file.

By nightfall they had reached the summit. Looking back at Lorum Bay, Kesira saw lanterns winking on and off throughout the village. The twilight cast an eerie gray over the Sea of Katad and turned it into a heaving, restless beast straining to break free of its bonds. And moving in from the south, devouring streets and buildings, sucking up human lives as it came, the oddly glistening magical fog dropped its tendrils and dug in for the night.

"Ayondela keeps a strict rein on her minions," Kesira

said, staring at the mist of death. "She enforces a curfew more stringent than any human watchman."

Molimo tugged at her sleeve, indicating a good place to camp. She shook her head, short brown hair swinging away from her face. "No. We will keep on. The baby grows hungrier, if I am any judge." She cupped her left breast, feeling the gathering weight of milk within. "He's missed two meals already. More and he will turn weak and die."

His birth in the middle of Ayondela's winter curse and his survival spoke of the baby's strength. The way he had endured the journey across the sea, the shipwreck, and all that followed told of more than strength. Kesira could almost believe that a demon *had* sired the boy.

Although their mounts had long since tired from the steep climb into the hills, Kesira pushed them on. Often she had to walk her horse to allow it a chance to catch its breath. Several times over the next hour Molimo looked back at her, an expression of concern on his face. Kesira saw the turmoil boiling within him. He wanted to speak and couldn't. Not for the first time, she cursed the jade demons and the affliction forced upon Molimo. She only barely understood how he must feel, wanting to speak to her, trying to make more than inarticulate gurgling noises. Everyone carried a different burden through the world.

Kesira had to admit that hers had compounded from simple revenge for all Lenc had done to her order to protecting the infant. If the baby had been her own flesh and blood, she wouldn't have felt more for him.

"What is it, Molimo?" she asked when the man stopped and just stood in the middle of the tiny path. He cocked his head to one side, as if listening. Strain as she might, Kesira caught nothing but natural sounds. *Trenly* crickets warbled and croaked their mating cries, a bit of wind whispered off the sea and carried with it the smell of salty water and fish, and tiny pops and creaks told where rock, heated by the summer sun, now cooled in the darkness. All natural, all expected.

Molimo came to her side and held out his tablet. He erased the words almost as quickly as he wrote them.

"Who could be following us?" she said, astounded. "Not the stable hand? Do you think he told the town constable of the horses we took?" Molimo shook his head. "What, then?"

"Steel Crescent" was all Molimo wrote.

Kesira heaved a deep sigh. Ahead rode the Emperor's Guard, and behind came the implacable Nehan-dir with his surviving mercenaries. Kesira experienced a curiously detached feeling, as if she floated atop the world and looked down emotionlessly on all that happened. Captain Protaro had the Emperor to command him, and Emperor Kwasian listened to the counsel of the demon Lalasa. Nehan-dir sold his sword to the highest bidder, the strongest jade demon. Lenc commanded him.

No one commanded Kesira Minette.

"What am I to do? How can I tell when I am right?" she muttered.

Molimo nudged her and pointed to his tablet. On it he had written, "Doubt others but never doubt yourself."

"One of your patron's maxims?" she asked. Kesira pulled back a step when Molimo started laughing. "What's so funny?"

"We must hurry on. We dare not be trapped on this stretch of trail," Molimo wrote, ignoring her question. Kesira saw the wisdom in the man-wolf's words. Nehan-dir's soldiers would slay them without effort here. The heavy wall of granite lay to their right, and a sheer drop of over a hundred feet vanished into darkness at the left side of the narrow trail. They had to keep advancing; to retreat—or to remain where they were—would bring them face-to-face with the Steel Crescent.

The horses protested but finally allowed Kesira and Molimo to push them at a faster gait. Soon the trail widened, mountain pastures stretching out to either side. And ahead Kesira saw tiny camp fires blazing.

"Protaro?" she asked Molimo. He solemnly nodded.

Kesira let out a low whistle, then sat astride her horse sucking at her cheeks. Now that they'd overtaken the Guardsmen she had no plan. The soldiers would not simply allow her to ride into camp to claim the baby. Even if Protaro did permit her in, he would never allow her to leave. She was the only source of nourishment for the baby.

Molimo made encompassing motions with his arms, indicating that they should circle the camp and approach from the far side. Kesira silently turned her horse to do so. If Protaro posted guards, they'd be alert on the trail leading back to Lorum Bay. She and Molimo spiraled in to the camp fires. As they rode silently she assayed their position and formed a plan.

Dismounting on the far side of Protaro's encampment, she tethered her horse and said softly, "We must move by stealth. I will enter the camp and get the baby."

Molimo protested but Kesira ignored him. "I do not mean to be cruel, Molimo, but you must stay behind. I can't chance a transformation. The other-breast is unpredictable. If only you controlled the shape-shifting better." She sighed. "You don't. I must go in alone. Watch and guard my back."

Molimo tried to stop her. He ran to his horse and pulled the tablet from the pouch slung behind his saddle, but the woman didn't wait to read his scribbled message. Kesira melted into the inky night that cloaked the mountain meadowland, her full attention turned to Captain Protaro's camp.

She measured every stride, tested every footstep before putting full weight down. No twig cracked. No leaf crumbled to betray her. Softer than any wind, Kesira Minette drifted through the trees, merging with nature to become a random sound, a dark shadow, a being more elemental than human.

"We'll be out of the mountains and onto the prairie by tomorrow noon," said one battered-looking man crouching near the fire. "I tell you, Cap'n, these hills aren't for the likes of me and you."

"Why not?" Protaro lounged back, propping himself up on one elbow. He gnawed at what meat remained on a small bone. "We've been through many mountain passes before, Tuwallan. You only ever get this edgy when we face up to magic."

The man—a scout?—chuckled. "I remember the Pinn Campaign. Couldn't kill those animated black boulders for love of the Emperor. Never did hear how you countered their attack."

"Pits. The men dug pits all night long. What makes you uneasy about this fine evening?" Protaro leaned back and stared up at the diamond points of stars in the sky. Involuntarily Kesira's rocked her head back and followed his gaze. Was the Guard captain staring at the constellations? The Jeweled Scepter just poking up over a dark mountain crag or the Throne of Azzica half turned in the sky?

"We ought to have left a few stragglers to guard our rear. We're traveling blind back there, Cap'n. Let me send a couple of the eager ones to check."

"Speed is more important. If we spent our time looking to our tails, the Emperor might not get his bundle before the Equinox Festival."

"What makes that brat so important?" Tuwallan duck-walked a few steps and peered down at a dark form in swaddling. "Doesn't even cry out."

"He's not taking the goat's milk too well, is he?" asked Protaro, concerned. Kesira felt some of the tension flow from her. The Guard captain at least cared for the boy and wasn't permitting him to be maltreated. But it sounded ominous that the infant refused to take the milk offered.

"When he gets hungry enough, he'll eat. But I never saw one so young that didn't cry out. He'll make a fine Guard in another fifteen summers."

"That's your trouble, Tu'lan. All you think about is the service."

"You do different, Cap'n?"

"No."

Conversation died down along with the fire. Kesira carefully studied the sentries, their posts, how they patroled, and when their watches changed. The Throne of Azzica made a half turn in the sky before Kesira moved into the camp, going directly to the baby.

Eyes so pale that they seemed luminous in the dark peered up at her. She smiled and stood the boy in her arms. Rocking him gently, she turned and began her slow journey back into the darkness.

Tuwallan stirred in his sleep, pulling his trail blanket up over one exposed shoulder. Kesira paused, thinking herself to be part of the night, willing her form to blend with dark shadows. But whatever it was that made the man Protaro's most expert scout alerted him. He rolled onto his back and stared straight at her.

Kesira knew better than to bluff her way out of this. She took three quick steps forward and dropped beside the soldier. The baby lowered to the ground, she struck with a short, hard punch to the prone man's throat. Tuwallan gagged. Thumb and forefinger closed his nostrils. Her other hand clamped firmly on the damaged windpipe. She squeezed. Not only her own life depended on it but also the life of the baby.

Tuwallan struggled feebly, trying vainly to get air into his tortured lungs. Then all movement ceased. Kesira held the grip for another minute to make certain that he wasn't bluffing, then released him. For all the battles he had survived, he had died relatively peacefully in the midst of his friends.

Kesira picked up the infant and forced herself to walk carefully into the darkness. Any sudden movement or incautious sound might alert the guards. Ten minutes later Kesira let out pent-up breath she hadn't known she held.

She looked down at the bundle in her arms. "You missed me, didn't you?" The baby's hands fumbled at her blouse. "No, you didn't miss me, you little imp. All you missed were a few meals." She sighed as the baby began to nurse greedily. "I don't blame you. Goat's milk can't be as satisfying."

The baby's appetite sated, Kesira continued on through the sparse mountain meadow, keeping low and taking advantage of the grassy contours. Only when she rejoined Molimo did she again feel safe.

That sensation passed.

"What is it?" she demanded, seeing the man's dour expression. He started to hold up his writing tablet, but an all-too-familiar voice stopped him.

"The negotiations will go more quickly if I deal with her directly, other-beast."

"Nehan-dir!" she gasped. Her hands opened and closed on nothing. How she wished for her stone-wood staff. Two quick spins, a thrust, and Nehan-dir's head would be crushed on both sides and the carcass knocked into a ravine.

The short, skinny leader of the Steel Crescent moved into view from the deep shadows that had hidden him from sight. He held his sword out and leveled it at Molimo, but Kesira saw no real intent to use it. Whatever weapon Nehan-dir wielded now, he thought it more effective than his vaunted steel blade.

"You ride well," he complimented. "We were hard-pressed to keep up with you. And to rescue the baby? A stroke of genius."

"You won't get him—not without a fight!"

She cast a quick glance at Molimo. The man sat slumped forward, as if he'd been defeated already. This was so totally unlike him, she wondered what Nehan-dir had done.

"I have learned my lesson, noble lady," Nehan-dir said mockingly. "I haven't come to fight you for the child, though the idea appeals to me. Lenc has ordered the baby delivered to him, and fighting you might not accomplish that."

"Nothing will," Kesira retorted. She clung to the baby with such fervor that he stirred and tried to push himself

away. Tiny fists gripped at her until she relaxed enough
to allow him to breathe again.

"There is a price for everything, even people," said
Nehan-dir.

"Power is yours. You have yet to find mine!"

"Ah, you are wrong. At least I have told my followers
that I have penetrated that facade of iron surrounding you
so totally." Nehan-dir reached into the front of his tunic
and pulled forth a handful of blue-tipped green feathers,
then cast them in front of him as if paving the way for a
tender-footed nobleman.

"So?" Kesira saw nothing in the mercenary's action to
menace her.

"Those are *trilla* bird feathers. From your friend Zolkan."

Kesira said nothing. Molimo let out a strangled gasp
that began deep in his chest and died in his throat.

"We have the *trilla* bird. If you do not agree to exchange
the baby for your Zolkan, well," Nehan-dir said, smiling
wickedly, "I have been told that *trilla* bird meat is quite
tasty."

Molimo's ebony-dark eyes filled with tears and then
overflowed. Kesira watched in silent horror as they stained
the dirt on the man's cheeks. She might have called Nehan-
dir a liar, but the sight of Molimo crying like this convinced
her that the Steel Crescent did hold the bird captive. Whatever communication existed between Molimo and Zolkan
had confirmed it.

But to give up the baby for Zolkan?

Kesira fought back tears of her own as she shook with
impotent rage.

Chapter Ten

"THE TRADE IS QUITE simple, even for one such as you."
Nehan-dir openly sneered at her now. "The baby means
little to you. How can it be any other way? It isn't even
your flesh and blood. But the *trilla* bird . . ." The mercenary leader's voice trailed off suggestively. Kesira had no
doubt that Nehan-dir would perform the vilest of tortures
on Zolkan, given the chance.

"A few tail feathers cast on the ground does not mean
you actually have him," Kesira said.

Molimo handed her his tablet. On it he had written,
"Nehan-dir speaks the truth. Zolkan is their prisoner."

Kesira didn't bother to ask Molimo how he knew. That
odd communication between him and the *trilla* bird might
have come into play. If so, she had to believe that the
worst had happened.

She took a deep, settling breath and forced calm upon
her turbulent thoughts. Panic now spelled death for those
she loved—and perhaps even herself. Nehan-dir did not
deal honestly if he could find a more devious path to
follow. Kesira imagined herself drifting on the gentle summer winds, tossed as lightly as one of Zolkan's feathers,
drifting, floating, coming to rest on the good earth. This
gave her the needed tranquillity for deeper thoughts to rise
within her for examination, thoughts otherwise hidden behind the static of her fear.

"I want to discuss this with Molimo."

Nehan-dir made a deprecating gesture. "Take all the

time you want. Just don't be longer than one minute." He gave an ugly laugh. "How you can discuss anything with a cripple is beyond me."

Kesira wasted no time on Nehan-dir. She huddled close to Molimo and pressed her trembling lips to his ear. "We cannot let Zolkan stay in *his* hands."

"Boy is important. Without him there is no way to defeat Ayondela." A tear fell from Molimo's cheek to spot the tablet. He brushed it away self-consciously.

"Zolkan is more than a friend to you, isn't he?" she asked. Molimo only nodded. Kesira looked at Nehan-dir standing indolently, his sword balanced on its tip near the toe of his right boot. She kept her calm—and knew she had the answer.

She stood in front of Nehan-dir. Shoulders squared, Kesira looked him directly in the eye. For a moment her attitude perplexed the mercenary. The cobweb pattern of scars on his face throbbed pink, and his eyebrows lowered in a frown. Whatever response he'd expected, it hadn't been such boldness.

"I won't turn the baby over to you," she said in measured tones.

This did surprise Nehan-dir. "Then the bird's life is forfeit."

"That gains you nothing."

"Satisfaction. Some small pleasure watching the feathered one die." The small mercenary shrugged. "It's a hard life. I take what enjoyment I can, where I can."

"You'd still not have the baby."

"There are other ways."

"I offer you one," Kesira said. She forced herself not to nervously lick her lips and so betray her fear. "Zolkan and the infant are to be the stake in a winner-take-both duel."

"Oh? They're the stakes, are they?" Contempt rippled through his words, but Kesira saw that she'd won. Interest glowed in the man's narrowed eyes. She had embarrassed him too many times in their past meetings for such an offer to go unheeded. His finest warriors had died at her or Molimo's hand during their cross-country flight. Their escape from Ayondela's Isle of Eternal Winter had been the crowning humiliation for such a proud fighter.

"Do you accept the challenge?"

"If I don't, the *trilla* bird dies."

"If you don't, the baby will never be yours," Kesira countered hotly.

Nehan-dir smiled wickedly. "That's not necessarily true. While I can't bring my full force to bear at this moment"— he tipped his head in Captain Protaro's direction—"there is nothing to say that I won't be victorious later, down the trail, after you have left the Guard's protection."

"I can always decide that the boy is better off in the Emperor's hands than in yours."

"You have already made that decision once. Why make it again?" he asked. His eyes darted to where the infant lay, pale eyes watching closely in an uncharacteristically old and wise fashion.

"Single battle. At dawn."

"Where? I do not cherish the idea of combat so near to the Guard's camp. They won't take the loss of the child easily."

"Down the trail. A few miles. The fight won't take long." Kesira hoped it would never come to pass. She was only angling for more time and the possibilities it might offer.

"There is a small well. Be there at sunrise." Nehan-dir vanished into the ebon night as silently as if he'd never been present. Kesira stood and stared at the emptiness— and felt an equally large hole within her.

"We cannot fight by his rules, Molimo," she said. They hurried to their mounts, her mind racing all the while. "I'll cut myself a staff and engage him."

Molimo shook his head.

Kesira ignored him. "While we're fighting, you sneak into his camp and steal away with Zolkan, just as I've done with the baby."

Molimo looked skeptical. Kesira didn't blame him. The idea seemed too fragile to bear close scrutiny, however, and it was the best she could come up with under such pressure of time.

An hour down the trail Kesira stopped and went to a small sapling about her height. She motioned. Molimo chopped and hacked at it with his sword until she had a smooth staff. Kesira shivered as she ran her fingers along the supple green length. Gelya would never approve. The wood had been hewn with steel, thus robbing the staff of any mystical power that might otherwise have been imparted to it. Its balance did not pleasure her, either. One end was heavier than the other.

Kesira ran agile fingers down its length, frowning as tiny buds popped out along it. She hacked them off, stroked over the wood to test its smoothness, and again found incipient limbs sprouting. On impulse, she held her hand over one recent amputation. Her touch restored life to the staff.

Molimo watched silently. She shook her head and carefully scraped away the new growth she'd inadvertently fostered.

"It will have to do."

"This plan will never work," wrote Molimo. He underlined his words with a quick flourish to emphasize his worry.

"Can you think of anything better? All Nehan-dir's followers will want to watch the fight. Only if they do will their attention shift away from Zolkan. You *must* rescue him then."

"What of you?"

Kesira ran one hand through her short brown hair. "I don't know. Maybe I can defeat him." She saw the man's sour expression. "I don't think I can, either, but you told me that self-doubt is the great killer. Let's get on with it. I want to be away from both Protaro and Nehan-dir before noon."

Molimo trailed and dismounted when they came to the

small artesian well Nehan-dir had mentioned. Already three
of the Steel Crescent soldiers stood by their leader. Their
attention turned to Kesira as she walked up. She laid the
baby down in a lightning-struck tree trunk, carefully filled
with a few patches of moss, to make a small, comfortable
cradle.

"Where's Zolkan?" she called to Nehan-dir.

"We have him. Do not fear on that point. I give you
my word of honor that he will be released if you defeat
me."

Nehan-dir slid his sword from its sheath. He accepted
a small, round shield from one of his men and turned down
the offer of a heavy helmet from another. Kesira smiled
at this. After almost drowning in the Sea of Katad, Nehan-
dir had learned that armor carried its own penalties. While
he wasn't likely to fall into the shallow pool of clear water
bubbling from the depths of the planet, he didn't want her
superior mobility to work against him. No armor.

Kesira thought that his sword and shield would prove
more than adequate against her unseasoned staff. Her eyes
flickered in Molimo's direction, then came back to Nehan-
dir. She could only hope that Molimo had sidled toward
the copse surrounding the well and was making his way
to Nehan-dir's encampment to rescue Zolkan.

"Haieeee!"

Kesira dropped into a defensive stance as Nehan-dir's
shrill war cry shattered the tranquillity of the morning. He
rushed her, sword held high. She deftly avoided his headlong rush, turning her back toward the rising sun. But she
found this did her no good. He used the brilliantly polished
shield to reflect light into her face. They circled warily,
looking for any advantage.

"Give me the baby and save yourself," Nehan-dir said.

"We fight. To the death, if necessary."

Kesira easily fended off his thrust and swung her staff
around to soundly thump Nehan-dir in the ribs.

The battle had begun in earnest.

* * *

Molimo watched as Kesira and Nehan-dir squared off. He began reciting the spell given him by Toyaga. Molimo saw the warriors' eyes blink and come unfocused as the magicks took hold and turned him into an object not easily stared at. The magicks made it easier for the mercenaries to watch their leader than to obey Nehan-dir's orders not to let Molimo out of their sight.

He worked his way up into the jagged rocks above the battle site, then across the face of a cliff, continually repeating the spell to keep prying eyes away.

Zolkan? his silent message went out. From below came the singsong speech Molimo had hoped to hear.

"Only two guard me," warned the *trilla* bird. "How degrading. They have me caged!"

Zolkan sounded more peeved than angry at his treatment.

"They pluck my feathers for their amusement! I will peck out their eyes for this affront! My lovely feathers, *gone!*"

Remain calm. Kesira fights Nehan-dir so that I can rescue you.

"Be quick about it." A loud squawk of protest allowed Molimo's sharp ears to pinpoint the bird in the Steel Crescent's campsite. One of the mercenaries had shaken Zolkan's cage to silence the bird.

Metamorphosis began inside Molimo. He stopped, sweat beading his forehead. He pressed himself into the cool, substantial rock, wincing at the slight pain as an outcropping cut into his flesh. He didn't want to transform into a wolf. Not now. He had to retain this form to rescue Zolkan.

His friend. Zolkan. Kesira fighting. Pain. Molimo fought to focus his thoughts on human concerns and not on animalistic ones. But the pain, the pain!

The dizziness passed, and he held on to the human shape. He gusted a sigh of relief, then turned his attention back to the camp. Two guards stood, one on either side of a crudely constructed cage. A dirty rag had been tossed over the top, but Molimo saw a long, brightly colored tail feather protruding from between the bars.

Carefully working his way down the rocky slope, Molimo came within ten teet of the guards before one turned and saw him. Gone was all hope of using Toyaga's spell to advance within striking distance.

Molimo whipped out his sword and took three quick steps forward and lunged. The tip of his blade found a bloody berth in the man's throat. Jerking free, Molimo slashed viciously at the other guard. She had time to respond.

Steel met steel.

But the contest ended swiftly when Zolkan got his head out between two of the wooden bars and fastened his beak firmly on the woman's leg. She yelped in pain as the serrated edges severed a greave and found flesh beneath. Molimo gave her no chance to recover. His blade arced up, down, into her shoulder, to sunder important arteries. She died without uttering a word.

Release her, Molimo commanded. *I can't get you out of the cage unless you do.*

"Satisfying," Zolkan said. "She tormented me constantly. Bitch. Pigeon-shit bitch!"

Kesira is facing Nehan-dir. We must get back and tell her you are safe.

"How are we to escape?" squawked the bird.

Molimo said nothing.

"Another of her fine plans, eh?" muttered Zolkan. "Great start, no finish. Pigeons plan better!"

Go, my friend. Show yourself to Kesira and let her know she can disengage.

Zolkan stretched cramped wings and legs, then waddled along clumsily until he found a downhill stretch. Racing along, flapping hard, the *trilla* bird became airborne. Molimo watched Zolkan spiral upward, then begin descending to warn Kesira. To his dismay Zolkan returned immediately, landing heavily on his shoulder. He knew the bird had only bad news to impart when sharp claws cut carelessly into his shoulder.

"They are gone. All of them," announced Zolkan, bitterness seeping into the words.

How?

"Why did you think Nehan-dir would fight fairly? He wanted baby, he took baby. Ground looks as if Kesira fought when all surrounded and took her prisoner."

They took her to insure food for the baby, Molimo said.

"Weakling child," grumbled Zolkan. "Not like *trilla* bird hatchlings. A few weeks in nest, then out. Only way to learn to fly."

Don't sit there, get aloft. Find them. They can't be more than a few minutes away.

"You run after them. I saw no horses."

Nehan-dir wastes nothing, said Molimo. *But I have two mounts. Theirs.* He pointed to the fallen soldiers. *Go. Find them and return to let me know where.*

"Others seek you. Squad of men coming from direction of Lorum Bay."

Protaro and the Emperor's Guard. Kesira killed one of them to recover the baby.

"Brat is going to get us slaughtered. Leave it with Nehan-dir."

No! You know why we cannot do that. Now go, damn your beak. Go!

Zolkan took wing again and strained up the meadows until he found morning thermals to ride. Quick black eyes scanned the ground for signs of Kesira and her captors. Zolkan found them in less than ten minutes. He wheeled to return to Molimo.

"Their horses tire," said Zolkan.

Kesira holds them back. See how she purposefully chooses the worst path?

The *trilla* bird cawed and hunkered down on Molimo's shoulder to watch. Molimo pulled his horse around abruptly and took a higher path through the meadow to keep a stand of trees between him and Nehan-dir's party. The man had been all too aware of the Emperor's Guard slowly narrowing the distance between them throughout the day. The collision of the Steel Crescent mercenaries and Captain Protaro's men was not something Molimo wanted to see again. If luck held, he and Kesira and the baby would be far away by the time the Emperor's fire mixed with the Order of the Steel Crescent's tinder.

"They stop. I hear sounds of dismounting," said Zolkan.

Molimo vaulted from the saddle and tethered both horses to a low shrub. He hurried into the lightly forested area bordering the meadow, feeling as if some force pulled him toward Nehan-dir.

Power fills me, he told the *trilla* bird. *It is a sensation similar to that I get when I use Toyaga's spell.*

"Compulsion magicks?"

I . . . it may be. It is so difficult for me to tell. If only I were stronger!

Molimo dropped to hands and knees and traversed the last twenty yards in this manner. Through bushes fragrant with blossoms and buzzing with pollen-dusted insects, Molimo peered out to see Kesira nursing the infant. Beside her stood Nehan-dir, hand on his sword hilt. The others in the band prepared fortifications.

They realize Protaro is close behind, he said. *They must not be able to outrun the Emperor's Guard.*

"Should I attract Kesira's attention?" asked the bird.

Wait. She . . . she knows we are here.

"How?"

The baby tells her. The baby summons me. Me! How is that possible?

"It has more power than the pink worm it resembles," Zolkan said with ill grace. "Trouble. It only brings us more trouble."

Molimo pushed Zolkan back into the wooded area and fell flat onto his belly. Even his sharp ears did not catch all that Nehan-dir said to Kesira. Whatever it was, the words obviously distressed the nun. She shot to her feet, only to be shoved back to the ground. Molimo closed his eyes and concentrated on retaining his human shape. As before, it did him no good to become his wolf self.

Power from without aided him. When he opened his eyes, he saw that Nehan-dir had sent away the others guarding Kesira. Only he stood over her.

Molimo began the magical spell that would allow him to approach unseen.

> The world about me,
> There are no eyes.
> Freedom of the air and sky,
> I fade into nothingness.

He inched forward as quietly as he could. One hand reached out and tugged at Kesira's sleeve while his other gripped his dagger. Nehan-dir died if he penetrated the veil of magic.

Kesira frowned as she looked down, then smiled. She shook her head slightly to indicate that this was not the most opportune time to escape. Molimo knew they had no choice. Protaro and his Guardsmen would arrive within the hour. If they were caught up in the ensuing battle, it would bode ill for everyone.

"They will not recapture the baby," said Nehan-dir to Kesira. "Lenc has ordered the infant's presence and promised vast rewards when we are successful."

"The Emperor will grant you equal riches," she said.

"Riches? Lenc promises power. What else is there? With power all riches can be mine." Nehan-dir half turned to survey the hasty construction work on the battlements. Molimo flowed upward, the hilt of his dagger aimed directly at the man's prominent chin.

Metal struck bone. The mercenary leader fell to the ground, stunned.

"No!" Kesira said as Molimo reversed the knife to slit the exposed throat. "Leave him."

Molimo was not going to obey. Never leave behind a weapon or a living enemy. Those were hard lessons recently learned. But he had no time to finish even a quick cut now. Nehan-dir's soldiers had seen him, and Kesira tugged at his arm.

"Leave him!" she cried. "We must get away. Why couldn't you have waited?"

Molimo shoved the woman toward the sparse forest. She stumbled but held on to the child. The rattle of weapons kept them moving until the thicker stands of trees sheltered them. Molimo jerked her to one side and pointed to a game trail running at a right angle to their current path. Without hesitation Kesira took it. Molimo started to continue on, then heard the uproar from behind.

None of the Steel Crescent mercenaries followed. The Emperor's Guard had attacked, successfully decoying the mercenaries into believing that their main body still rode the trail. This diversion might be enough to let him slip away with Kesira.

Zolkan! he cried, reaching out to find the *trilla* bird.

"They won't be after you for several minutes," the bird responded. "Stay with Kesira."

Molimo darted along the trail, feet pounding heavily until he overtook her. He looked at her dirty face, the matted hair, the scratched arms and battered clothing and had never seen any woman as pretty.

The baby's pale eyes fixed on his dark ones. Power flowed. Molimo croaked, but no audible words came.

Kesira halted and stared curiously at them. "Are you all right?" she asked Molimo. The man nodded. Kesira reached out and touched his cheek. "You're flushed. You're not running a fever?"

Zolkan battered his way through the overhanging branches and perched on a slender limb just above their heads. "Horses dead. Protaro's soldiers killed them."

"What? Why?" Kesira asked.

"Thought they were Nehan-dir's. Battle goes against Steel Crescent. Nehan-dir still unconscious." Zolkan looked disparagingly at Molimo. The mercenary leader ought to have died with a quick slash of the dagger.

"Without horses, what are we going to do?" Kesira asked. "We must go back and steal some. That's the only way. The confusion, we can——"

Molimo took her by the elbow and turned her to face a shallow depression in the side of a low, rocky hill. He went to it and began digging, dirt and greenery flying. In a few minutes he revealed a low cave entrance. Molimo pointed.

"Well, it might work," she said, frowning. "If we hide long enough, they'll think we escaped. But I don't like the idea of hiding in a cave." Memories of all that had happened to her in the Abbey of Ayondela returned with haunting force.

Molimo scooted in on his belly. Reluctantly Kesira followed close behind—and just in time.

The heavy tread of boots echoed down the game trail they'd just abandoned. Zolkan awkwardly pulled loose bushes up to cover the entrance, but he didn't work fast enough.

"There," called a loud voice. "There they are. In that cave!"

Kesira and Molimo exchanged looks. Fighting in the narrow confines of this rocky shaft was out of the question.

"Let's get on with it," she said. "I don't like it, but we have no other choice." On hands and knees Kesira Minette crawled deeper into the cave. From the sides and above she felt the ponderous weight of rock waiting to crush her to a bloody pulp.

Chapter Eleven

"WAIT! STOP! Don't leave me!"

Kesira looked back over her shoulder the best she could in the low-ceilinged rock passage and saw a green lump of rumpled feathers waddling along behind.

"Zolkan!" she cried. "Why didn't you fly off?"

"Trapped. Pigeon-shit soldiers trapped me!" The *trilla* bird hopped up and landed on Kesira's back. She sagged under the additional weight. With the infant slung under her, so that she could barely move, and the large bird's bulk pressing her down, Kesira felt as if she truly carried the weight of the world on her shoulders.

From the pursed mouth of the cave came the sounds of pursuit. Kesira took a deep breath and continued after Molimo. No matter where this passage led, it would be paradise compared to being captured by either Captain Protaro or Nehan-dir. Both would share her death for what she'd done to them.

An eternity later Kesira banged into Molimo. The darkness had turned absolute, and claustrophobia closed in on her, making it difficult to breathe. She knew that this was only a failure of her mind, not of the air itself, but that did not make the problem any less significant.

She snapped at Molimo, "What are you stopping for? Keep going!"

He crawled another few feet. Kesira sensed a widening in the tunnel, as if it turned into a large chamber. She rushed forward as fast as she could on hands and knees,

then cautiously explored with her hands. The low ceiling
vanished abruptly. Like a blind beggar, Kesira started feeling for the limits of this chamber.

She shrieked when she found Molimo.

"You startled me," she said, trying to still her racing
heart. When the pounding in her temples died down, she
heard the scratchings of metal on rock back in the passage.
Someone came for them—and she had no idea whether
it was the Steel Crescent or the Emperor's Guard.

Even worse, it didn't matter. She had to fight to the
death to keep them from taking the baby. Kesira cradled
the infant and rocked it gently, soothingly. She felt one fat
little fist clutch at her, but no sound rose from those lips.
Weights even greater than before descended on her. The
child had to be afflicted in some fashion—possibly by the
evil power of jade. All her troubles stemmed from Lenc
and the others. All Molimo's did also. It seemed only
reasonable to blame any problems of the baby on the jade
demons.

"We don't have much time," she said. "They're not
more than five minutes behind us. How long do you think
we can hold them back, Molimo?"

She tensed when the man fumbled at her pouch, then
relaxed when she saw what he wanted. He withdrew the
last of her magical powder used for starting fires.

"Do you have any fuel?"

The sudden blinding flare of white answered her question. He had found some dried cave moss. It burned rapidly, but the ample piles of it in the medium-size cave
provided fuel for all the time they'd need. She closed her
eyes and tried to calm her raging emotions. All the time
they'd need: less than five minutes now.

Sounds of pursuit came closer.

"That," squawked Zolkan. "Move it! Move it!"

"What?" Kesira swung around to see what the bird
meant. At the rear of the cave a large, circular stone plug
filled—what? A new passage? To where?

Kesira went to the plug and ran her hand over it. In

the guttering light cast by the burning moss all color vanished. She squinted and ran her fingernail across the surface.

"*Tulna* stone. This cost an Emperor's treasury to make!"

"Open it, open it. No time to steal it. Hurry!" urged Zolkan. The bird waddled back and forth nervously. "They come soon, too soon. They eat *trilla* meat!"

Kesira's fingers tensed, and her shoulders ached from the attempt to push the stone door, or pull it, or move it in any direction. Sweating, eyes burning with acrid smoke from the burning moss, she sank to the floor.

"Too heavy," she said.

She glanced up at Molimo, who stood strangely transfixed. Kesira started to touch him, to urge him to resist the shape-change to wolf. But his expression was subtly different from that seizing him prior to a shape-altering. She thought a change was occurring but not of form.

Molimo walked to the orange *tulna* stone, widened his stance, and put his hands flat against the smooth gateway. Muscles expanded along his upper arms and shoulders, knotting so hard that his tunic began to bulge. Sweat popped onto his forehead, but his face kept the same odd lack of expression.

The stone door moved inward. Molimo shifted, and the door swung away to reveal a corridor walled in ceramic tiles decorated with intricate dancing figures, finely drawn geometric patterns, and colors so brilliant, they almost hurt Kesira's eyes. It took her several seconds to realize why.

"The tiles glow!"

Molimo stood motionless, eyes fixed on something at the far end of the newly revealed corridor. But on what Kesira couldn't tell.

Zolkan had already flapped his way into the passage, cawing loudly. Kesira followed, taking Molimo by the hand and gently pulling him after.

"Can you close the door?" she asked. Her eyes darted to the low tunnel soon to be filled with the soldiers pursuing

them. Having the door between them and the soldiers
would further hinder capture.

Molimo did a smart about-face and leaned against the
orange door, getting it into ponderous movement once
more.

Kesira put her weight against the door, too, when she
saw the first soldier stagger upright in the smoky chamber
they'd just left. A loud battle cry rang in her ears—almost
as loud as the slithering of steel against sheath.

"Oh, faster, faster," she moaned, straining. Kesira
doubted that her efforts aided Molimo one iota, but she
had to try. All the power she had felt when she fought
Esamir pulsed through her, but it was still too small an
effort to move so ponderous a door. She saw that the
advancing soldier, one of the Emperor's Guard, evaluated
the problem facing him and acted instinctively. He threw
his sword forward to prevent the door from smoothly meeting the jamb. By the time they got the blade free to lock
the door, his comrades would have joined him.

The shiny steel clanked noisily as Molimo pushed the
stone door closed.

Kesira watched in mute horror as the blade began to
smoke. It melted and ran down the walls to form a puddle
of hissing, molten metal. She danced away to keep the
metallic spray from burning her.

"What caused that?" she asked.

Molimo motioned for her to accompany Zolkan down
the corridor.

"They'll have the door open soon," she said. "You're
right. We must be away when they get through."

For the first time Molimo's expression changed. He
smiled, then laughed silently. With a soot-smudged finger
he wrote on one of the snowy white tiles lining the walls.

"No one opens that door."

"But you did."

"I am feeling stronger now. I heal. Away from jade I
heal!" His words trailed into illegibility as the soot finally

rubbed free of his fingers, and Kesira couldn't read the rest.

Molimo may have felt stronger, but Kesira's legs buckled under her. She sagged. Molimo caught her and half carried her along the glowing hallway. The pictures flowed beside her as if they had taken on a life of their own. Kesira fought to stay alert and failed.

"Rest," ordered Zolkan, hopping up beside her. "We can go on soon. When it arrives."

"It? What are you talking about? What *is* this place?" she asked. But her strength faded more and more. Kesira lay back, the baby snuggling serenely at her side. She drifted off to a deep, dreamless sleep, the last thing she remembered being Molimo saying, *We can reach Ayondela before dawn*.

Kesira stirred and opened her eyes. Molimo sat just a few feet away, watching her. His expression defied her powers to describe, but it was a tender look. Love? She couldn't say for certain.

"Hello," she said, stretching her arms and legs to get circulation back. "I had the strangest dream—or not-dream—just before I went to sleep. I thought you spoke to me."

Molimo looked at Zolkan, then back at her. He shook his head slowly, thoughtfully.

"Not likely, not likely," the *trilla* bird squawked. "When do we eat? So hungry. Can't stay clean, don't get fed. What life is this to lead?"

"One of us gets fed," she said, picking up the infant.

Molimo dropped to the floor and pressed his ear against the cool ceramic tile. For long minutes he listened, then quickly motioned to Zolkan. The bird let forth a long string of the singsong speech that excluded Kesira before saying to her, "Ride comes. We go faster now. Be sure to hang on."

"Ride? Our horses are outside—dead, you told me."

"No horses. Faster. We go to Ayondela. Come along, hurry, hurry!"

Kesira settled the baby over her shoulder and gently patted him as she went to stand beside Molimo and Zolkan. The bird cawed and vaulted to her right shoulder.

"Put it away. No time for hobby."

"Zolkan, he's not a hobby."

The sudden change in air pressure made Kesira clap hands over her ears. She cried out and neutralized the inner pressure, and finally a long, wide yawn finished the job. Kesira stared in amazement at the device causing her the discomfort.

"It's like a wagon," she said, "but there aren't any wheels. What manner of magical device is it?"

"Demons hate travel among humans," said Zolkan. "This is demon's private transport system."

Kesira examined it carefully. The short, padded bench mounted on a circular plug of *tulna* stone had come through an irising hole in the wall. Other than this she saw nothing at all. Molimo took her elbow and guided her toward the bench. With some trepidation she sat down, Molimo beside her. Zolkan muttered to himself, then jumped to the seat, wedging himself between them.

"Hate this. Why can't we fly?" the bird grumbled.

The sudden acceleration took away Kesira's breath, even as a scream formed on her lips. The bench and circular stone behind it shot forward toward a solid wall. A fraction of a second before they'd have become jam, the wall irised open to a diameter large enough to accommodate their strange vehicle. They blasted through and into a long, dark shaft. The sense of speed mounted, and wind seared at the woman's face.

"I can't see anything!" she shouted past the rush of air. "What if we hit something?"

"We die," came Zolkan's hardly cheering words. "Hate this. Better to soar and look down on miserable humans."

Kesira gulped as a tiny point of light grew and grew. Another doorway irised open; they stopped as quickly as

they had started. Kesira tumbled forward, not prepared for
the braking. Molimo grabbed her in time to save her from
a nasty fall.

On shaking legs Kesira walked away from the bench.
A gust of wind blew past her, and the magical vehicle
vanished on its imponderable way beneath the ground.

"Who conjured that?" she asked, staring at the empty
space where the vehicle had been. "It must have been a
mighty demon."

"Not so strong but a good demon," said Zolkan. "Merrisen honeycombed world with these pigeon-brained things
for his own use. Other demons use them sometimes."

"He waited for one of those carriages to come, then
just rode it? How'd he control where it went?"

"Merrisen powerful enough to summon, then direct,"
explained Zolkan. "But no longer. Some roam, going from
spot to spot. We caught one of those."

Kesira shook her head in amazement. She had never
suspected that such a network existed. "Do these tunnels
reach into the Yearn Mountains?"

"Within ten miles of your nunnery," said Zolkan.

"How do you know this? You've never shown such
knowledge before."

"No need to tell all I know, is there?" The *trilla* bird
jumped from her shoulder and flapped a few feet to land
in front of another large diameter of *tulna* stone. He made
pecking motions at it, anxious to be under way. Kesira
went to the stone and laid her hands against it. Try as she
might, the stone door refused to budge. Only when Molimo
came over and began pushing did it move slowly.

Kesira boldly walked through to the chamber on the
other side, not expecting the reception she received. Hairy
arms grabbed at her hair and face. Clawed hind feet came
up to savage her belly. And the creature's bulk made her
stagger backward into Molimo.

An inarticulate cry erupted from Molimo's throat. The
almost human sound turned to a wolf's snarl. Kesira
slumped to the floor, hands clutching her belly, thankful

the claws had missed the baby. In the center of the chamber Molimo and the ape creature faced each other, snapping and dodging, venting noisy challenges, looking for the other's weakness in order to end the battle.

"Zolkan, help him!" she cried.

But the *trilla* bird perched on a broken tile, not moving. Disgusted with her friend, Kesira shucked off the sling holding the baby and put him out of harm's way. She rushed to Molimo's discarded clothing, her hand almost closing on the sword hilt, but though her indoctrination had faded, she could not ignore Gelya's edict against using steel. Instead she grabbed Molimo's tunic and rushed forward, swinging it in front of her.

The ape creature turned large, luminous brown eyes in her direction. Yellowed, broken teeth clattered together, and an unearthly howl filled her ears. She didn't wait to see what further devilment this monster might give. She tossed the tunic as if it were a fisherman's net. It spun open, then fell over the creature's head, momentarily blinding it.

A gray streak passed her. Molimo's fangs found the beast's throat. Strong neck muscles bulged as Molimo ripped and tore, even as the ape creature's claws opened bloody streaks on the wolf's flanks. That raking motion weakened, then stopped when the last of the creature's life fled its carcass.

Molimo threw back his lupine head and howled in triumph. Kesira watched, sick to her stomach. Even though she would have died without the other-beast transformation seizing Molimo, she wished it could be otherwise. It was so difficult to care for someone who might view you as dinner.

The howling cut off in midnote. Quick green eyes darted about. The sensitive wolf nose sniffed the air.

Kesira almost fainted when she saw the bat fluttering crazily into the chamber. She had never been afraid of bats—real bats. This one robbed her of all feeling but dread.

A human girl's face had replaced the usual ratlike one.

"Kill you, kill you!" cried the bat, swooping low. Tiny fangs opened and closed just a fraction of an inch away from Kesira's nose. She swatted at the odious other-beast, then saw that it flew directly for the baby. Kesira's feet slipped on the blood-slickened floor and sent her sprawling facedown. She screamed and fought to get to the baby before the bat-thing.

Zolkan dropped like a stone, talons catching the bat just behind the neck. The *trilla* bird jerked sideways, lost airspeed, and fell heavily to the tile floor, still clinging to the bat. Another hard jerk produced a tiny snapping noise. The other-beast shrilled and died. Zolkan cast it away with obvious distaste.

"Jade infects too many," he said.

"That had been a little girl? A child?" asked Kesira in shock. The idea that the baby—*her* baby—might end up like that stunned her. "I've seen adults caught in the transformations but never a child. Why?"

There had been no reason for her to exclude small children from her mental image of those afflicted with the jade evil, but she had. Those either switching totally, like Molimo, or permanently caught or trapped halfway, had all been adults.

"This is a travesty," she muttered between clenched teeth. "Ayondela will pay for this. And Lenc—curse you, Lenc! If I desired your death before, it fades before the hatred I hold for you now!"

"Shush," cautioned Zolkan. "Jade power lets them hear anything, anywhere."

"Come for me now if this is so," Kesira challenged. "I'll meet you!"

A hand on her shoulder broke her insane rage. Molimo had undergone the transformation once more and had donned his clothing. The tunic had been tattered by the ape's claws, and blood soaked everything. He went to the white tile on the walls and wrote in blood, "Do not summon them until we are ready. Please!"

"But this is awful." Kesira sat cross-legged and stared at the girl-faced bat.

"Bad," agreed Zolkan. "Worse if we die."

"Did Merrisen always guard his chambers with the likes of that?" she said, forcing herself to look away from the bat-thing and toward the ape.

"It is other-beast too. Great power flows nearby. Ayon-dela is atop her mountain."

"We'll be battling their ilk?"

Zolkan's head bobbed up and down.

"Then let us get to it. My nerve might not last much longer." Kesira saw that the baby had watched their struggles with inhuman calm, but then, what did a mere babe in arms know of such atrocities against nature? She slung the boy comfortably and followed Molimo down the glow-tiled corridor.

They passed another of the orange *tulna*-stone barriers and into a cave. Kesira Minette left the cave to emerge into the bright light of day.

She gasped at the sight dominating the landscape.

Chapter Twelve

"THAT'S IMPOSSIBLE," Kesira Minette whispered. She took a step forward and stood, arms hanging at her sides. The single spire rose up with beauty so breathtaking, it couldn't be real. Pure white snow decorated the ebony trail spiraling up the dark red granite column like a portrait lifted from a master painter's canvas. No detail marred the perfection, but the mountain itself accounted for only a small portion of Kesira's awestruck gaping.

A tiny toy of a jade palace capped the peak. Sunlight reflected off the green sides in a dazzling display that highlighted the other stark colors.

"How large must it be?" she said, her voice returning to normal. "It looks so small, but the peak is immense. The palace must be larger than the Emperor's!"

"More, much more," agreed Zolkan. "Deadly too. Everywhere Ayondela has traps. No one invades. Thousands died constructing her hideaway." The *trilla* bird turned bitter. "She had birds fly up much. All died. All."

"Do you mean *trilla* birds? You're not large enough, Zolkan."

"Magicks made many large enough. Many thousands. All dead. The spells killed all, noble hearts bursting from effort." Zolkan made a spitting noise. "She is shit. Worse! Ayondela not fit to live."

Kesira wobbled slightly, light-headed. Her inchoate plan to offer the baby to Ayondela in exchange for her neutrality

135

seemed naive. But her rune sticks had indicated that as
the solution to the problems posed by the female demon.

"I can't comprehend such magic," Kesira admitted. For
the first time she had an inkling of the forces she opposed
and how lucky she had been to defeat both Eznofadil and
Howenthal. Wemilat had given her some protection, and
Kesira had to admit that only demons unseen and unmen-
tioned opposing Ayondela had brought victory.

Who were her allies now? Wemilat the Ugly had died.
Toyaga had perished. Left were a molting *trilla* bird and
a young man whose tongue had been ripped out. Kesira
wanted to cry when she looked down and added Raellard
and Parvey's infant.

A bird, a baby, and a mute, together with a nun from
an order whose patron had perished. The mighty con-
querors!

Molimo snapped his fingers in front of her nose and
broke her self-pitying reverie. In the dirt he etched the
words, "We can do it. Doubt yourself and fail. Believe
and succeed."

"You're sounding more like Gelya all the time," Kesira
said, smiling weakly. "But there's not much choice, is
there? If we don't try—and as bad as it looks, we've got
the best chance—no one will. The Emperor is off in Limaden tending to the concerns of running the Empire.
We've defied him because we thought we could do a better
job of fighting the jade demons."

Kesira looked again at the majestic spire rising to stab
the very clouds. White, fluffy cumulus clouds built below
the summit, then rose.

She frowned when she noted the odd swirling of those
clouds. They looked more like the product of a tornado
than mountain-wind-whipped clouds.

"Those," she said. Molimo nodded.

Zolkan said, "Worse than mist in Lorum Bay. That was
just practice. Those clouds are deadly. No one flies to the
summit, not past clouds."

"Can we even climb the trail?" Kesira knew she had

received power enough from Cayabbib to dissipate small clusters of clouds—but those! She witnessed hurricane-force winds churning at a mile-deep layer of cloud ringing the mountaintop.

"We must."

Visions of the clouds surging around her, crystalline knives slashing at her face and hands and arms and any exposed portion of her body rose in the woman's mind. Such magical protection provided Ayondela more security than legions of soldiers. Who could mount an upward assault on the jade fortress in strengths enough to conquer?

"Stealth is our only hope. Can we sneak past the clouds?"

"Only go through. Very, very dangerous," said Zolkan.

The slick granite walls of the shaft hadn't formed naturally; they had been scoured clean by the slicing action of the clouds.

"We have a long way to go on foot," Kesira said. "I've lived in mountains all my life and know how deceptive distances can be. This looks so close—and lies so far away."

They began the trek to the base of Ayondela's fortress.

"The other-beasts haven't bothered us for the past four days," Kesira said. "Any reason why not?"

Molimo drew the answer in the dirt. "They fear Ayondela's power. No one stays this close to the heart of her magicks."

"But her power created them—or at least the power of the jade did."

"Come too near jade and it twists you," spoke up Zolkan. "Even I feel its awful influences when I wing closer. What must those with true power feel?"

"You mean other demons?"

"The jade pulls them like lodestones draw iron. Then it destroys." The bird shifted uneasily on her shoulder. Kesira reached down and plucked a blueberry from a bush and held it for Zolkan. His quick beak snared it from her palm without even touching her flesh. "Berry unripe.

Phooey!" Zolkan spat the skin and a few seeds out and
rubbed his beak against her blouse.

"You complain too much."

"You complain more if this gives me shits." Zolkan
wiggled his tail feathers above her shoulder to make his
point.

"Do you feel the power of the jade? If it holds the other-
beasts at bay, it must be immense." She glanced around
nervously. Kesira imagined pressures mounting, but they
were all in her mind. No physical pressure assailed her,
and she didn't detect any magical one.

"I don't. Molimo might."

"Do you, Molimo? Feel Ayondela's magicks?"

Molimo had been leading the way down the winding
trail. He stopped and looked back. Kesira swallowed hard
when she saw his normally dark eyes flashing jade-green.
Only when he transformed into wolf did he have such a
feral, predatory look. But even as she watched the light
died, and midnight eyes peered up at her.

Molimo shook his head, but Kesira knew he lied.

The other-beasts had dogged their steps, but she worried
more about Protaro and Nehan-dir. While the quick transport under the mountains and far to the south had given
her and the others many days' lead on both the Steel
Crescent and the Emperor's Guard, she did not doubt that
their determination and wrath at her would goad them into
inhuman speeds. She had never made any secret of her
destination. Protaro had to know—and Nehan-dir need
only inquire of his jade patron.

"Is Lenc up there with Ayondela?" she asked.

"Who knows? We find out when we knock on front
door," said Zolkan.

Kesira jumped when a bass voice said, "Such information might be had for a price."

She spun, whirling the pitiful staff she had fashioned
from a small sapling. Like the other she had made, this
one's wood proved too green for real strength. She needed
hardness, not suppleness. And every time she tried to strip

off the fledgling limbs, new ones grew. Her slightest touch generated life, not the death she wanted.

But this accounted for only a part of her problems. The baby slung in front of her body hindered her too. She silently thanked Molimo for his quick retreat along the path. The man-wolf stood at her side, sword drawn.

Kesira frowned. How had the stranger escaped Molimo's keen senses? And her own were scarcely less acute.

The man sat cross-legged on a boulder, looking down at them. The amused expression on his face irritated Kesira more than anything else. He wore a long, dark brown robe embroidered with silver-thread-contrived beetles. On his head he wore a floppy cap pulled down low over his left eye at what he no doubt thought a jaunty angle. From beneath the hat poked shocks of sandy hair.

But his expression, those laughing blue eyes, that damnable way he had, all made her feel inferior.

"Who are you?" Kesira demanded.

"Such manners. One expects more from a nun of your order. Gelya's order, is it not? I detect the fine nuances in your speech, the way you walk along the trail—most delightful when observed from the proper angle, I might say." He leered at her openly.

"Molimo, Zolkan," she said. She began backing away and motioned for Molimo to do likewise. Zolkan buried his head under his wing and refused to look from his perch on her shoulder.

"Don't leave. Please! Have I offended you? What did I say? I get so lonely in these hills. No one comes along this way anymore, not since *she* built *that*." He pointed at the jade palace on the summit of the spire.

Kesira didn't follow the man's gesture. She had grown suspicious and noted that many warriors used such a motion to distract. From the corner of her eye she saw that Molimo didn't look away, either. Kesira felt vindicated. Molimo suspected this man, too, but of what?

"You live nearby?"

"Oh, yes, of course I do. For many years. It is so

peaceful in the hills, except during the winter months. Then there're continual snowstorms. Nasty ones but you grow used to them. I have. I even like them a little now. But for this time of year! Ah, nowhere in all the realm is there a finer spot."

"Who are you?"

The man slid down from the boulder and landed lightly. He made a bow Kesira thought more mocking than courtly.

"I supposed everyone knew me. How could I have been so mistaken, eh? I am Norvin. There are other names that go along with it, but you'd never remember them, so why bother?"

"Pleased to meet you," Kesira said insincerely.

"Your friend must be the doughty Zolkan, this one without tongue is Molimo, and you are Kesira Minette. And the baby." Norvin started to touch the child, then stopped, his face losing all expression. He glanced over at Molimo. "This one's power is . . . ample," Norvin said. Before Kesira could ask what he meant, the brown-robed man danced away.

"You must come and dine with me. Such a feast it will be. Never has anyone tickled your palates like I will."

"How do you know our names?" Kesira asked.

"You are famous throughout the realm. Aren't you the sister of the Mission? Yes! The gold sash, while the worse for wear, shows it. I was right!"

Kesira saw that she'd get no straight answer from Norvin. She tried a different approach. "You mentioned paying for information."

"But of course. All is for sale. I am the ultimate broker of any and all information. You need to know of Ayondela's palace? I have explored far into the cutting clouds and can sell you a map. Farther? You need only ask— and pony up the appropriate amount of coin. *I can be bought!*"

Norvin made it sound like a virtue.

"I'm not sure you have anything worth purchasing,"

Kesira said. "Come, let's be on our way. We still have a few hours of sunlight before the mountains rob us of day."

"It is worth more than the mountains themselves, what I can sell you. For, you see, I am a mage of some power. Some *immense* power."

"Why do you stay in Ayondela's shadow?"

"It . . . feeds me. I take what she discards and grow wiser from it."

"You," Kesira accused, "are not a demon?"

"I? Hardly. Oh, that is rich. She thinks I am a demon." Norvin shook his head and laughed at her. "While I am powerful, I am not *that* powerful. Except in one way."

"We have no need to listen to his blitherings," she said, turning to leave. If he intended to stab them in the back, Kesira decided that this might be better than having Norvin bore them to death with his egotistical bragging.

"You might have noticed that I use words well. I am a very oral person."

"I'm sure," Kesira said, tiring rapidly.

"I speak well, I sway the masses, should I ever encounter any—and I offer Molimo the power of speech. I have the power. I can restore his tongue."

Kesira stopped dead in her tracks. Turning slowly, she stared at the self-proclaimed mage in amazement.

"Yes, Lady of Gelya's Mission, it is true. Every word of it," Norvin said.

"You can give Molimo back his speech?"

"I can—and I will. For a price."

"No price can be too high for this."

What Norvin named was too high. "I want the baby," the mage said, his blue eyes gleaming.

Chapter Thirteen

"IT'S EVER SO SIMPLE. I would think even one as clever as you could understand my proposition." Norvin stood with arms crossed and a superior look on his face. "You give me the child, I give back Molimo's tongue and his power of speech."

"That's not possible," Kesira said in a low voice.

"But of course it is!" exclaimed Norvin. He bounced around. "The power is mine. I am a mage and very good at what I do. Or," he said, cocking his head to one side as he stared at Kesira, "do you mean you won't surrender the baby?"

"Both."

"It can't be both," the mage said firmly. "No, absolutely not. I get so lonely out here. I see you wandering through with a child you don't really care a whit for, and I think to myself, 'Norvin, you master mage, what is missing from your life?' The answer is ever so easy to come by. Companionship."

"Get pet," grumbled Zolkan, daring to look out from under his wing for the first time.

"I had a *trilla* bird once," Norvin said lightly. "I ate him."

"He'd do same with baby," said Zolkan. "Never trust any who eats bird flesh. Cannibals! All are cannibals!"

"A young one to learn my trade, to grow with me, to share the experiences of this wondrous life. Imagine living in such splendor *and* being trained by the foremost mage in all the world." Norvin swept his arm around to indicate the panoramic beauty of the countryside. Kesira couldn't help but follow that arm—partway. Her eyes stopped at the base of the spire holding Ayondela's jade palace. Slowly she studied every rock, every imperfection in the column until she came to the jade structure atop it.

Living in the shadow of such evil was no fit life for anyone, even a braggart like Norvin.

"Ah, you fear the young one's life because of Ayondela. Do not. She never notices that which is so close at hand. Her gaze goes out to the rest of the land. She fails to see me. She overlooks me as she looks over me. The baby would be safe to grow into manhood here."

"What magicks do you control that you can restore a tongue magically sundered?"

"My patron is noted for healings. You've certainly heard of him. Dunbar?"

Kesira said nothing. Close ties with a demon explained Norvin's knowledge. She had no doubt that the elevated society of demons buzzed with all that happened concerning Lenc and the others. Their existences were threatened, but most were powerless to fight the jade. She had considered most demons' desire to ignore all that happened and decided that the demons were just like humans—all too willing to believe conditions would improve without their help. Was Dunbar different?

Molimo caught her eye. He slowly shook his head. Kesira wondered if the man-wolf read her mind. At times it seemed so. At times it seemed that she read his thoughts.

"What use is the child to you? A burden, nothing more. He'd be a cherished part of my household. But come, I promised dinner such as you've never tasted before. Come and see how I dine in gourmet style every night."

"Eats *trilla* birds," complained Zolkan. "Eat shit before you dine at his table."

Norvin laughed in delight. "No *trilla* meat on this day's menu. Come and see for yourself."

The brown-robed man almost danced down the trail.

Kesira tried to understand his motives and failed. He seemed a happy enough sort, even addlepated, but she detected undercurrents of something more. No man in his right mind lived this close to the bastions of Ayondela's power without being touched—adversely.

"Come and look, see the sky? Those clouds mean nothing to the sky. The vast azure vault is limitless, Ayondela's power limited to a few paltry clouds of crystal knives."

Kesira let Norvin rattle on with his pointless speech. The beauty of the Sarn Mountains affected her, but her mind kept returning to the spire and the jade palace atop the spire. *That* was her goal; *that* might be her death.

"Wait," the mage said, thrusting his arms out straight on either side of his body. From behind he took on the aspect of some brown-winged bird of prey. "There is movement all around us. Evil stalks us."

Molimo shook his head and tapped his ears. He saw and heard nothing. In her ear Zolkan whispered, "Crazy as pigeon shit. Let him be. We can go on without him. Lies about Molimo's tongue."

"What is it you see?" Kesira called to Norvin. "We don't see anything."

"What?" the man bellowed. "How is that possible? You, the demon killers, do not detect them? They're everywhere. Everywhere!"

Even as the mage stomped around, flapping his arms and making odd gestures, Kesira sensed the presence of *others*. Not other-beasts but something deadly—and magical.

Whirlwinds exploded into flesh-searing violence all around. Dust blasted forth to blind and sting, and feathery fingers of mobile air ripped at Kesira's clothing. Her wolf-skin skirt flapped wildly and tripped her, bringing the woman to her knees. Zolkan was blown off her shoulder in a spray of green- and blue-tipped feathers, and the baby's hands clutched at her with as much strength as any full-grown adult.

"Molimo!" she shouted into the teeth of the wind. "Where are you?"

Of the man-wolf there was no trace. Kesira squinted into the dust storm and sought out Molimo. Zolkan could find shelter behind a small rock; Molimo might change to wolf form. She wanted to avoid that transformation in the mage's presence. While Norvin probably knew of this additional affliction, Kesira wanted it kept secret if he didn't. People reacted with instinctive hatred for the other-beasts.

She found Molimo and clung to him. But even through the cloaking of the brown dust she saw the man's eyes change from coal-black to glowing jade-green. Power emanated from his body in palpable waves, but he fought the shape-change. Kesira felt his body quivering as he used every ounce of his being to prevent the animal metamorphosis.

"Good, Molimo," she shouted. "Fight it. Fight it!"

Even as she spoke Kesira thought she heard Molimo say to her, *Wind devils. Norvin summoned them!*

Hands grabbed for her. Kesira struck out and landed a fist on her unseen attacker. Molimo's arm snaked around her waist. Together they stood against the wind's onslaught.

"It's getting stronger," she cried. "Find shelter."

There is none.

Kesira wiped dust from her face and stared at Molimo. "You spoke," she said, not quite believing it. The man-wolf shook his head. Kesira was distracted by the baby trying to crawl up the front of her blouse. She held the infant in her arms, astounded at the baby's strength. Only a few months old and he possessed the coordination of a three-year-old.

Pale eyes stared at her and turned her queasy. Was it Molimo speaking or the baby? Intelligence shone from the child's eyes. She believed in that instant that he was the offspring of a demon father and a human mother.

"No!" she cried. Metaphor turned to reality. The whirl-

wind of dust developed visible teeth, snapping, opening
and closing ever closer. Teeth of rock and dust and debris
surged up and plummeted to engulf her. Kesira screamed,
turning her back and hunching over to protect the child.
Molimo twisted around and interposed his body between
her and the disembodied teeth.

Kesira cringed, waiting for the impact. It never came.
She opened her eyes and saw nothing of the churning dust.
Cautiously relaxing, she discovered nothing but a tranquil
trail.

"What happened?" she asked.

Molimo sat down heavily, green eyes fading to a more
normal black. He shook, and sweat soaked his clothing.
Whatever effort he had expended, it had been prodigious
to drain him like this. From behind a rock a few yards
distant came a familiar squawking noise. Zolkan pulled
himself up to the top of the rock, unhurt but minus a few
more feathers. The *trilla* bird staggered around as if drunk,
then righted himself.

"There," came Norvin's satisfied voice. "Took care of
the devils. Awesome expenditure of magicks on my part
too. Did you not cherish the skill with which I wielded
the spells?"

"You didn't get rid of those . . . things. They just went
away."

"Nonsense. Of course I dispersed them. Frightful strain,
but there's no mage who can honestly call himself my
peer. One sorceress might be able to claim an equal skill,
but that is neither here nor there. Come along. I did promise you a fine dinner."

"Do these whirlwinds come often?"

"Only since Ayondela finished her jade palace. I think
they might be the souls of some of the workers killed
during the construction. Thousands died. Then again, it
might be nothing of the sort. What's the difference? With
me you are safe. Come, come!"

Norvin skipped down the trail like a schoolboy. Kesira

and Molimo followed, more fearful of disobeying the demented mage than anything else at the moment.

"Here. Isn't it lovely? All mine. Years to build but worth it; well worth it, yes!"

The quaint house did have a certain charm. Norvin had used the side of a mountain for one wall and followed the contours of the land with the rest of the structure. Tasteful, sedate, it seemed at odds with Norvin's flamboyant—and insane—nature.

"Come in. We'll be perfectly safe from those terrible wind devils. They never stray too close to the mountain slopes. Breaks them apart into eddies."

The inside of the house was as neatly appointed as the exterior. If Kesira hadn't met Norvin she would have thought this house belonged to a prosperous farmer or landowner.

"Your rooms are at the top of the stairs. Go clean up. Pick whichever rooms suit you—or room, eh?" Norvin winked broadly, a lewd leer rippling along his full lips. He left them standing in the entryway without uttering another word.

Molimo fidgeted, but Kesira took his hand and led him up the stairs. "We might as well enjoy this," she told him. She opened the first door on the right and gasped. Even the Empress's bedchamber couldn't have been so sumptuous.

"Look at the bed. It . . . it's so comfortable. And there's a bath!" Hot water steamed in the ceramic tub. "And the wardrobes have clothing." She took out one Imperial ball gown and held it up. If a tailor had spent days working on this gown, it couldn't have been more perfectly suited for her in style and color and fit. "It's as if we found paradise."

Molimo shook his head. He went to the full-length mirror, dipped his finger in a washbasin next to it, and quickly wrote, "Norvin is not to be trusted."

"I know that. The whirlwind? He caused it?"

Molimo nodded. Kesira didn't ask how the man knew.

He sensed magicks more easily than she, having been touched by the worst of the jade rains when Lenc destroyed Merrisen.

"You will not give up the child?" wrote Molimo.

"No," she said. "I do not deal in human flesh. Not even if it restores your tongue."

"I heal faster now," Molimo continued. "Soon I will be able to speak again."

Kesira worried at this illusion so dearly held by Molimo. Bodies did not regrow severed organs or limbs, yet he no longer appeared the fuzzy-chinned youth. He had developed—aged—rapidly. Kesira frowned as she realized for the first time that Molimo now looked years older than she, rather than years younger. This had occurred within the span of a few months.

"Good water," came Zolkan's squawk. The bird dived into the warm bathwater and washed the grime from his feathers. When he emerged to perch on the edge of the tub, what feathers he had left shone with a brilliance that dazzled Kesira. "Now to eat. No decent meals on the trail. Blueberries, pah!"

"They kept you alive," chided Kesira. "Be thankful for them. A hungry person never listens to reason—not that you do even when your belly's full."

"Listen to reason," Zolkan declared. "Seldom hear it, though."

From below came Norvin's loud shout, "Dinner is served in one hour. Don't be late or I throw it to the animals."

"Your big chance, Zolkan," said Kesira. "Keep us locked in and you get all the meal."

The bird didn't appear pleased at that prospect.

Bathed and clothed in finery from the wardrobes provided by Norvin, they sat down to dine at the elegantly appointed table. Candles burned with fragrant softness, delicate china and silver flatware graced each setting, and effervescent wine bubbled in crystal goblets.

"It is so seldom that anyone blunders in my direction.

A feast to celebrate!" Norvin clapped his hands. Floating unattended from the side of the room came trays heaped high with steaming viands of every description. Zolkan hopped to the table and pecked at one suspicious dish presented in a circle of *trilla* bird feathers. He turned a beady eye toward Norvin but said nothing. Zolkan settled down and began eating, making no attempt to show good manners.

"This is all so elaborate," Kesira said, "for you to have prepared by yourself. You must have a staff of a dozen or more to maintain the place."

"Just myself," Norvin said. "And a spell or two to aid me."

Norvin waved his hand indolently and brought forth a new round of floating dishes. Kesira watched, remembering the dust storms that had come upon them so suddenly. She knew nothing of magicks and spell-casting, these being rare traits even in such power centers as Limaden, but it struck her that only a matter of degree separated this display from the miniature tornadoes.

"My patron is quite generous in imparting spells to me," Norvin went on. "That's why I am so sure I can restore Molimo's tongue."

"In exchange for the baby."

Norvin lifted his crystal goblet and inclined his head in Kesira's direction. He sipped, the bubbly wine apparently tickling his nose. Norvin smiled, then laughed. "I do so love this wine."

"Trading a life for Molimo's tongue is not to my liking," Kesira said.

"Ah, I detect Gelya's light touch in your answer. Human dignity, nobility of soul, never trade a life for a life. What a bore Gelya was. Not that I am glad to see him go, mind you." Norvin finished off his wine with one large swallow. "Go rest, sleep on this weighty matter. Come the morrow, you might see differently."

Norvin looked from Molimo to Kesira. "Imagine what

it would be like hearing his lover's lies whispered in your ear at night, eh?"

Norvin stood and left abruptly, not giving Kesira time to retort.

"Food tastes like shit." Zolkan spat out a mouthful on the intricately woven gold tablecloth.

"It took you three helpings to decide that?" Kesira said, her mind on Norvin's offer. She dismissed it. While she felt some responsibility to Molimo, he had healed enough to be able to look after himself. The infant was another matter.

"Pah!" Zolkan wiped his beak on a napkin and fluttered to sit on her shoulder. "Time to sleep." With that, the *trilla* bird tucked his head under a wing and dozed off.

Kesira and Molimo ascended the stairs, self-consciously hand in hand. "Sleep well, Molimo," she said. He started to protest, but she gently pushed him away. Inside her room she closed the door and leaned against it, tears in her eyes.

"Duty," she said. "I have my duty to perform. Revenge. Nothing else must intrude." Kesira hated the idea that she would ever consider trading another's life for Molimo's tongue, yet Norvin's offer tempted her sorely. It showed the depths of how much she did care for the man—love? Dare she deny that it was love that produced such thoughts? And how badly she had been disturbed by all that had happened since Lenc destroyed her nunnery, her friends, her patron, her universe.

She went to the baby and gently rocked him. He slept soundly. She placed him back in the wood cradle, thinking that here he would be safe and cared for. Surely Norvin's magicks could feed the baby.

Kesira forced such images from her mind. The boy was not hers to barter with like a sack of oats. And the rune sticks had said that Ayondela's rampage would be halted because of the baby.

She reached into her battered leather pouch and pulled out the bone box containing the five carved rune sticks.

With a quick toss she sent them flashing across the slick bedspread. They landed with soft plops, their pattern meaningless. Again Kesira cast. Again no reading was possible.

"Too close to Ayondela?" she wondered aloud. "Too confused on my part to read? Or is it Norvin's meddling?" She had no clear notion which of those answers might be true.

Tired, she took off the elegant gown and hung it in the wardrobe. Kesira slipped between the satin sheets on the soft bed and let her body relax totally. She floated off to a deep sleep, resting better than she had in weeks.

When she awoke the next morning, the baby was gone.

Chapter Fourteen

KESIRA MINETTE LAY in bed staring at the empty cradle. Her mind tumbled and spun without direction until she forced herself to sit up. No emotion rose. All feeling had become deadened by the loss.

Molimo burst into the room, sword in hand.

What . . . ?

Kersira looked up, her listless attitude such that she didn't even question that she'd heard Molimo speak.

"Norvin must have kidnapped the baby. They all want him. Why is he so important? Captain Protaro had him kidnapped. Nehan-dir tried to steal him away. Now a mage without a sane thought in his head takes him from under my nose." Kesira spoke in a voice devoid of emotion. "It might be best to let Norvin keep him."

"No!" squawked Zolkan, fluttering around. "Rune sticks say baby is needed for Ayondela's defeat."

Kesira stretched to where she'd placed the carved bone box. She tossed out the engraved sticks again. This time they fell into a readable pattern.

"The baby is the key to Ayondela's rampage," Kesira said. "That's what the runes tell me."

Angrily she jumped from the bed, throwing back the covers. She stormed around, emotions flaring uncontrolled now. "Why do the runes sometimes speak to me and other times say nothing? What is *wrong?*"

Zolkan landed on her shoulder and dug in his talons

152

until she calmed down. "It is art, not science. You cannot always expect total success."

"I feel as if someone is *sending* me the messages. I am not responsible for them. I only act as a conduit." She slumped to the bed, head in hands. "It's as if the times I am unable to read the rune sticks are when the sender is not noticing me. Other times, the message is clear. That must be it. It must be!"

"Demons communicate in odd ways," muttered Zolkan. The *trilla* bird looked over at Molimo, who crossed the room and sat beside Kesira, his arm snaking around her shoulders.

"They all want the boy. The boy. We haven't even given him a name. Why don't I call him Raellard after his father?"

"Boy's father was a demon," pointed out Zolkan. "Raellard and Parvey Yera both agreed on that."

"Or Masataro or something else?" Her voice turned shrill with mounting hysteria. "He deserves a name. He's being used as a punting ball in this madness. Why shouldn't he have a name?"

Molimo's arm tightened. She fought, but the man proved too strong for her to easily break away. Instead she turned and buried her face in his shoulders. Hot, salty tears dampened his shirt. Molimo held her awkwardly and made soothing sounds deep in his throat.

It will be all right.

Kesira jerked away, eyes wide. "You spoke!"

Molimo shook his head.

"I *heard* you."

"I heard nothing," said Zolkan. "You imagined it. You are distraught by loss of baby. If we are to recover pink wormy thing, we must seek Norvin's trail. A mage will not be easy to track down."

"I didn't imagine it. I *heard* him speak. Molimo, you did speak, didn't you?" She looked into the dark eyes. Tiny sparks of green danced in the depths, unreadable in their meaning. "Not with words for my ears, but I still *heard*. Didn't I?"

Molimo took her by the arms and lifted her. Gently he pushed her toward the pile of her travel clothes draped over a chair, then he spun and left the room. Kesira heard him rattling around, fastening his sword belt, preparing his pack for the trail. She sank back to the bed and simply stared after him. She had reached a point where nothing made sense, everything confused her, and she didn't have the slightest notion of what to do. Gelya had not given any succinct maxims to cover her present condition. Kesira realized, perhaps for the first time, how alone in the world she was.

She had slipped out of the neat order imposed by society. No longer did she have an order to provide stability and guidance. By denying Emperor Kwasian's soldiers when they came for the baby, Kesira had dissociated herself from an even greater social structure than family. She had disobeyed the Emperor's direct order.

To whom did she go for guidance? Where did she turn for reassurance? Kesira knew now she had clung to the baby with the feeble hope that this might turn into a family for her. The structure the child gave to her existence far outweighed any usefulness against Ayondela.

"We are your family," said Zolkan, as if understanding perfectly what troubled her. "Molimo and I and baby are all family."

Kesira dressed silently, her mind still in turmoil. Life had turned into a giant puzzle for her, with most of the pieces missing. Worst of all, she had no idea where the boundaries were anymore.

Every footstep cost her that much more of her precious energy. Kesira felt she had come to the end of her life's journey. Too tired to think, she settled down and began humming to herself. Zolkan craned his head around and stared at Molimo, who listened.

"Your death song?" asked Zolkan.

"It will be completed soon," she answered. "I had only a few lines written before. When I left the nunnery to go to Blinn, three lines had suggested themselves. Now I've added ones about the Quaking Lands and Wemilat and Eznofadil and Howenthal. And Rouvin, yes, about him— and my own failure."

"Failure?"

"Something prevented me from loving him as he loved me. He died with my name on his lips. I mourned his loss but nothing more."

"He was a braggart," said Zolkan. "He loved only himself."

"He was a hero."

"Molimo is hero. He faces with courage his affliction every day. You do heroic things and you have no idea of what is heroic. *Pah!*" The *trilla* bird launched himself from the nun's shoulder and flapped hard until he became a tiny green dot in the cloudy sky. Then even this reminder of the bird vanished.

"I've insulted him. Why?" she asked.

Molimo dropped to the ground beside her and rapidly wrote, "A useless life is an early death. Yours has meaning."

"What meaning? Sister Fenelia and the others are gone. I have disobeyed the Emperor. I can't even properly tend an infant."

"He is the focus of much power. Power beyond our comprehension."

"Mine, yes," Kesira said thoughtfully, "but yours? I often wonder."

"My power returns after being caught in the jade rain, but slowly, too slowly," Molimo wrote.

"What power? Speech?"

He nodded. Kesira sighed. Molimo was deluding himself; just as she was, trying to convince herself that the world would return to the peacefulness she had known within the Order of Gelya.

Molimo pointed to the faint scuff marks on the dusty trail they followed into the hills. Every step took them closer to the base of the spire holding Ayondela's jade palace. For this Kesira felt some small relief. Norvin's hurried flight had been in the direction they needed to go.

"The boy is getting hungry by now," she said. In spite of her intention to name the baby, she hadn't. Something stopped Kesira short of actually putting to voice the "proper" name. It had to be more than the idea that a name bound them together. As far as Kesira was concerned, the baby might as well have been her natural-born son.

"Norvin's magicks might hold hunger away," wrote Molimo. "The mage goes to meet another."

"How do you get that from the spoor?" For the first time in the three hours since leaving Norvin's neatly appointed house, curiosity got the better of her.

"The baby is of no use to a mage, any more than he is to Emperor Kwasian."

"You're saying that it was the Emperor's demon Lalasa who wanted the baby and therefore it must be Norvin's patron who does also?"

"Yes," Molimo wrote. "The baby is a focal point for demonic interest."

"Norvin's patron," mused Kesira. "Dunbar, he said. Do you know this one?"

Molimo shrugged. What this gesture meant Kesira couldn't say. She heaved herself to her feet and told Molimo, "We'd best be on our way. There're still many hours of light left, even here."

High peaks to the west shortened the summer day by several hours. Kesira knew that Molimo could track as well at night as in the daylight, but she preferred to be able to see the tracks herself. She believed implicitly in the man-wolf's ability but saw no reason to take chances; on herself she could always depend.

The loud warning caw from above brought Kesira's green staff whipping around and into a defensive pose. Beside her Molimo drew his sword. Zolkan flashed into sight, beating his wings so hard in a braking action that his pinions creaked and snapped with effort.

"Many other-beasts ahead!" he warned. "Norvin has made them angry. They come along trail. Flee! Hurry, hurry!"

Kesira had just pulled herself onto a dusty boulder when the first of the loping jackal creatures came into view. It stopped and turned to look at her and Molimo standing on the rock. Jet-black, the jackal looked more like a shadow come to life than a living, breathing animal. It threw back its head and let forth a mournful cry that stirred hidden emotions within Kesira.

"That sounds so much like the 'Lament of Lost Souls,'" she said wistfully. "We used to sing it when we were depressed." The jackal looked up at her, agony in its eyes. The howling took on more musical overtones—this other-beast remembered its human origins.

"Is it afflicted like. you?" she asked Molimo. "Can it change back into human form?" So many of the other-beasts had become trapped in mid-transformation. She thought of the bat with the small child's face and repressed a shiver of dread.

Kesira saw a legion of the beast-humans lumbering along the trail. One man pulled himself along on arms; from the waist down he had become a diamond-patterned snake. Another's body had remained untouched by the changing evil of the jade; her head was that of a *prin* rat. All members of the pack showed both animal and human features. Only the jackal seemed to have made a complete metamorphosis into animal—and Kesira wondered. Did the brain still function as human?

She found that it did not matter. No matter what condition these poor creatures had been cursed with, they all had one thought in their brains: *Kill*.

The jackal yipped sharply, then leapt. Kesira swung her staff around, off-balance. The woman realized that she had become so used to carrying the baby that she now compensated for his weight—and the weight was gone. Kesira fell to her knees, skinning both of them, but the hard end of her staff crashed soundly into a lupine head.

No real damage was done, but the jackal fell back to the ground, piteously yelping.

The other creatures attacking did not yelp in pain or surprise. They attacked with a silent ferocity that startled Kesira.

Molimo's blade swung in a red arc, blood spraying as he defended her right side. Zolkan dipped and darted, talons seeking eyes, beak ripping at any flesh exposed overlong. But the three of them together could not hope to withstand the onslaught of so many other-beasts.

"Leave us, Molimo," she shouted. "Use your spell and get away. You must save the baby. Please! Do it!"

Zolkan's strong neck twisted and ripped off a bit of fur, part of an ear still attached to it. The *trilla* bird spat it out and ducked, fluttering away from a snake beast that struck and landed heavily, split tongue flicking in anger at its failure.

"What of me?" the bird protested. "Do I matter so little?"

"I hoped you would stay with me for a while longer," the woman said. "Then you can go."

Kesira's elbow snapped as she swung her staff around as hard as she could, missing her target. Impact of wood on rock sent a shock up into her arm that caused pain every time she moved.

"Go now," she urged.

Kesira felt a curious mixture of relief and betrayal when she noticed that Molimo had vanished. Irrational as it was, she hoped he would stay with her. But that would only have meant his life also. She had no way to escape; he did. One of them should survive to continue the fight against the jade demons.

Still . . .

Kesira swung her staff low and broke a *chillna* cat's leg. It tumbled off the boulder and disturbed the attack of two other creatures. She took the brief respite to gasp in deep lungfuls of air. And then the attack came again, from two sides now that Molimo had left.

She forced calm onto herself. As she fought she concentrated on her death song. Kesira hadn't thought it quite finished yet, but she knew she had to be wrong. A final verse, then death. If only she could have included one about Lenc's demise and how she had exacted revenge for his killing of Gelya.

Kesira shrieked in surprise as the huge boulder beneath her feet moved. Slowly at first, then with increasing speed, it rolled forward onto the attacking other-beasts. Like an acrobat at the Spring Fair, she danced along quickly to keep her balance atop the rock. Cries, human and animal, and a mixture of both human and animal, echoed up as the rock caught many of the attacking creatures by surprise. Others, including the jackal, darted out of range, but their spirit had been broken. Not even the most vicious of nips and barks from the jackal rallied his forces to stir up the attack to its former intensity.

Zolkan pecked out an eye. Kesira broke one creature's neck with a vicious swing of her staff and kicked another in the belly. Molimo scooped up a creature and snapped its spine.

The jackal eyed her, then backed off. Turning tail, it ran down the path.

Kesira carefully walked along the top of the boulder and looked behind it. Some immense force had moved the rock at the precise instant it'd do her the most good. At first Kesira saw nothing. She frowned as sunlight caught faint depressions in the bedrock. Sliding down and scraping her knees further, Kesira bent to look at the depressions.

"Footprints," she said in wonder. "It's as if someone pushed against the boulder so hard, he left footprints in solid rock."

Zolkan squawked and alighted on her shoulder. "Molimo's strength grows," the bird said.

"*He* did that?"

A presence made her spin, staff ready. Molimo smiled broadly. Kesira's eyes dropped to the man's boots. The soles had been worn off—by the effort of pushing a boulder as large as a peasant's hut?

"How did you do it?" she asked. "You *did* move the rock?"

He nodded, then motioned that they must hurry. Kesira agreed but still wanted an answer. It wasn't forthcoming. No human could have started the rock rolling.

"Did Toyaga give you more than the non-noticeability spell?" she asked. Molimo turned slightly, the slight smile on his lips both ethereal and mocking. Kesira went cold inside when she saw that his coal-black eyes burned with emerald brilliance.

"He does not partake of jade," said Zolkan, seeing her frightened reaction. "Do not worry about Molimo. He is . . ." The *trilla* bird's words trailed off. Another joined them.

Kesira stopped to glare at Norvin. The mage held the infant as if the child were nothing more than a sack of potatoes. In spite of what must have been an uncomfortable position, the baby did not cry out. If anything ever disturbed his calm, Kesira had yet to discover it.

"You really ought to have stayed and savored the hospitality of my manor," Norvin said. "The magicks would have kept you comfortably for many years."

"I want the baby back." Her words snapped out, as brittle as glass and as sharp-edged as a knife.

"Now, Kesira, you know that's just not to be. We all have our mission in this world. The game must be played to its end, and I have taken the marker. Do return and let us be."

"Your pack of other-beasts didn't stop me. You won't, either."

"That bothers me." Norvin frowned. "Usually they are very proficient. Not too many returned from this foray. You are more than you appear, Kesira. And your friends surprise me also." Norvin's eyes fixed on Molimo.

Kesira gave the mage no chance. She shoved down hard on her staff, using it to help launch her attack. Four steps, five, six. The staff whipped around at knee level. Seven steps, then eight, and the wood rod impacted on Norvin's thigh. The mage dropped, howling in pain. She used the recoil off his thigh to whirl the other end back around to crash into his upper right arm. From the way it turned flaccid, she knew she'd meted out a good blow.

A foot planted in the middle of the kneeling man's chest sent him tumbling onto his back. She reached for the baby. Pale eyes looked up at her with faint displeasure.

"You can't take him, you can't!" shouted Norvin.

"You won't," came a softer, more menacing voice. "I have plans for the boy that do not include one of Gelya's proselytes."

Kesira found herself frozen as she reached for the infant. Molimo came to her side, unhurried, and helped her straighten up so that she could face the newcomer.

The old man's long white beard came to his waist. Warts and mottled skin made him uglier than any other human Kesira had seen, and gnarled hands with knuckles the size of pecans reached for the baby. Insane thoughts flashed through her mind. What dice those knucklebones would make!

"Stop," the old man commanded. Kesira glanced around to see Zolkan fall from the sky as if dead. The heavy bird crashed to the ground a few feet away.

"He can do the same to you if he wants," said Norvin, painfully getting to his feet. He leaned heavily to protect his injured thigh, and his right arm still dangled uselessly. "My patron Dunbar is a greater mage than I."

"You fool," the demon Dunbar said without rancor. "All you know I have taught you."

"You can't take the baby. He'll starve."

"This is a matter of some interest," said the old man-demon. "How is it that you nurse the infant? But this is of only passing importance. I can suspend its life function to prevent starvation."

"But why? What is so vital that you'd do this to a poor orphaned child?"

"I expected more from you." Dunbar dismissed her out of hand.

Kesira saw that argument would not sway either Dunbar or Norvin. She reached down inside herself and found the old faith engendered by a lifetime of adherence to Gelya's teachings. Wemilat's kiss burned on her breast. And all that she had obtained from Cayabbib as he died now rose within her. She felt like a cauldron with uncooked portions of stew boiling around inside. Kesira pushed aside any confusion that might weaken her—and she acted.

Her staff arced up and came down squarely on the top of Dunbar's head. Even though the demon appeared to her as an old man, she showed him no mercy. The magicks locked within his frail-appearing body more than offset any physical disability.

The impact caused her to drop her staff. Pain lanced into her injured elbow and made her stagger slightly. But Dunbar dropped to the ground, unconscious.

"My patron!" shrieked Norvin, all pretense of urbanity peeled away. The mage swung on her, right arm shaking. He dropped the baby and used his left to steady his damaged right.

Molimo interposed his body between the mage and Kesira just as the miniature tornado took form. Teeth of wind and dust snapped and clacked and tore at Molimo's frame, but Kesira avoided the worst of the magical attack.

She rubbed her elbow and picked up her staff. They fought demons and mages and won! For an instant this revelation disabled her more than her injuries. Then she rejoined the battle. Norvin sent his whirlwind against Molimo; he couldn't break it apart and send it after both of them. Kesira attacked the mage with fervor, all her anger coming out as her staff rose and fell on his arms and shoulders.

"You can't do this!" screamed Norvin. "Stop this instant!"

"The baby," Kesira said with grim finality. "We're taking the baby."

A quick blow to the back of Norvin's knee sent him sprawling. While Molimo kept the whirlwind at bay she scooped up the baby.

"Come on. Let's get Zolkan and get away from here!"

Kesira took two steps toward the fallen *trilla* bird when all sensation left her body. She fell facedown in the dust, almost crushing the infant. Eyes focused on the rock beneath her face, but nothing else seemed functional. Kesira wanted to scream, but her lungs held no air. She suffocated by slow measures.

The vibrations in the rock told her that someone took the baby from her nerveless arms.

"Do you wish to live?" came the demon's angry words. "Yield to me!"

"I . . . I yield," she said in a voice almost too choked to be audible. Her lungs filled with life-giving air, and her limbs responded. The paralysis that had fallen over her like the first chilling snowfall of winter vanished.

Dunbar held the baby in his arms in a more reasonable fashion than Norvin had. The infant did not look happy at this turn of events, but neither did he cry.

"For what you've done I ought to kill you out of hand."

"Do it and be cursed," flared Kesira, angry at both the demon and her own failures. "You can't steal the baby!"

Bars of flame surged skyward between angry woman and demon. "Starve in there," Dunbar shouted. The demon stalked off, baby in his arms. Norvin licked his lips nervously, then hobbled after his patron. Through the shimmering, intense heat of the fiery bars Kesira saw the mage look back several times before rounding a curve in the trail and disappearing from sight.

Within the circle of flame both Molimo and Zolkan lay, unmoving. Kesira approached the barrier and cringed from the fierce heat. They were truly prisoners in Dunbar's magical prison. She saw no way to escape. None.

Chapter Fifteen

KESIRA MINETTE TURNED from her futile attempts to breach the flame barrier and knelt beside Molimo, hopelessness rising within her. Whatever spell Dunbar had used to paralyze her also held Molimo in thrall. She sat, legs crossed, Molimo's shaggy head in her lap. Ebon hair spilled out to cover the wolfskin skirt. She softly stroked the man's forehead, reflecting on how fate had doomed Molimo. He so easily became the wolf wearing a skin similar to her skirt, a hunter's prize, unable to control the animalistic instincts.

But Kesira wondered at the man. Both Norvin and Dunbar had hinted that Molimo's powers were not to be taken lightly. All evidence pointed to him pushing the boulder over onto the other-beasts. No amount of effort on a dozen men's parts could have budged such a massive stone, and yet he must have been responsible.

"Does the jade possess you so?" she asked softly. The blazing emerald in his eyes hinted that it might.

His eyelids fluttered; dark eyes stared up into her softer brown ones. "Welcome back to the world of the living," she said. "Don't try to move. Just rest for a few minutes. The spell wears off quickly enough, but you'll be a little queasy. I was."

Kesira knew that the effects passed almost immediately. She just didn't want for this moment to pass. But it had to. Molimo forced himself to a sitting position, studying carefully the flame bars holding them to this spot.

He quickly wrote in the dirt, "Have they left? I no longer *feel* Dunbar nearby."

"You sense him?"

"Not now."

"No," she said, "that's not what I meant. You mean, you can detect him in some way other than seeing or hearing?"

Molimo nodded, then pointed to his tongueless mouth. Kesira understood.

"A talent you can now use because of the action of the jade rains," she said. "If something is lost, there must be gain elsewhere. Balance, symmetry in the world, always exists. Gelya said that this was the fate of the universe."

"Fate?" he wrote.

She laughed. "My interpretation. If all things balance, then the sum must always be zero. Isn't it distressing to think that the best one can average between birth and death is mediocrity?"

Molimo stared at her curiously, then turned to examine the tiny columns of fire rising a hundred feet and more into the air. The extent of their circular prison came down to a diameter of less than ten paces. Molimo cautiously moved closer and closer to the dancing tubes of orange flame, testing every inch of the way. When he lacked but a few inches of touching, he winced and moved away. Blisters sprang up on the palm of the venturesome hand.

Kesira started to tend it, then stopped, watching in surprise as Molimo glared at his injured hand. The blisters sank back into the skin, and pinkness marking the sites of the wounds deepened and melted into the tanned area until no trace of damage remained. Molimo looked disgusted at the time wasted tending such minor problems, then began walking the circular area, less than an arm's distance from the flaming bars.

"Molimo, how'd you heal yourself so quickly?" Kesira asked. "Answer me!"

"I just do," he wrote. "Do you know how you heal yourself?"

"No, my body does it through its own knowledge. But I don't do it as fast. Why, you healed in seconds!"

He shrugged. "A second, a day, what's the difference? I still have no idea how my body does it." He continued his circling.

Kesira stared at him, then shook free of her mounting dread. Molimo changed daily—hourly. This hardly seemed the same man she knew a few months earlier lying beside the road, more dead than alive from the showering jade. This one moved boulders as large as huts, commanded spells given him by demons, and healed with a glance. He had aged visibly, now approaching middle age, but with this added age came power and ability. He had been touched, but how?

The imprint of evil jade burned too brightly for Kesira to bear it. She turned from Molimo and his surliness.

Kesira bent down and gently turned Zolkan over onto his back. The *trilla* bird lay as if dead. She tried to pry open one of his beady black eyes and failed in the attempt. While Molimo stalked around more like a wild beast than a man, she stroked over Zolkan's feathers and gently probed for some sign of injury. The bird still breathed; she thought he only experienced the effects of Dunbar's paralysis.

"Zolkan, are you awake?" she asked softly.

Wings twitched, then fluttered. Instinct took over. The bird curled his head under one wing. Kesira carefully pried the wing up and found the familiar black eye peering up at her.

"Let this bird die in peace." Zolkan moaned like one nearing death.

"The demon used a spell on you. You're all right, just a bit battered from the fall. You were twenty feet in the air when he paralyzed you with his magicks."

"Pig-shit demon," muttered Zolkan. Kesira knew then that he'd be fine. With a twitch of the tail feathers and an awkward twist, Zolkan got to his feet, then settled down like a hen roosting. He still lacked strength to do more than glare.

"Fry us," he grumbled. "Dunbar tries to cook us inside his oven and eat *trilla* bird meat. Damn cannibal!"

"You'll be able to get free," Kesira told him. "When you're strong enough, you can fly straight up and over the top of the flames."

"Catch fire and die," insisted the *trilla* bird. "Dunbar wants me fried, that . . . that product of diarrhea!"

"Calm yourself," soothed Kesira. "Molimo and I might be caught here, but you can get away." In a more desolate tone she added, "You might be our only hope for escape. I see no way for either Molimo or me to get through those bars."

The orange flames danced and licked at one another, scant inches apart. The heat reddened her skin and caused her to sweat profusely. Kesira took only one look at the ground to know that tunneling free was out of the question. They had the misfortune to be trapped in a particularly rocky stretch of the trail.

Kesira sat heavily in the dust and began running it through her fingers. Every time a tight, dry clump of dirt landed, a green sprout poked up. Curious, she stroked over the buds and saw new growth. Her touch accelerated growth.

"Sister Kai would have kept me in the fields all summer if I'd been able to do this at the convent," Kesira said, a little awed at how her mere touch seemed to foster life. It finally occurred to her that the staff hadn't grown its new limbs by itself; she had aided the growth.

"Isn't this amazing?" she asked of Zolkan. "It must be part of Cayabbib's legacy to me." She ran more dirt through her fingers and produced neat rows of weeds foolishly attempting to survive on the rocky path. This was a gift of great importance, but it did no one any good now. They were still trapped within the flaming prison.

Zolkan sputtered and swore, talons clicking against rock as he paraded around. Kesira started to lash out, to tell him that he made her nervous with his restless pacing. Gelya had always preached that those with patience received all that they desired. She failed to understand how simply sitting and waiting proved anything in her present situation.

The woman shifted the blue, knotted cord around her waist and took off the golden sash, now tattered almost beyond recognition. With loving care she straightened it the best she could, then wove it around the blue cord of her order. Idly she pulled out the bone box containing her rune sticks. A quick casting could hurt nothing.

Kesira's attention focused immediately on the result of the fall.

"Molimo, Zolkan, look," she said.

Zolkan waddled over, but Molimo continued his tireless circuit of their prison. "What do you read?" the bird asked. One wing reached out tentatively to point at the stack of five sticks.

"Ayondela. I see a female jade demon," she said. Kesira's face furrowed as she concentrated. Words and images bubbled up inside her head, unbidden. The casting of the rune sticks worked to free her inner senses, the ones she had such small control over.

Eyes closed, Kesira said, "I see myself facing Ayondela."

"Where?"

"In a room constructed entirely of jade. It might be inside her jade palace. I meet her, but there is no fear. Confidence rides at my shoulder."

"What happens?"

"Ayondela fears me. No, not me, but someone with me. I cannot see who it is. Perhaps Molimo."

"She does not fear him," Zolkan said with finality.

"The picture wavers." Her entire body floated with sweat now. Kesira kept her eyes screwed shut so tightly, her face began to ache with the strain. "I see no more of the confrontation. But the fear on her face!"

"What else?" prompted Zolkan.

"I . . . nothing. I can't see how to escape this imprisonment, but I must have if I am to meet Ayondela in her palace." Kesira opened her eyes and felt the sting of perspiration running into them. She wiped at the corners of her eyes, then peered through the flame bars to the majestic tower of granite holding Ayondela's jade palace.

Somehow she would make the journey to the top of that mountain. And Ayondela would fear her once she arrived.

Bleakness replaced her little thrill of precognition. Kesira Minette realized how tantalizing this glimpse had been and how it only served to make her more depressed over her imprisonment. Life had always been this way for her, ever since her parents had been slaughtered by brigands. The elder Minettes had been on their way to market. Their bountiful harvest insured an easy winter. With the profits from their grain they'd be able to stock in enough supplies from Blinn's fine merchants to weather any snowfall in the Yearn Mountains. But the brigands had foolishly struck as they went to market rather than waiting until they returned. With no solid coin or luxury goods to buy off the thieves and only a wagonload of grain to offer, both Rudo and Jensine Minette had been slaughtered by the brigands. All the while Kesira burrowed between the sacks of grain, fearfully peering out.

She had seen one thief slit her father's throat. What the rest had done to Jensine Minette had been forever burned into Kesira's memory.

Catatonic, she had sat and stared long after the brigands had left. Sister Fenelia had found her late that day and taken her into the Order of Gelya.

As kind as the sisters of the Order of Gelya were, nothing erased the evil memories of that autumn day. Kesira had spoken again and even laughed and frolicked with others her own age in the order, but the underlying sense of despair had been a constant companion, reminding her that Gelya's teachings were ideals and not necessarily attainable in a world populated with brigands. Now that emptiness rose within her and cast her into an arid desert without end.

"Can't fly over," squawked Zolkan.

"Eh? What's that?" she said, turning to the *trilla* bird.

"Spell turns flames inward near top. No flight out."

Kesira stared upward but failed to see what Zolkan meant. Her despair mounted, however, and she did not question him further. If he said he couldn't escape, he couldn't. And what good would the bird's escape do either her or Molimo? They had run out of allies. Toyaga had perished; so had Cayabbib; and Wemilat the Ugly had died defeating Howenthal. This Merrisen Zolkan spoke of so highly had been vanquished by Lenc in the battle that had robbed Molimo of his tongue and dropped bits of jade across the land; she had even been given a vision of Merrisen's destruction. Worst of all, her patron was no more.

"Dead," she murmured. "Gelya is dead."

"Despair doubles strength," said Zolkan.

Kesira turned her listless brown eyes to the bird. She frowned. "What are you talking about?"

"Did not Gelya say as much? Do you surrender this easily? You escape. You know that."

"But how?"

"You do," insisted Zolkan. "Runes say so."

"The rune sticks," Kesira said, shaking her head. "I have no idea what to make of them. Ever since Gelya was killed, the power seems to have grown within me, but what credence do I put on my interpretations? It's as if someone else is telling me what to say, slipping clues into my mind."

"Not all demons are strong," said Zolkan. "Most cannot oppose jade demons openly. Some sly. Some sneaky, but good too."

"You're saying there might be demons aiding me by giving hints through the rune castings?" Kesira almost laughed at this. "Why do they choose me? I am the last member of a dead order. The jade demons cannot fear me."

"Howenthal and Eznofadil do not fear you."

"They're dead."

"All more reason for Ayondela and Lenc to oppose you. No one else battles them. Human Emperor chases own concerns. Nehan-dir wants only power. You have slain two jade demons."

Kesira tried to force away the tenuous threads of Zolkan's ensnaring logic. So what if she had been successful to that extent? The most powerful of the demons rampaged throughout the land, usurping power and tightening control.

But she had aided Wemilat well. And Toyaga had been destroyed before Kesira battled Eznofadil. The power grew within her.

"Never mind," said Zolkan. "Nothing you can do. Sit, wait. Let Dunbar have baby."

"Damn your feathers," she snapped. "I am honor-bound to protect the baby. His father and mother died because of me." Kesira didn't question the truth of this. She used emotion to whip herself up into righteous indignation. "How dare Dunbar try to prevent me from following the honorable course through life? How *dare* he!"

Kesira shot to her feet and walked directly to the flame barrier. Her eyes watered as she stared unblinkingly. Resolve firmed—and something hidden deep inside stretched and stirred and came to life. Kesira reached out, her hand trembling. Then all nervousness passed. She knew what had to be done and how to do it.

She *knew.*

One hand gripped a bar. No flesh seared. No pain drove her back. Fingers wrapped around the flame bar; the woman began to tug. The stirring deep inside her soul became a writhing, seething, churning creature that gave her renewed determination. She thrust out her left hand and gripped the adjacent bar of pure orange flame.

Kesira sensed Molimo and Zolkan beside her. They added to her strength through their presence, but the true power came from reservoirs inside. Kesira began drawing the flame bars apart, not through force of muscle but through force of spirit. She was greater than any spell Dunbar might cast. Duty drove her. Honor demanded performance.

The bars parted. An inch. Two. Five. A foot. More.

Kesira looked past the barrier and to the mountain cradling Ayondela's palace. Surges of will allowed Kesira to separate the bars further. The nun saw a gray body jump past her: Molimo. A loud squawk, followed by a cascade of bright feathers, echoed back to her: Zolkan.

She took a step forward until the bars arched on either side of her body, bending at fluid angles never attempted by iron. For a moment she stood and stared in wonder. She had done this. Kesira Minette, orphan, alone in the world, her sisters slaughtered by powers beyond her comprehension. She had battled back and won.

Kesira took another step forward and dropped her arms to her sides. A loud hissing behind her caused her to yelp and jump away. The wolfskin skirt had begun to smolder and stink.

The brown-haired woman turned and stared in disbelief. She felt as if she had come out of a lifelong coma into a world brighter, more vibrantly alive, better. Kesira stared at the flame bars and saw how Dunbar had performed his magicks. While she could not duplicate the feat or destroy it, she knew full well how it had been accomplished.

"So simple, so elegant," she said, more to herself than to Zolkan, who fluttered down to land on her shoulder.

The *trilla* bird peered at her, then said, "You learn of worlds beyond your world."

"What do you know of that?" she asked. "You seem to know so much more than you reveal. Tell me! What's happened to me? How can I walk through spells of such potency?"

"Cayabbib. Wemilat. You accumulate demon power. You will never be demon, but now you use their gifts. You glimpse their world."

Kesira spun around, almost dislodging Zolkan from his perch. She narrowed her eyes and pointed down the trail. "They return. Dunbar and Norvin are coming back."

"Dunbar might have sensed your escape," said Zolkan. "Let's fly."

"Go on without me," Kesira urged. "I am going to get the baby back. I've not escaped from Dunbar's prison simply to turn my heel and flee like a craven."

"He is demon. Too strong!"

"You're the one who said I've accumulated Cayabbib's and Wemilat's power. Zolkan, I *feel* it within me. If I don't use it, I'll never know. Better to oppose Dunbar now than to meet Ayondela later and be unsure of myself."

"Wait for . . . Molimo." Zolkan sidestepped back and forth along her shoulder. His beak clacked when Dunbar and his tame mage, Norvin, holding the baby, walked into view.

Dunbar frowned when he saw Kesira and Zolkan outside the spell prison. "I sensed something amiss with my prison. It is good that I returned. You astound me with your resourcefulness. Or am I congratulating the wrong one? Where is your companion?"

"Molimo had nothing to do with our escape."

Dunbar laughed, obviously not believing her. "It is of no concern. I misjudged your ignorance of demonic matters. I shall tell you this once and only once. Do not attempt to interfere. You awaken angers best left slumbering."

"In the jade demons?" Kesira tried to hold back her own anger and failed.

"There, yes," said Dunbar. He shuffled forward until he stood squarely in front of the nun. "The order of the universe is shifting. These are uneasy times. If you find yourself a hidey-hole, you might weather the storms of change and survive in your pathetic way. Otherwise . . ." The demon shrugged thin shoulders to indicate that Kesira would be killed without any thought of mercy.

"You've been kind once," she said, her words laden with sarcasm. "You will be again."

"No." Dunbar missed her meaning, but Norvin caught it. The mage stepped forward and whispered hurried words into the demon's ear. Dunbar brushed him away as if the mage were nothing more than an annoying fly buzzing around.

"Now that the baby is in my control I have no need of anyone." Dunbar pulled himself erect. Kesira felt twinges in her joints. The demon cast another spell to immobilize her.

"What is the baby to you? To the jade demons? If they fear an infant so, why haven't they killed him before now?"

"Insane pride, belief that they were invincible. Lenc and the others refuse to believe that we enter the last days of their power. We have long debated the Time of Chaos, those of us who even dare mention it. Lenc does not believe it will ever happen—especially not with him in total power."

"You claim that Chaos is gripping the world now?" asked Kesira.

"Not yet." Dunbar glanced toward the baby. "Soon, unless the proper order of life is restored."

"Please," pleaded Norvin, holding the baby as if the child might turn into a snake and squirm free at any instant. "Let's not carry on like this. Please!"

"He is useful—to a point," Dunbar said of Norvin. Kesira blinked. The demon spoke to her as an equal and to his mage as if Norvin were nothing more than a menial laborer. "He does yeoman's work tending the child until I can instruct it properly."

Dunbar heaved a deep sigh. "Enough of idle chatter. Even a worm like Norvin can be right. I have suffered your presence too long."

Kesira fell to her knees as pressure engulfed her. From all sides came crushing planes, compressing her, trying to compact her to Zolkan's size. The full power of a demon turned against her.

Chapter Sixteen

KESIRA MINETTE GROANED in agony from the magicks compressing her. Nowhere did she find succor. Zolkan lay as if dead, one glassy eye staring up at the azure sky littered with fleecy, rapidly moving clouds. Of Molimo she saw nothing. And the pain! It mounted gradually, but simple twisting and turning did nothing to alleviate it.

"Norvin," she called. Her teeth clacked shut as Dunbar increased the pressure to the point that she almost passed out. "Norvin! The demon only uses you. Listen to his words. He scorns you!"

Her eyes blurred. Curtains of dark drew silently at the perimeters of sight, but still Kesira fought. The depths of her strength did nothing to fight off the crushing insistence of Dunbar's spell, but she detected weakness in the demon's rank: Norvin.

"Wait. She can be useful," said Norvin.

Dunbar waved his mage away, shooing him away like a noisome puppy following too closely.

"See?" Kesira grated out between clenched teeth. Her innards turned to jelly. Bones protested and threatened to break. Worst of all, her head felt as if Dunbar had placed it within the jaws of a vise. Every pass of his hand clamped down that much more firmly.

Had it all come to this moment? Kesira's death song lacked verses. She had composed many new ones to tell of her travails, but of Ayondela she had written too little.

And what of the baby? Nothing. She had concentrated on Eznofadil and Howenthal.

How could she die when she wasn't prepared? It wasn't Cayabbib's energy or Wemilat's protection that held back the demon's spell now; it was her own innate courage and strength of character. Dunbar tried to force her into early death, but she had obligations to meet.

Revenge had to be taken on Lenc for what he had done to her patron. Only Kesira Minette remained to do it.

Dunbar's eyebrows arched when he felt the stiffening of her resolve and the failure of his spell to further crush her.

The elderly appearing demon swung around when the sleek, gray form of a wolf flashed past. Kesira's eyes were filled with stinging sweat, but she caught sight of Molimo's vicious jaws closing on Norvin's throat. The mage gurgled hideously as he died. Molimo tossed his head and sent a spray of blood over Dunbar.

"He was mine!" shrieked the demon. "You . . . you're not an other-beast! You're—"

Dunbar never finished. Molimo whirled around, lithely stepped over the baby lying in the dust, and launched himself at the demon. Whatever spells Dunbar commanded held Molimo at bay. But the break in the demon's attention freed Kesira from her crushing, invisible prison. For a moment she fell forward onto hands and knees and panted, doglike.

Then she rose.

Within her burned anger fed by mistreatment at Dunbar's hand. Energies surged *through* her from no discernible source. She acted as a conduit and diverted them at Dunbar.

"Aieee!" The demon's beard exploded into wild, consuming orange flames. Dunbar staggered away. Molimo tried to follow but hesitated, then fell back to stand guard over the baby. The infant's pale eyes watched with intelligence and interest too old for such a small child. No sound came from his lips. He let Molimo's growls speak.

"You are no different than Lenc and Ayondela," accused Kesira. "While you have not followed the path offered by the jade, your intentions are evil. You'd deal in human life as if it meant little more than this." She snapped her fingers. Power erupted from within her, and Dunbar's long white hair turned to ash as the dancing blue-orange flame worked up toward his chin. The demon shrieked and tried to beat out the fire.

"Stop it! My head! Inside, it burns. My brain burns!"

Kesira had no idea what she did, what magicks she commanded or how this transformation had come about. Something about the punishment she had endured triggered an artesian well of strength and ability far surpassing even a demon's.

"Your lack of caring betrayed you," she said. "You sought only safety for yourself. Selfish lives deserve selfish death."

Dunbar fought now. Kesira turned gelid inside as the pressures from all sides mounted once more, but this time the spell lacked true conviction. With a careless toss of her hand she pushed aside the invisible planes seeking to crush her like a leaf placed between the vellum pages of a book.

The coldness left Kesira as she fought on. She came to realize that she was a match for the demon. But the nun battled only to a draw. Dunbar's initial panic had faded, and the fires adance on his head had sputtered out. Demon and woman faced each other, realization slowly dawning that neither would triumph in this battle. For all her newfound powers, Kesira could not vanquish Dunbar, nor could the demon make any further headway against her.

From her left came the sputters and squawks she knew so well. Zolkan rolled onto his side and used a shaky wing to regain his feet. The beady black eye slowly focused. The sound of his voice shocked Kesira. The *trilla* bird cut loose with singsong so rapid and high-pitched that she winced.

"Zolkan!" she shouted. "Quiet!" Her warning did no good. If anything, the bird's shrillness increased. Kesira felt as if he drove white-hot needles through her eardrums.

"He works for me," said Dunbar, a smirk crossing his ancient lips. "The bird is mine!"

The demon sought only to unnerve; no truth rang in his voice. Kesira saw the effect of Zolkan's words on Molimo. The wolf shape flowed and faded, human arms and legs and torso reappearing. In seconds Molimo had fully transformed into human. He came to stand beside her. Kesira, in spite of the continuing duel of magicks with Dunbar, blushed as she saw Molimo's nakedness. While nursing him to health after the jade rains, she had seen him thus many times. Now it was . . . different.

Before, he had been a boy. Now he had become a mature man.

Energies of subtly different composition filled her. Sexual energies. They merged with the magical energies instilled in her by Cayabbib and Wemilat. Molimo held the baby. New dimensions came into play. Her heart went out to the poor child left an orphan by the jade demons. Pale eyes bored into her softer brown ones. As steel is tempered by fire, so did her powers become tempered by the infant's penetrating gaze.

Dunbar toppled face-forward, like a tree with its trunk sawed through. The demon lay twitching feebly, arms and legs aflutter as if he were the newborn and not the ancient.

"You rightly oppose the Ayondela and Lenc," Kesira said to the fallen demon, "but your methods were doomed to failure. You placed personal concerns above those of duty and honor." She let out a long, gusty breath. "If only Gelya had lived instead of you."

"My body is afire." Dunbar moaned. "Put out the fire, I beg you!"

Kesira had no idea what she had done to him. As a hose only carried liquid, so she had been a pipeline for the magical energies debilitating Dunbar. She made a few passes with her hand but sensed nothing. Dunbar's agony did not lessen.

"This is your punishment for kidnapping the baby, for treating Norvin so shabbily, for not living up to your responsibilities."

"Please!"

Kesira turned and jerked her head toward the mountain of granite dominating the landscape. Atop it gleamed the green dot showing where Ayondela awaited them. Without further word to the fallen demon she and the others started on the journey that could only end with a far deadlier confrontation.

"Ayondela," she said softly, "I am coming for you." Kesira's eyes narrowed as she saw the path winding up the side of the mountain.

"How do we know Ayondela is in her palace?" asked Kesira, panting from the long day's hike up the steep, rocky road carved from solid stone. She sat down heavily, rested her staff against a boulder, and unslung the baby from his position in the pack on her back. She rocked the infant until he drifted off to a peaceful sleep.

How she envied the child. His world was so simple, hers so complex. In the nunnery Kesira had lived a peaceful life uncomplicated by concerns basic to others outside Gelya's walls. The farmers nearby would never let them starve, even in lean years, taking away any fear on this account, not that such aid had ever been needed. Their own farming efforts had been blessed, and their charity kept many others alive. Of politics and the affairs of the Empire, Kesira knew vanishingly little. The Emperor commanded their loyalty. That basic tenet had been driven home repeatedly. Duty to family was second only to duty to Kwasian.

For Kesira her sisters in the order were her only family.

A tear formed as she thought of them, dead. Kesira brushed the tear away and heaved a deep sigh as she thought of how she had disobeyed the Emperor's Guard

captain. Family—sisters—gone, open flaunting of the
Emperor's command, all she held most basic had vanished.

The baby nestled against her breast, eyes screwed shut
in sleep, one tiny thumb thrust into his mouth. Zolkan and
Molimo rested a few paces away. The *trilla* bird harangued
Molimo constantly with the singsong speech. Whatever
he said did not make Molimo any happier. The man-wolf
frowned and gestured, dark eyes buried under a squint that
turned him bestial.

She rose and joined them, her legs protesting any movement at all. The steep climb had taken its toll on her, yet
they had covered only a quarter of the distance to the
mountaintop.

"Don't you like the view?" she asked, trying to lift the
others' spirits. "Look. There's the valley leading back into
the mountains. Somewhere in that direction is the mar-
velous transport we used to get here from Lorum Bay."

Molimo began writing in the dust. Zolkan hopped down,
and quick claws obliterated the words. More singsong
protests erupted from the *trilla* bird's beak until Kesira
lost her temper.

"Speak so that I can understand!"

Both bird and man turned to stare at her.

"I will *not* be excluded like this." Tears began misting
her vision again. "We are in grave danger and might find
ourselves confronting Ayondela at any instant. I do *not*
want the last thing I hear to be a deafening, shrill bird."

"Sorry," said Zolkan, but his tone carried no hint of
contrition. "Ayondela knows we come."

"How are you so sure?"

"At the end of road she awaits us." The bird shivered.
Tiny puffs of green feathers dropped from his body. He
quickly preened and then canted his head around to peer
up at Kesira. "Going to die looking a mess. No good. No
good. Hungry too."

"How you look when you die has nothing to do with
it," she said tartly. "How you've lived your life is all that
matters."

"Want to look good when I die."

Kesira turned away. The vista spread before her would have brightened her spirits under other circumstances. She hadn't been lying when she commented on the stark beauty of the mountains, the burgeoning green of the stunted summer growths, the vibrant yellows and velvety browns of wild flowers in bloom months late. Kesira sighed as she drank in the sight. Those were the flowers sacred to her patron. But the vision of paradise held those flowers as only a small portion of true loveliness. The air came crisp and sharp and clean in her nostrils, and the gentle stirrings of birds far off in the trees rode the wind to her ears. All this and a myriad of other details stretched away from her. Along the road she found only rock—and more rock. The chunks of gravel along the road had been designed to give purchase to draft horses and large wagons, not foot travelers. Kesira had to be continually on guard or she'd turn an ankle on the too-large gravel. But what troubled her the most was the lack of vegetation. Everywhere else she looked, blushes of summer finally touched the land. This ominous, dark red granite mountain jutted above the other mountains, devoid of life. The only hint of green was Ayondela's palace at the top of the road.

Jade green. Death green.

"We've come so far, and I'm still unsure of what we will do when we find Ayondela." She sank down to a rock beside Molimo. "What can we really achieve?"

"Do not doubt," he wrote on a small portion of dusty rock. "Ayondela can be stopped. She and Lenc consolidate their power. Zolkan is wrong; she does not know we come. Not yet."

"How do you know? How does Zolkan know Ayondela is even in her palace? She might have fled to another. Didn't she abandon the Isle of Eternal Winter? Perhaps she's somewhere else now, leaving this palace behind."

"Lenc's flame faltered," wrote Molimo.

Kesira nodded. She had interrupted its magical continuity, but why was this enough to drive away Ayondela?

There were so many unanswered questions. The source of her new power troubled her. She did not feel—*feel*—that the power stemmed from evil, but how could she know? The ways of magic had not been her training. No one in the Order of Gelya knew such things. The casting of the rune sticks had been the most remarkable ability among all her sisters, and she was the one capable of the reading.

Where did her interpretations come from? Kesira had always felt that the vivid pictures, the subtle hints, the niggling uneasinesses had originated outside her mind and not from within. Who or what planted those beguiling glimpses of the future?

Unbidden, she turned and studied Molimo's strong profile. Scars marred his handsome good looks, and he appeared to carry burdens as great as hers. Gone was all trace of the callow youth she had known. And replacing it?

Power? Yes. Worry? Definitely. Was he the source of her rune-casting skill? If true, that only raised more questions than it answered. Molimo had been touched by the jade and become an other-beast, but she knew that he transcended that affliction often enough to alert her to a strength of character surpassing most humans.

"Molimo, you deal so easily with demons. Are you one of them?"

"Ridiculous," piped up Zolkan. "He is caught in jade curse. You see him change to wolf. Would a demon permit that?"

"Toyaga gave him a spell he has no trouble using. Ayondela acted as if she recognized him. . . ."

"Not so. She did not recognize him. Impossible." The bird waddled around self-importantly. Kesira saw this as an attempt to turn her away from the topic. "Why would jade demon know mere mortal?"

Kesira stared hard at Molimo. He took no notice. She shook her head. Molimo was more than a poor, afflicted farmer unable to control the other-beast changes. He had a nobility lacking in others, and there was a mystery too. She wanted to pull away the veils of mystery surrounding him and reveal the true nature behind the lies and half truths and misinterpreted appearances.

"Molimo," she said softly, touching him lightly on the arm. "I don't care what you are. I love you." Emotions within her stirred and fought for supremacy. She feared for him; she feared him. Dominating everything else, she loved him.

A small smile rippled Molimo's lips. His dark eyes sparkled for a moment, then turned icy. He gestured, indicating that they must continue their climb.

Kesira kept the baby slung in front of her. She hefted her staff and leaned heavily on it as she began the tedious journey upward. They traveled for another hour before Kesira called out for Molimo to rest.

"Just a few minutes," she begged. "I tire quicker now." She considered letting Molimo carry the baby but always stopped short of asking. Molimo had not offered, either, which struck her as odd. Always before, he had been solicitous of her.

Kesira reflected. Molimo didn't show the outright contempt for the baby that Zolkan did, but the man also seemed leery of the child. Protective, yes, but also . . . frightened?

"Hurry," urged Zolkan. "We must go upward quickly. Night comes. We dare not be on road after dark."

"Why not?" she asked. "We haven't seen any other travelers, much less guards."

"What need does jade demon have of human guards?" demanded Zolkan. "Magicks abound. All around, all around!"

"What are you blathering on about?" Kesira said. "There's nothing." Both up the curving road and back along the bend she saw only rocky emptiness. Now the road presented a much finer view: hundreds of square miles of heart-stopping beautiful land stretched before her. Kesira could almost imagine herself Empress, commanding all this terrain.

But of guards or ward spells she saw no trace.

"Clouds!" The *trilla* bird flapped his wings in real agitation. Molimo shied away from the pummeling.

"We've climbed high enough to be among the clouds," Kesira admitted. "While it's getting chillier, we're clothed heavily enough to keep from freezing. Are you cold, Zolkan?"

"Clouds!" the bird repeated. "So soon you forget. Like the mists in Lorum Bay."

Kesira stopped and stared at the green bird. Of ordinary clouds she held no fear. Mists of invisible razors that slashed at her flesh filled her with dread, even if she had successfully walked through them in Lorum Bay after laying with Cayabbib. Anger at Zolkan's secrecy burned away fear.

"Why didn't you say something sooner? We could have made better time. Come along!" Kesira placed staff to rocky road and levered herself forward. She hadn't taken a dozen paces when the first wispy tendrils of fog drifted down from above. They had reached the spot where low-scudding clouds had appeared level with them out over the valleys and drifting into other peaks in the Sarn Mountains. Now she found the slightest hint of those soft, wetly caressing puffs frightening. Gentle reminders of summer changed to fanged, vaporous dragons intent on killing.

Kesira shook off the fantasy building in her mind. "Don't distract me," she told Zolkan. "Give warning when necessary but don't build this into something it's not. See?"

Kesira thrust out her hand. One gray finger of mist swirled downward and wrapped around her wrist. Even though she tensed at the touch, no burning came. Only clammy dampness.

"It is nothing more than fog. As you pointed out, the day is almost at an end, and mountains draw clouds like lodestone pulls iron. Come along."

With a boldness that she didn't really feel, Kesira strode off through the gathering fog. Quickly enveloped in its gelid arms, she fought the insane urge to break into a run.

At her breast the baby stirred, one tiny hand gripping her blouse so that he could turn and see what was happening. Behind her, Kesira heard Molimo and Zolkan. The bird rode on the man's shoulder and protested vigorously such blatant foolhardiness.

The fog chilled but did not cut. Kesira hurried on before her courage flagged.

"Look out. To the left," she said to Molimo as the man came level with her. "The sunset. Doesn't the mist make it all the more lovely?"

Rainbows gleamed, and one began to form a perfect circle behind them, as if forming a colorful exit. In front, the setting sun turned the mist gold and silver and, in places, ominously dark.

"There!" squawked Zolkan. "Ahead!"

Kesira stopped and gripped her staff, ready to fight. Then she relaxed. "It was only a trick of the light," she assured the *trilla* bird. "Nothing is there." Kesira brushed the sweat from her upper lip. She had also seen the dark, swiftly moving phantasm. But she and her friends were the only beings of substance in the fog. What both she and Zolkan had glimpsed had been, as she had explained, a trick of the setting sun.

Only a trick. Over and over Kesira told herself that until she believed it. In gathering darkness they continued up the road, often not able to see more than a few feet ahead because of the dying light and the blowing waves of gray fog.

The baby stirred. She placed a hand on his head to soothe the boy, but for the first time since she had "adopted" him, the child fought. Weak struggles made Kesira rock him and say, "There's nothing to worry about. Nothing, nothing." Her voice calmed Zolkan; the baby's fists pounded futilely against her chest.

Kesira frowned. Something disturbed the infant. She looked behind her, down the road, past gravel and granite to the emptiness of the verge. One misstep would carry her thousands of feet to her death. But the road was wide. Such a mistake couldn't happen, even in pitch blackness.

From ahead drifted more clouds.

Molimo let out a gurgling sound that almost put his pain into words. A feeble tendril of the fog reached out and swirled around his leg. Where the cloud touched appeared lacerations.

"The clouds!" she cried. "Zolkan, get away. Hurry. Save yourself!"

"Cannot. Look above! Cloud banks everywhere. We are englobed. They eat our flesh!"

The *trilla* bird fluttered around, wings whipping at the clouds, dispersing them a little—but not enough. Overhead, behind, ahead, the crystal clouds billowed with deadly, silent intent. Even as Zolkan tried to fly, the invisible razors within the clouds slashed off portions of wing and tail and crest. The air filled with feathery debris from the bird's futile escape attempt.

Molimo had ripped off his tunic and flapped it wildly. The sudden breeze, pitiful as it was, forced away a tiny portion of the clouds. Kesira rushed forward, staying as close to Molimo as she could. The woman didn't even protest when the heavy *trilla* bird alighted on her shoulder. The burden of the child and the bird caused her knees to buckle, but Kesira fought every step and kept pace as they forged ahead.

But Molimo's arms tired, and the insidious fog wormed its way past his gusty shield.

Tiny incisions bled with increasing profusion on exposed arms and legs and faces.

She closed her eyes and tried to summon whatever power it was that allowed her to walk through the fog unscatched. Kesira winced as her pitiful spell failed and new cuts appeared on her hands and face.

"Back, back down the road," Kesira urged. "There's no way we can reach the summit. Not fighting these damnable clouds." A quick swipe removed a tiny rivulet of blood from her forehead and kept it out of her eyes. Molimo shook his head. "Why not? Let's retreat and try again later."

Again Molimo shook his head. He kept a steady pace upward. Zolkan spoke for him, saying, "We near top. More chance to die retreating."

Kesira protected the baby the best she could, but the fog slipped through her fingers and found tiny fists and bare arms and silken-haired head. The baby stirred more and more. Kesira found herself hard-pressed to control such a small child.

"We can't!"

"Must," insisted Zolkan. The bird cut loose with a shrill singsong that Molimo understood. The man picked up the pace even more but at a price. More of the fog slipped past his flapping tunic. All around them hideous figures loomed. Kesira swallowed hard as she thought she saw direbeasts of impossible size opening and closing their fiercely fanged mouths. Darting shadows like wolves nipped at her legs until her boots turned slippery with her own blood. She stumbled and would have fallen, but for Molimo's arm supporting her.

"No!" she gasped, fighting to regain her balance. The clouds had swirled around in such a way that the woman thought she fell headlong into a gaping mouth lined with diamond teeth. As Molimo's tunic sent gusts toward the apparition, the teeth changed into water droplets and the mouth became nothing more than dark rock.

Illusion it might have been, but their wounds were all too real. Kesira felt herself weakening by the second. The trek up the mountain had depleted much of her stamina; dying the death of a thousand cuts pushed her closer to collapse.

Zolkan's claws added to her injuries when the bird tightened down on her left shoulder. Blood flowed in twin rivers.

"Stop it!" she cried. "You're worse than the clouds!"

"Stay on road. I can fly. You cannot."

Kesira wiped blood away from her eyes. Sweat stung

and made her blink. The blood blinded her as surely as if a dark silk bandage descended over her eyes. She saw how close she had strayed to the edge of the rocky road. Another step and she would have been tumbling for many long seconds until she smashed into the base of the sheer cliff.

"Thanks," she murmured. "But it'll take more than this to get us away." She sobbed as a damp finger of cloud-stuff stroked over her eyelids. Pain. Blood. Blindness. Kesira reached the end of her endurance. No amount of faith in Gelya and his teachings readied her for this insistent, all-pervasive torture.

"I can't go on. I can't, " she sobbed as the cloud billowed with increasing insistence around them. It was as if Molimo fanned the deadly clouds into existence now, rather than chasing them away.

"Can't go on. Can't, can't." Kesira sank to her knees.

Agony assailed her from every direction. Eyes bled. Her blouse dripped blood. Every square inch of exposed skin had a dozen tiny scratches, a score, hundreds.

Breaking the eerie silence of the crystal clouds, a small voice rose. Wordless, crying in pain and rage, it mounted in intensity. At first Kesira thought it echoed from ahead. Then she imagined that the cries came from Molimo's sundered mouth.

She shook when she realized that the baby cried for the first time.

"Poor thing," she said, trying to soothe it. But the child had passed the point of being so easily calmed. The frustration locked in that tiny voice tore at Kesira's heart. Shrill, the thin, young voice rose until it passed the limits of her hearing and made her flinch away. Zolkan cawed in protest, and Molimo clapped hands over his ears to hold back the awful, penetrating cry.

"The clouds! Molimo, keep..." Kesira's voice trailed off. Molimo had stopped waving his tunic, but the clouds no longer encroached upon them. They stood as if enclosed in an invisible, protective bubble.

Louder, ever louder, came the baby's cries. Face screwed

up tightly, fists clenched, the baby turned red with the effort of crying.

The bubble around them expanded.

"It . . . the crying is driving away the clouds!" Kesira struggled up from her knees. The baby's voice strengthened. "To the top. Hurry. We can reach the palace. Hurry, oh, please, hurry!"

Zolkan no longer weighed her down. Molimo aided her. And the baby cried. Never before had a child cried so loudly, so powerfully, with such stunning effect. The jade demon's deadly crystal-edged clouds parted and made way before such might.

Chapter Seventeen

"THE JADE PALACE," Kesira whispered in awe. She clutched the baby to her breast as if he would sprout wings and fly away but fixed her full attention on the slender towers at either end of an immensely tall, intricately carved jade wall. Those towers, also of white-veined jade, moved in subtle, eye-confusing ways that disturbed her. From the corner of her eye Kesira saw movement. The tower to her left. Spinning to face it, she saw only the solid, dully phosphorescent green, but she had the impression of sinuous twisting. As soon as she faced it and confirmed its solidity, more motion attracted her. The tower to the right.

No matter how she turned, the tower on the other side of the palace moved.

"The jade is alive," she said, louder. Zolkan flapped from Molimo's shoulder to hers. She gripped her wooden staff more tightly. As her fingers pressed to the wood she felt tiny buds sprouting. How she envied them their mindless life. If only she could keep from thinking, from knowing her fate! Inside those walls Ayondela awaited her. But as she had foreseen in her rune casting, she felt no fear for herself. For Molimo and Zolkan and the baby Kesira fretted, but not for herself. The power had come to her.

But the woman had no inkling as to its source. All Kesira knew for certain was that the power opposed that of the jade and that it would have been given Gelya's blessing, had her patron lived.

"Clouds try to cut us," the *trilla* bird protested. "We must escape soon."

"The baby's crying holds Ayondela's foggy messengers at bay," said Kesira, more interested now in getting inside the palace. She walked to the wall and examined the carving. Untold workmen had spent lifetimes on these decorations—perhaps even lifetimes cut short by Ayondela's wrath.

"Palace built on bones of workers," said Zolkan. The bird clucked nervously. "Too near jade. We must hurry."

"For once I agree with you." Kesira started walking along the wall, eyes seeking the slightest crack that might indicate an entrance. As she approached the tower at the corner her steps slowed. She cast her gaze upward. From the slit windows cut high in the jade tower gushed forth more of the deadly clouds. The stars twinkling in the darkening sky played hide-and-seek through those crystalline billows, beguiling her, holding her captive to her own imagination.

Kesira saw creatures both mighty and pathetic trapped with the clouds. Some were punished with hideous cuts while others romped with wild abandon, feeding off the souls of those dying from the magicks. Ayondela's clouds soared into the vault of the sky and carpeted the heavens with death. And always, no matter how the winds dissipated those clouds, the slits in the tower pumped out more of the killing vapors.

Kesira jumped when Molimo placed a bleeding hand on her shoulder. He pointed to the clouds gusting forth and shook his head.

"I didn't think we could get in those windows," she assured him. "But what a favor we would do the world—and ourselves—if we could plug the vents."

Again Molimo startled her. He reached out and used a bloody forefinger to write on the jade wall. Wherever his blood touched, the jade came alive, burning with an intensity almost too great for human sight. Kesira slowly read the blazing words.

"I agree," she said. "Ayondela must know we have
reached the top of her mountain. Why does she always
seek mountaintops for her place of power?" Kesira glanced
back through the bubble of cloud around them. Just beyond, she knew, the edge of the granite spire looked down
on a five-thousand-foot precipice.

"Demons prefer privacy," squawked Zolkan. "For
Ayondela this is perfect. She can work her evil and see
all."

Clouds of shining crystal continued to spew forth from
the tower. Kesira shivered at the thought of the death and
suffering those slashing puffs of mist might cause. Uneasily she looked around and saw that those very clouds
edged closer. The baby's angry cries had quieted to more
contented mewlings now—and the clouds crept up on
Kesira and the others.

Molimo wiped away more blood from his forehead and
etched more flaring letters into the jade. "Only demons
can enter this palace," he wrote.

Kesira sensed undercurrents boiling within her. She was
no demon, or even half-breed, such as Rouvin had been.
But entry posed no problem for her. She had seen the
runes. She confronted Ayondela. Inside the walls of jade.

"How would a demon enter?" she asked. Kesira stiffened as she saw Molimo write out the instructions. Whether
the words burned in eye or brain, she didn't know. The
swiftness of his answer reinforced what she had come to
suspect.

"Very well," the nun said. "We shall attempt an entry
through the use of some minor magic." Molimo had indicated that this small token separated the curious—and
mortal—from those of more exalted—and demonic—
birth.

Kesira faced the carved wall and tapped her staff against
the solid jade. Dizziness assailed her. She felt Molimo's
supporting arm, but she brushed it away. A curious de-
tachment filled her like water fills a jug. Magicks previously untapped welled up and spilled over. All that Cayabbib

had imparted now aided her. Wemilat's kiss burned hot on her breast. The skills used to read the rune sticks came into play, and the nun began reading the hitherto random carvings on the wall. Just like the runes, they spelled out messages to her. Patterns shifted; she altered them, read them, exulted in them.

"Only demons may pass?" she asked quietly. Kesira's laugh echoed forth. The solid jade dissolved into mist. She stepped forward *through* the wall, just as Wemilat had traveled through solid rock. A coldness brought out goose-flesh. Kesira took another step and passed into the great hallway leading to Ayondela's throne room.

Beside her stood Molimo. On her shoulder Zolkan quivered in fear, the physical proof of the *trilla* bird's fright running warm and liquid down her back. And cradled in her left arm quietly rode the baby, eyes wide and cries stilled.

"My staff may not be of Gelya's sacred stone-wood, but it appears potent enough when I use it." Tiny limbs again sprouted from the shaved wood rod, leaves a living green countering that of the cold jade surrounding them.

Molimo wiped away more blood from his eyes. On impulse Kesira reached out. The fire of magicks burning within her had not yet died down. Sparks arced from her fingertips to the man's open cuts. He winced as fat blue discharges played along his wounds, but as Kesira's hand passed, the effects of the crystal clouds vanished. He was healed.

Kesira stepped back, as surprised at this as Molimo. She started to speak, to tell him of all the things burning inside her. Molimo motioned her to silence, pointing down the long corridor to the doors opening onto Ayondela's audience chamber.

"You're right," she said softly. "Later. After we speak with Ayondela."

"Speak?" protested Zolkan, his heavy body shaking as if he had the ague. "She will not *speak!* Ayondela will *destroy!* Can you match her power?"

"I no longer fear her." Kesira had read the runes; it had been difficult to believe that facing Ayondela would not instill great fear in her, but Kesira now experienced powers beyond her comprehension. She had lain with demons and absorbed their powers. And had there been more, a dormant seed within her, that only now came into full blossom? Kesira drifted along on winds too strong for any mortal to fight. Where that gale was taking her, she didn't know.

Staff thumping soundly with every other step, Kesira walked boldly toward the lofty arch and the jade doors. Beyond them awaited Ayondela.

"Foolish," muttered Zolkan. "We cannot go on."

"The runes told me I had nothing to fear."

"Runes?" shrieked Zolkan. He batted his wings against her face and head. "Lies! You have no power to see the future. All that was sent by Merrisen."

"What?" Kesira swung about and poked at the bird with the tip of her still-blossoming staff. "Merrisen is dead. I saw the battle with Lenc. Merrisen died."

Molimo grabbed for Zolkan, missed, sent the bird awing. Zolkan squawked in fright and continued up, wings straining.

Kesira rapped her staff against Molimo's shoulder. "Explain his words. Does Merrisen live?"

Molimo solemnly nodded.

"Why doesn't he aid us directly? Is he afraid?" Kesira lost some of the bravado she'd felt. "Does he use us as a cat's-paw while he performs other deeds? Or is he sacrificing us to weaken the jade demons?" Fear gripped her heart tightly, keeping it from beating. Kesira's mouth turned to cotton, and she found it impossible to swallow.

Molimo's stricken look did nothing to restore her confidence. He grabbed her by the upper arms and pulled her close. The light brush of his lips against hers sent an electric thrill throughout her body. She jerked back, the baby stirring restlessly. Tiny fists gripped her blouse and demanded her full attention.

Molimo glared angrily at the baby.

"It's too late, Molimo," she said, her voice harsh and alien in her ears. "Before, yes. But not now. Not here." The words grated even more as she said, "I *do* love you." Tears ran down her cheeks. She resumed her steady progress toward the huge doors.

Outside the doors she had only the sense of vast rooms and sullen quiet. Passing under the arch and into Ayondela's chamber took away her breath. The room had no walls. Kesira looked out into infinity in all directions. She staggered slightly, vertigo seizing control of her senses. She quieted herself using techniques taught by Gelya. All that was of substance around her allowed Kesira to focus. Her staff. The baby. The sound of Molimo's harsh breathing. Distant flapping of Zolkan's wings. Faint, musty scents caused by the sealed room.

Sealed?

Hesitantly Kesira opened her eyes again. This time she mastered her giddiness. Each wall presented a different view. Directly in front of her, framing a jade throne that seemed to float in midair, she saw a vast plain, checkered with green and brown squares of farmland. Clouds jetted to and fro, touching lightly before soaring back into the azure sky. Everywhere those clouds touched they left deep, ragged furrows. Closer examination showed Kesira the misery locked within the beauty.

Peasants died in Ayondela's deadly clouds. The land itself was raped and ravaged by the slicing actions of those deceptively innocent puffs of moist white.

Kesira shuddered slightly, turning to the left. A city cloaked in night and streets lighted by occasional gas lamps lay like a perfect jewel. But the perfection contained no joy. Dark clouds gusted between buildings like a vaporous assassin seeking out victims. One tiny figure ran pell-mell along the street—only to be cut off.

No sound reached Kesira, but she knew that the small child died with shrieks of total agony on his lips.

The vista to the right proved even stranger but not less

appalling. Darkness as complete as any mineshaft turned the wall into a mystery. Gradually Kesira realized that she did indeed peer into the bowels of the planet along a cruelly driven tunnel. Cowering at the far end of the shaft like rats chevied by terriers was a small group of people, too indistinct for individual recognition.

They shared the fate seen on the other two walls. Crystal clouds glittering in their deadliness, billowed along the tunnel and brought a slashing, vicious end. Again no sound reached Kesira's ears, but she fancied that she could smell the fear, the death.

And above? Kesira Minette looked aloft to seek out Zolkan. There in the heavens arched not a roof or the sky but a view of the Emperor's palace in Limaden. Kesira recognized it from descriptions. What mortal dwelling could be so grand? Clouds lunged like a master swordsman, only to vanish in wetness before reaching the walls of the Imperial city. Fascinated, Kesira craned her neck to watch. Long minutes of the duel convinced her that Emperor Kwasian still resisted, that Ayondela had yet to force the ruler to abdicate.

Odd thoughts drifted through her mind. Was Captain Protaro safely within the zone of protection used by the Emperor, or did the guard Captain still seek out the baby? Why did she care?

Kesira jerked in surprise when Molimo pointed downward. Kesira had resisted the urge because of the new waves of vertigo it produced. No solid floor existed beneath her feet. She floated, just as Ayondela's throne seemed to be suspended in thin air. Miles below bobbed a fleet of ships flying garish banners decorated with animal totems.

"A barbarian invasion fleet?" She looked at Molimo, unable to come to any other conclusion. The man solemnly nodded.

"They take advantage of the unrest throughout Kwasian's realm," came a soft, pleasant voice. "They think to gain ascendancy, but, of course, that is absurd. *I* am victorious. *On every front!*"

"Ayondela!" Kesira hadn't seen the female demon enter the room, but amid the confusing jumble of pictures, such an entry could have been made easily.

"You enjoy the display? I am pleased with it. The . . . magicks are so easy for me now." The demon sat on her jade throne, icy blue scepter in hand. The long canines had become even more pronounced, turning her once considerable beauty into a travesty. Even as the demon spoke, those fangs grew in length and pulsed with a soft inner light; the teeth were of the purest jade.

Before Kesira could respond, Ayondela went on in her conversational tones, "Lenc had no difficulty convincing me of the power of the jade. Why hadn't any of us seen it before? It is so simple to embrace its power. You come to join me?" For the first time Ayondela focused her full attention on Kesira and Molimo.

She frowned, as if trying to remember the answer to a difficult question.

"I know you," she said. "You are not demons. *You* are not!" The scepter of blue ice pointed directly at Kesira. The woman staggered under the magicks pouring forth from that gelid wand.

"Ayondela, we come to plead with you. There is no need to bring such misery to the world. Lenc only uses you. He—" Kesira was slammed back by the force of a spell cast by the female demon.

Kesira watched in abject horror as Ayondela's aspect altered from one of tranquillity to total insanity.

"You murdered my only son. *You* killed Rouvin." The demon's entire body pulsed with a pale verdant light. She rose, arms crossed over her breast. Water ran down her arms from the melting scepter. Ayondela took no notice. She stepped forward, away from her throne—and grew.

Kesira tried to convince herself that the rune casting had been accurate, that she would meet and defeat Ayondela. She put all the magical power into her words that she could, hoping they might sway Ayondela. Kesira had to repeatedly thrust away the mind-numbing fear that

threatened to seize her. But the effort became increasingly
difficult. Ayondela had been crazed when they'd met before. Kesira saw nothing but burning, jade-fueled insanity
in those demon eyes now.

"Lenc lies to you," Kesira shouted. "You visit your
clouds on the land and create death and destruction—and
the people hate *you*, not Lenc. He uses you for his own
purposes!"

"Rouvin died. You killed my son!"

Whatever shred of sanity that had lingered in Ayondela
after her son's death had fled. Kesira knew better than to
explain the circumstances. True, Molimo had ripped out
Rouvin's throat with wolf fangs. But the jade gave birth
to Molimo's other-beast transformations. And Rouvin's
death had been necessary to free Wemilat. Only with this
kindly demon's aid had it been possible to combat another
jade demon, Howenthal.

"No amount of suffering among the mortals brings Rouvin back to me," Ayondela raged. "But the jade gives me
the power to make the suffering continue for all eternity."
Ayondela staggered slightly, righting herself.

"For all eternity?" shouted Kesira, taking a different
tack. "In human terms you were immortal—but not now.
Don't you feel the jade sucking away your vitality? Your
life is drawing to an end because of the jade. The more
you rely on its power, the sooner you will die."

"Lies!"

"Lenc is the liar. He knows that he will perish quickly
if he relies heavily on the jade to subjugate humankind.
That's why he lets you do it. He is duping you, Ayondela.
Reject him. Reject both Lenc and the jade. It's not too
late!"

But Kesira knew that it was. The green pulsations
bathing Ayondela's body told as much. The addiction
to power was great, but the insidious nature of the jade
had worked its way into every nerve, every artery, every
brain cell of Ayondela's being. Removal of its power
would reduce the female demon to a mere husk.

Kesira summoned her newfound energy, coaxed it, nurtured the sensations of power, and then loosed it.

Ayondela staggered, but Kesira couldn't tell whether from the potency of her magical thrust or simple infirmity brought about by the jade.

"You killed Rouvin," Ayondela said single-mindedly. "For that you will suffer. Oh, how you will suffer! No mortal has ever felt what you will endure. You will beg me for death."

"I beg you for life, yes," said Kesira, trying to reform her thoughts and devise a new method of attack. She had hoped her power had grown to such an extent that the thrust would have ended the conflict. Ayondela had shrugged it off. Now Kesira needed new ploys. But what? She realized with a sinking feeling in the pit of her belly that she knew so little about such warfare—or any warfare.

"Worm! Slut!"

"For the rest of the world. Take my life, do what you will to me, but let everyone else live. Stop your assaults on the farmlands, on the Emperor, on the people."

"On the barbarians sailing so diligently for the coasts of this continent?" Ayondela's lips curled into a sneer around the deforming tusks of glowing jade.

"Even them. The Emperor can deal with them. Return to the old ways, Ayondela. Think how it used to be." Kesira felt the imponderable weight of Ayondela's spells crushing her. She shifted the baby so that she could sling him on her back and leave her hands free. Kesira's knuckles turned white on her staff as she hoisted herself back to her feet. But even this simple movement took more effort than she had expected. Ayondela battered at her strength constantly, and Kesira had no effective way of fighting back.

"The old ways?" Ayondela's madness faded slightly. "The old ways," the female demon mused. "They were so nice. Separate from the annoying presence of mortals, dealing among ourselves, demon to demon with our concerns."

"Yes!"

Ayondela snapped from her reverie. "That has passed. A new order must be imposed. The other demons—other than Lenc—are fools! We have power. What good is power unless it is used?"

"The jade perverts your power," Kesira said. Where was Molimo? How she needed his support now!

"The jade *gives* the power," bellowed Ayondela.

An invisible hand pulled Kesira into the air and tossed her toward the far wall, the one showing the ravaged farmlands. She shrieked as she knew she would fall miles to her death. Kesira groaned as she smashed into invisible—and substantial—walls. She sank down, bleeding from nose and split lip.

"The jade gives me the power to see what effect I have on the land. Me! Ayondela!"

For an instant the image just beyond Kesira's nose shimmered and turned into the solid green of jade. As quickly as the flickering had come, it vanished and again showed the destroyed farms and ruined lives produced by Ayondela's clouds.

Kesira mustered what power she could. Dimly she heard the baby begin to whimper. The woman pushed aside such worries. She would die quickly unless she found the power to resist the jade demon. But try as she might, Kesira failed to find the proper combinations of power from Cayabbib and ability from Wemilat. The kiss Wemilat had placed on her breast burned with manic fury, making her sob with lancing pain every time her heart throbbed another frenzied beat.

"You resist?" asked Ayondela. "There is power within you—where does it come from?" Ayondela pointed her scepter at Kesira, and the woman lost all sense of time and space. She hung suspended in a world of her own, blackness wrapping her in numbness, her senses gone.

One by one Ayondela restored those senses. Pain shot through Kesira's body in ways hitherto unknown to the woman. She thought she had known suffering, but real pain visited itself on her now. Odors so hideous that she flinched away assailed her nose, and tastes combining bitterness and acid tang gagged her. Light burst with painful brilliance, flaring jade-green to remind her of her tormentor. And then sounds returned, choking cries from the infant, strangled gasps from Molimo, outraged squawks from Zolkan, and another sound, unrecognizable.

Finally Kesira knew that those awful noises were produced by her own throat, that Ayondela's tortures wrested the ultimate in protest from her.

Then Ayondela began the punishment for her son's death.

"The flesh that sprang from my loins is no more," she heard Ayondela say. "You robbed me of a millennium of pleasure from his company. He was more than half demon. Rouvin was special. He was my son!"

Kesira's back arched as needles of white-hot pain shot into her belly, seeking out the most sensitive of her nerve endings, over-stimulating until she wanted only the surcease of death. Ayondela did not grant it.

"My precious crystal clouds. See them? See how they love to caress your fine body?" Cackles totally lacking in mercy or sanity echoed in Kesira's ears. And then she felt the misty dampness washing over her body. The clouds had cut and slashed physically before. Ayondela added a psychic dimension to the torture. Not only did the cloud flay Kesira's skin, they also tore at her deepest-held beliefs.

She bled and hurt—and doubted.

The crystal clouds cut away at her most cherished desires, her belief in Gelya and herself, her position in society. She doubted herself and Zolkan and even Molimo.

Kesira Minette began to curl in upon herself. At first she only pulled her body into a fetal position. Then her mind contracted, struggling to fend off the feathery touches against her consciousness. She retreated to the darkness of catatonia even as a distant, buried part of that living spirit that made her *her* protested.

But no effort on her part held Ayondela at bay. Kesira began to die physically and emotionally.

"Molimo," went out her thought. "I *do* love you. And you, too, Zolkan. And my baby, my baby . . ."

The clouds dragged mistlike tendrils across the fringes of her mind, forcing her to collapse ever inward. A hard, bright spark burned as she made one last effort to fight. Then even this spark faltered and diminished until it was only an ember.

The runes had lied. She had not defeated Ayondela. And she had known soul-numbing fear.

The last thing Kesira Minette experienced was the crying of the baby. This only added to her defeat. She had failed not only her order and herself but even an innocent child.

Chapter Eighteen

SWADDLED IN HER own madness, Kesira Minette sank deeper and deeper into her own mind. She wandered lonely corridors, blind and lost, but strangely she experienced no fear. Fear had assaulted her, but now Kesira existed in a realm beyond mere terror.

Or had Gelya's teachings prepared her for this isolation? Never in her life had Kesira imagined such punishment. Seldom had she ever been alone. Her sisters in the order always had been there to help and cajole, to aid and amuse. And after Lenc's destruction Kesira had found solace in Molimo's company. And Zolkan! The *trilla* bird never failed to entertain her with his odd ways and insistence on hurrying, no matter how delicate or precise the matter.

Solitude was alien to her. Kesira found out exactly how frightening it could be to someone so dependent on others.

She curled up tighter, retreating further into herself. Ayondela's crystalline clouds had slashed and maimed, but their effect on Kesira's mind far transcended physical abuse. Kesira recoiled from the clouds in the only way she could.

Oh, how she had approached Ayondela with great faith in her own abilities! How she had erroneously assumed that the power gained from Cayabbib and Wemilat would be adequate. Kesira had misjudged Ayondela's insanity, fueled by the death of her son—and the jade.

The jade. Kesira wondered how she had ever believed it possible to confront the power of the jade and triumph.

Now she paid the price with total isolation from the world. All senses were stolen from her, and she was alone, *alone*, ALONE!

No sight, no taste or touch, no smell, no sound.

Except . . .

Some part of Kesira seized on the tiny sound filtering down the corridors of her mind to find her in the absolute blackness. It came as a cry, hardly more than a whisper. But it mounted in intensity. Kesira's hopes rose like a geyser surging toward the heavens. She was alone, but the sound had to be . . .

. . . the baby.

The infant's wailing cut through the barriers around her. Kesira dared to believe that escape from this inner prison was possible. She turned and followed the whimpers and choked cries—and met resistance.

Ayondela's clouds battered against the periphery of her mind, trying to force her back down into herself. Feathery touches, vicious slashes, drifting insanity all crashed against mind and body in a never-ending onslaught. Kesira used techniques learned over a lifetime to ignore, to accept, to continue on. She sought the baby and its dear cries. Once the child had repelled the clouds with his cries, Kesira had to believe that he could do it a second time. How, she didn't know or care. That it happened was enough.

Dim light. Touch. The feel of the wiggling child in her arms.

"I'm not alone," she whispered, almost crushing the child in her embrace. She blinked and saw the familiar room. All that had changed was the expression on the female demon's face. Before she had forced Kesira into lonely inner exile, madness had run rampant. Now fear touched the greenly complected face.

"Fear!" shouted Kesira. "Know what it is like, Ayondela. Renounce the jade. Do it and you need never fear again." Even as Kesira spoke she knew that the female demon was too deeply influenced by the magical green stone. Ayondela's tusks shimmered and burned with intense green light. The shadows cast on the planes and ridges of her face gave her a curiously mixed expression: fear and triumph.

It was as if Ayondela had realized what the jade did to her and yet still reveled in the power, unable to follow any other path.

"What is that *thing?*" the demon demanded, pointing her scepter at the baby. The air froze in a solid bar between scepter and child. Kesira interposed her body to prevent the icy thrust from reaching the infant. Such solicitude was unnecessary. The baby's sobs and whimpers shattered the column.

Tinkles of ice against jade filled the chamber as a small rain began. No matter how Ayondela cast her spell at the infant, his crying thwarted the effect.

"No!" Ayondela blasted to her feet. Green tusks working up and down as she tried spell after spell, Ayondela betrayed stark fear. Kesira took advantage of the she-demon's preoccupation to rise and approach. As the runes foretold, Kesira felt no panic, held no fear of a jade demon who had locked the world in winter, then slashed and cut it with her devastating clouds. Kesira squarely faced her adversary.

"Stop your attacks against those below," Kesira ordered. "We have come to help you, Ayondela, not to harm you. Your son's death was unfortunate, but the jade caused it. The *jade*. Forsake its corruption."

Ayondela sidestepped, moving away from throne and Kesira, then let out a shriek and bolted. Kesira grabbed for the demon, but the baby slowed her reactions. Ayondela escaped.

"Doors!" Zolkan warned from above. "Beware all doors. Traps. Ayondela has set traps everywhere!" Zolkan spiraled down and landed on Kesira's shoulder.

"Where have you been?" she asked. "I needed you, and you abandoned me."

"Saw it all," admitted the *trilla* bird. "Could do nothing. Such power! All turned against me. I . . . I defecated in fear! Like frightened pigeon, I shit everywhere!" Zolkan tucked his head under one wing, mortified at his craven behavior.

"Her power is immense, isn't it?" soothed Kesira. "But she fled when the baby cried. Just as her clouds were held back, so is Ayondela."

Zolkan peered out from under his wing, glaring at the baby. Even when the child saved him, Zolkan appeared to hold little affection for the child. Kesira hugged the baby closer to her breast where Wemilat's kiss pulsed and warmed her.

"Where's Molimo?" She looked around the chamber, head spinning in confusion at the scenes flashing by. She still felt disorientation every time she glanced at the floor— or where she knew the solid floor to be. Only emptiness stretched under her feet. Kesira forced the thought away. She would show no fear. The casting of the rune sticks had told her that she would show great courage facing Ayondela.

"There," said the bird. "There he is. Oh, wounds! Molimo is wounded!" Zolkan flew over to land beside Molimo. Kesira approached more cautiously. The man looked unharmed, but the green light burning in his half-opened eyes warned of the other-beast transformation. The nearness of so much jade pushed Molimo's control to the limit, but did it push him beyond that limit?

"Molimo," she said gently. "We are in grave danger. Ayondela has fled. But I know she will return as soon as she has regained her composure."

"Jade," said Zolkan, shuddering. "Jade gives her back determination. We must flee. Now!"

"If we go now, there'll never be another chance," said Kesira. She wobbled as blood rushed from her head. Feeling faint, she sat down beside Molimo. "What happened to you?" she asked Molimo. "I . . . I needed you, and you were gone."

The man drew an index finger across one of the new wounds that had appeared on his arm and dripped the blood seemingly onto the scene stretched out so far below. Every spot where a drop of his blood touched, burning jade appeared. Molimo quickly wrote, "I used the spell Toyaga gave. The jade weakens me. It is dangerous for me to be here. Dying. I am dying."

At that, Kesira had to laugh. "It's dangerous for anyone to be here," she pointed out. Anger flared on Molimo's face; she reached out to lightly touch his cheek. "I meant nothing by that."

"You can't know the danger," he wrote. Turning to get new space, he continued. "Ayondela can destroy me, in spite of my returning strength."

"Worse," cut in Zolkan, "she might identify him because of power."

"She knows Molimo?"

The *trilla* bird squawked. Molimo nodded.

"How?"

"Every second we stay in this palace adds to our danger. We must kill Ayondela if we can." Molimo's face turned paler. Kesira stroked over the wounds caused by the latest onslaught of the maiming clouds and eased some of the hurt. Beneath her fingertips she felt power surging, and, as she healed his cuts, so did a measure of his strength enter her, patching over the festering wounds left by her brief isolation.

Shivering, she pulled away. The healing was almost as bad as the loneliness.

"Ayondela's pretty pictures are fading," she said, looking around. From the burning droplets of Molimo's blood spread wave after wave of solid green: the floor returned to normal. When those ripples of solidity struck the corners, the scenes of farmland and Imperial capital and the night sky began to flicker.

The baby let out a tiny shriek that snapped off all the pictures and gave an unrelieved view of only shiny green walls. For the first time since entering the chamber Kesira got a good look at the way it truly was. Unlike the exterior walls to the palace, these walls carried no ornamental carvings. Only the delicate veining of jade broke the monotony of three-story-high walls and ceiling. The floor showed some small traces of scuff marks—and the place where Molimo had burned in his message. Those fiery letters still blazed with eye-searing intensity.

Ayondela's throne stood atop a foot-high pillar of jadeite, whiter and less intricately marbled than the walls. Of the female demon who had so recently occupied the throne Kesira saw no trace.

Zolkan pointed one bedraggled wing in the direction of an arched doorway. "There. She went there. Traps! Everywhere!" Zolkan didn't have to tell Kesira how frightened he was. She felt the continuing stream of semi-liquid warmth down her back. Her nose wrinkled at the idea of her blouse being further defiled, then pushed such thoughts away. Ayondela had fled; she must be found and stopped.

Kesira stood and stared at the archway Zolkan indicated. She saw not only with her eyes but also with senses other than sight. More important than the snippets of information she gleaned, Kesira's confidence built again. Doubt had assailed her when she had confronted Ayondela. Her pride and mistaken belief in her own abilities had led her to the brink of disaster. Now Kesira put the newfound powers into perspective. She might face a jade demon, but defeating one single-handedly was impossible.

For her it was impossible. Kesira looked down into the infant's pale eyes.

"You've kept from crying all this time, haven't you?" she asked softly. "You saved it for the moment when it mattered most. You saved me, you know?"

The baby gurgled contentedly, hands opening and closing on her blouse. Kesira lifted the infant and kissed him on the forehead. A smile wrinkled the corners of his lips and crinkled his nose and eyes.

"You've done well. Now we must continue the battle. Rest," she told the baby. To Molimo and Zolkan she said, "How do we track Ayondela? Any traps she's constructed would be the end of us if we sprang them."

Molimo swayed slightly as he walked. Kesira frowned, worrying over his endurance. All the way up the mountain—even through the deadly clouds on the road—Molimo had been a tower of strength. Entering the jade palace had taken more than a small toll on him; he looked as weak as when she'd first come upon him after the jade rains.

"We must hurry," said Zolkan. "He cannot take more. And if Ayondela discovers him . . ." The *trilla* bird's sentence trailed off. Kesira didn't ask him to finish it.

"If the doorway is booby-trapped, how do we find her? She might have gone to summon Lenc. The pair of them will be far more than we can cope with."

"Lenc has worries of his own," said Zolkan. "He would come only as last resort."

"Another door?" asked Kesira. "Do we have to directly follow Ayondela?"

Before Zolkan could answer, Molimo stumbled forward—through the arched entryway. From lips that had forgotten words came a shriek that froze Kesira as surely as any magical spell cast her direction by Ayondela. Molimo arched his back, head tossing from side to side, that hideous sound pouring from his lips. Flaring green bathed his body, causing his limbs to twitch spastically, turning him into a crazed marionette.

Kesira started forward to rescue him, but Zolkan prevented her by leaping from her shoulder and deftly spinning in midair, his wings pounding at her face. She was forced a step back to keep the bird from harming the infant she so lovingly cradled in her arms.

"What are you doing? We've got to save him. Look at him!"

Zolkan said nothing. The *trilla* bird whipped around and dropped downward slightly, claws fastening into Molimo's shoulders. Bloody spots sprouted on the man's tunic at every puncture spot—and tiny emerald fires blazed as the blood met and mixed with the magical curtain holding Molimo in thrall.

The bird's feathers began to smolder as he struggled amid the magicks to pull Molimo free. The bird finally twisted and flapped with his long wings, using both weight and flying power to jerk Molimo free. They fell into an unmoving heap on the floor.

For the span of a heartbeat Kesira didn't move. She stared at them. Zolkan lay on his back, eyes open and sightless. Molimo lay facedown. She saw no sign of life in either.

Shock gone, Kesira hurried to Zolkan's side. The bird's breast rose and fell softly. She ignored him as she rolled Molimo supine. The green witch-fire that always accompanied his shape-change to wolf blazed in his glazed eyes. She stroked over his forehead, using what power she could summon to restore him.

"Live, Molimo. Live as a man. Reject the other-beast inside you. But live, damn you, live!" Tears dripped onto Molimo's chest; Kesira didn't bother to brush them away. More rolled down her cheeks and onto his body until she viewed the world through wavering vision, as if water rippled between her and Molimo.

Molimo's lips moved silently now, voice again lost. Kesira started to speak, to give thanks, but the baby reached up to silence her. Molimo nodded. He mouthed the words, "Play dead. Ayondela will return now. Lie beside me."

Kesira slipped to a prone position, her hand clutching Molimo's. The man gently squeezed back. Kesira had to rearrange her position several times until she found a comfortable one on the the hard floor, the baby nestled between her and Molimo. Again Kesira wondered at the man's reaction. He didn't quite flinch away from the baby, but he definitely showed aversion.

She had no more time to consider this odd behavior on Molimo's part. The echoing click-click of sandals against the jade floor filled the chamber. Through partially opened eyelids Kesira saw Ayondela return to the throne. The jade demon strode with assurance again, secure in the mistaken belief that her booby-trapped doorway had done its job.

Kesira worried as to the next step. Ayondela had returned. But how did they go about attacking her? Molimo
had been drained by the force of the magicks guarding the
doorway. Zolkan stirred restlessly, but the bird's abilities
had never amounted to that much.

Kesira Minette knew the full burden of doubt. No fear—
the rune casting held her away from fear—but how was
she to combat Ayondela's evil? Kesira felt sympathy for
the people's lives blighted by the crystalline clouds Ayondela visited upon them. She even sorrowed for the destruction wrought on the land. The elements of nature had
been disturbed; nature had never been unfaithful to humanity, but the power of the jade had changed that. Now
only perversion of nature existed in the world. For all that,
Kesira felt her anger rising.

Was anger enough? Kesira doubted it. Even relatively
rested, she had not possessed sufficient skill or power to
turn Ayondela from her wanton course.

All Kesira could do was try.

She mustered her strength, prepared herself as Gelya
himself would have, and waited for the precise instant.

Ayondela shifted on her throne, nervously switching
the ice-blue scepter back and forth in her hands. Kesira
thought that the demon peered too intently at her—or at
Molimo.

Ayondela rose to her feet but did not leave the throne's
small platform. "Who are you, you who endure my fiercest
magicks? You who are so familiar? You!" Ayondela thrust
out her scepter. Frosty spears launched themselves from
the rounded top to fly directly toward Molimo. The man
moaned loudly as the ice penetrated his body. He propped
himself up on one elbow, staring at Ayondela.

His eyes burned with a green deeper and purer than
Ayondela's own. Her tusks began to pulsate, and fear cast
a dark shadow over her once again.

"This cannot be," the female demon muttered. "You
did not die. But the magicks, the spells—you did not die!"

Ayondela's scepter began to melt under the energy she

funneled through it. Kesira dared wait no longer. She threw up what barriers she could against the spells. For a moment hope flared. Then Ayondela's superior power and skillful conjuring ripped apart Kesira's feeble efforts at defense.

To Kesira's surprise the demon did not attack her. She focused her assault entirely on Molimo. Before Kesira's eyes the man withered, diminished. Whatever the spell, it sucked away Molimo's vital forces like pulling juice from a succulent fruit. The green glow in the man's eyes dimmed. No longer able to support himself, even on one elbow, he collapsed back to the jade floor.

Kesira shouted, "Stop it! You can't hurt him. You can't!"

"He is weaker than I," gloated Ayondela. "There might never be another opportunity. I loved once but no longer. I will accomplish more than Lenc ever dreamed of!"

All around Ayondela's throne billowed her frightening clouds. The vaporous masses huddled together, hesitant at first, then with growing boldness. They floated at knee-level across the broad floor, leaving behind a shimmering on every bit of jade they touched. Kesira saw creatures writhing in the clouds, half seen, totally frightening. Did those beasts produce the savage cuts with bared talon or were they only products of Ayondela's demented mind sent to horrify her victims even more?

Kesira tried her feeble powers against the clouds and failed. They roiled with internal storm winds now. Then they crept away from Ayondela's throne, stalking Zolkan, Molimo, Kesira.

The *trilla* bird let out a muffled cry that stopped as soon as the clouds boiled over him on their way to Molimo. Again Kesira tried to halt that advance. Again she failed.

Clouds rustled wetly on her arms and cheek and neck. Blood sprouted in red rivulets. She struggled to her feet. The clouds encircled her, then rose. Of Molimo she had no sight. The man had been covered totally by the shining magical mists.

"These are a perversion of nature," Kesira called out.

"Is there anything you do which isn't against the normal flow of the universe?"

Ayondela laughed, dementia seizing her in its grip once again. Green tusks throbbed with inner light. Her scepter pointed, and the clouds obeyed.

Kesira steeled herself not to cry out in pain. Her resolve vanished the instant the clouds stroked up the insides of her thighs and blood ran in torrents down her legs. Her cry lifted and reverberated in the audience chamber.

And was drowned out by another.

The baby began to cry again.

Chapter Nineteen

KESIRA MINETTE HELD the baby close to her body, but insistent, small fists beat against her. She relented, and the baby cried even louder. His rich, oddly full voice rose to drown out Ayondela's chanted spells. The intensity mounted until Kesira was forced to put the baby on the floor and clap protective hands over her ears. And still the cry grew.

Ayondela stopped gesturing with her scepter and fell silent. Her spells died. The clouds trembled and began creeping away from baby and nun. The expression of fear that came over Ayondela heartened Kesira, but the woman found it difficult to explain. What was it that the female demon feared so? The way the baby's cries repelled the clouds? Or was there more to it?

"Stop it." Ayondela groaned.

She staggered back and sat heavily on her throne. Weak hands failed to lift her scepter. The ice wand fell from nerveless fingers and shattered to glistening shards on the floor. "The sound. Stop it, stop it!"

"Release the land from your spells," demanded Kesira. "Bring back your clouds. Stop the death and destruction."

"I can't stand it. I . . . I curse you!" Ayondela lifted one trembling hand of gleaming jade and pointed at Kesira. Once, this would have terrified Kesira. Not now. She saw how debilitated the demon had become. And still the baby cried.

"That accomplishes nothing," Kesira said. "Give up the

power given you by the jade. Only by returning to the old ways can you live happily."

"Rouvin," the demon whispered. Anger—insanity—returned to Ayondela's face.

The baby's cry reached a crescendo.

Ayondela exploded, scattering fragments of jade in all directions.

Kesira dropped over the baby to protect him from the shower. Off to one side Kesira heard Molimo whimpering as the new jade rain cascaded on him. Her heart went out to him, but to protect the infant she had to stay where she was. When the fragments of jade demon stopped falling, she straightened. Zolkan tended Molimo; Kesira took the baby in her arms and slowly walked to Ayondela's throne.

Huge cracks had appeared in the solid jade where Ayondela had touched it. Kesira stared in mute amazement at how completely the demon had been destroyed—by an infant's cry.

The baby tugged at her blouse. She looked down into his pale eyes and failed to read the emotions churning there. Elation? She doubted it. Fear? Not a trace. It was as if the child had done a workmanlike job and was content with the result.

"What are you?" she asked softly. The baby turned his head as he tugged once more. Kesira looked away to a spot just behind the throne. One of Ayondela's tusks lay on the floor, softly pulsing with green light. She bent and lightly ran her fingertips over the tusk. Power rushed into her body, renewing her, making her whole once again.

Kesira backed away from it, but the baby protested.

"You want me to take it?" she asked. The baby nodded, showing mature intelligence in his infant's body. Kesira gingerly reached out and touched the long tooth. Pleasure filled her, but she had grown. She had tasted the power of other demons and knew that, somehow, this remnant of the jade demon posed no threat to her.

If anything, it offered solace—and hope.

Gelya had given strict orders against carrying steel

weapons. Kesira hefted the tusk like a knife blade. It lacked much as a slashing weapon, but as a thrusting one, it carried good balance and a point both deadly and seemingly unbreakable. She tucked the jade tusk into the knotted blue cord and gold sash at her waist. The baby smiled at her and all was well.

"Zolkan," she called out. "Is Molimo all right?"

"More dead than alive," came the grim words. "Hurt. Jade hurt him badly."

Kesira rushed to Molimo's side. The man's face was drawn and the pallor frightened her. She helped Zolkan move the man; he had fallen uncomfortably over her staff. Kesira pushed the staff to one side and stroked Molimo's forehead, summoning what healing powers she could. The wounds caused by the crystal clouds vanished, but the grayness remained, making him appear as if someone had cut his throat and drained all the blood from his body.

Molimo's eyelids flickered, then opened. His lips moved, but Kesira made no sense of what he tried to say.

Zolkan dropped between them and beat her back with his wings. "Jade tooth!" the *trilla* bird protested. "It kills Molimo."

"What?" Kesira looked down to her waist where Ayondela's tusk still pulsated a soft green. She reached for the tusk to throw it away, but the baby's cry stopped her. Kesira found herself caught between Molimo's infirmity and the baby's insistence that she keep the artifact. Before she could sort it all out, a clap of thunder filled the jade chamber. The shock wave bowled her over. Kesira grabbed frantically for her staff, only to find herself rolling along the floor slick with blood. She slammed hard into one wall.

Groggy, she turned to see what had caused the thunder.

Kesira Minette had experienced no fear facing Ayondela. She quaked inside now that she faced Lenc. Around the remaining jade demon's feet burned small white flames, flames akin to one desecrating the altar of Gelya in her nunnery. Lenc, powerful and arrogant, stood with arms crossed, wearing an expression of complete disdain.

"*You* have caused Ayondela such . . . discomfort?" His mocking words were accompanied by a slow, dramatic sweep of a heavily muscled green arm.

Kesira fought to get to her feet. Using the staff helped, but fear robbed her of true steadiness.

"You turned her against the world. You used her."

"Of course I did." Lenc laughed at Kesira's surprise. "You thought I would deny it? Hardly." His booming laugh rivaled any thunder in the Yearn Mountains. "For every use of the jade power a few seconds is nibbled away from a demon's lifespan. The others—Eznofadil and Howenthal and poor, troubled Ayondela—all performed their tasks well while I stood by and supervised their efforts."

"You do not mourn their passing?"

"Mourn? I *sought* their deaths. No one dares oppose me now. I alone can rule supreme. No demon remains with a fraction of my power. And Ayondela has virtually completed subjugation of the mortal world with her delightful clouds."

"Emperor Kwasian still opposes you!"

"So? His power is limited. All his farmlands are destroyed. How does he feed those who are still loyal? They will drift away when I offer them food."

"In exchange for what?"

"Why, in exchange for worshiping me, of course!"

Lenc laughed boisterously. Kesira fingered Ayondela's tooth in her sash. The warmth of the jade might have perverted Ayondela, but in a mortal's hand it might return the world to its natural order. Kesira took a few steps forward, thinking to draw the tusk and use it as a dagger aimed directly at Lenc's heart.

Jade destroying jade. It seemed to satisfy the symmetries of the universe.

"Hold!" bellowed Lenc. White flame replaced the demon's fingers. The leaping tendrils of cold fire pointed directly at her. Ayondela's ice scepter had sent freezing

waves up and down her spine; now Lenc's fire burned her
every nerve ending.

"You are only a poor mortal. One of Gelya's pets.
Nothing more. You cannot hope to harm me, the supreme
ruler of this entire world!"

Kesira started to boast of the other three jade demons'
demise, then bit back her hot words. For all she knew,
Lenc had maneuvered her into the position of killing pawns
he found no longer useful.

"Ah, you see something of my schemes. Do you enjoy
the visitations I have made upon you through the rune
sticks?"

"You?" The revelation was almost more than Kesira
could bear. "You sent me all those visions?"

"All? I can hardly claim all. Some. The ones I found
most beneficial. It hardly mattered whether you showed
fear or not in front of Ayondela, but it amused me if you
destroyed her."

"I didn't," Kesira said before she could check herself.

"Oh?" Lenc looked around the room. Molimo lay like
a corpse on the floor, Zolkan nested down on his chest.
The baby quietly rested a foot away. Kesira ran to the
child.

"He destroyed Ayondela? My son is more powerful
than I had thought."

"*Your* son?" Kesira refused to believe it.

"It happened soon after the full power of the jade filled
my arteries. The sexual thrill couldn't be denied. I visited
dozens of peasants along the Pharna River. I think I recognize something of this one's mother in him."

"You can't take him!" Kesira swung her staff around
and planted her feet firmly for the fight.

"Take him? Why should I even *want* him? My bastards
will overpopulate the world. I can have any mortal I want—
and any demon!" Lenc leered and stroked along one cheek
with his flame-tipped forefinger. "I can even have you."

Kesira didn't respond. She would die defending the
baby and herself.

Lenc appeared to know her every thought. "Die you will, foolish mortal. But I waste precious time. I must consolidate all that my three late allies have so graciously created for me and left as their dutiful legacy to the one destined to reign."

"Lenc, stop!" shouted Kesira.

"Thank you for destroying them for me. You saved me some little annoyance." Lenc flashed out of existence, a second peal of thunder filling the jade chamber.

Kesira stood like a statue, the enormity of all that had happened seizing her mind and emotions. Deadened inside, the nun simply stared at the empty spot where Lenc had been. The jade had ignited, and tiny white flames licked at the floor.

"We must flee! Feel it! Feel it!"

Kesira shook free of her shock enough to ask Zolkan, "What are you talking about?"

"Palace crumbles. We die if we stay!"

Kesira looked up and saw huge cracks widening in the ceiling. Smaller fractures from the walls joined them. The sound of stone *tearing* filled her ears.

She scooped up the baby, noting that the child wasn't responsible for this added destruction. He looked up at her with a quiet confident smile that warmed her.

A huge chunk of jade smashed onto the floor not ten feet away. The fragments, more brutal than those from the Emperor's artillery shells, ripped at her flesh. She winced and stumbled over Molimo. Kesira righted herself and slung the baby in the harness around her shoulders so that both her hands would be free.

"Up, Molimo, up! I can't carry you!" She tugged at the man. His eyelids fluttered and opened, but the stricken look showed that all his physical strength had vanished. Somehow the jade had sapped him totally. Molimo lay closer to death than life.

She dragged him along for a few feet before realizing how futile this was. Pieces of Ayondela's audience chamber rained down all around them. When the throne exploded and sent shards arrowing outward, Kesira knew they were doomed.

Hugging the baby close, she said, "I'd hoped for more for you. I'm sorry it has to end this way." But the baby smiled and pointed a pudgy finger toward her staff.

Kesira frowned, then dodged another large cross beam falling from the roof. The baby showed no fright. Was he really Lenc's son? Kesira couldn't doubt that, but if so . . .

She had no further time for reflection on the baby's lineage or the father's motives. The immense jade walls started to shatter, to explode, to send jade bullets throughout the room. The small injuries she and Molimo sustained would soon become major ones as the destruction mounted. Instinctively Kesira fended off a flying hunk of sharp-edged jade with her staff. She missed by fractions but still deflected it when a willowy branch sprouted.

The baby cooed. Pale eyes locked with her brown ones, and Kesira *knew*.

She planted the staff firmly on the floor and turned her healing powers on it. At first nothing happened. She brushed away the blood and jade dust settling on her and concentrated. Wemilat. Cayabbib. Even the tusk taken from Ayondela. All contributed to her flow of energy from deep inside to her staff. Just as she had once caused tiny leaves to spring forth, now she urged the limber wooden staff back to life.

Branches sprouted. Leaves popped out. The staff thickened and became a true trunk. And the fledgling tree grew. Almost faster than she could comprehend, the limbs turned bigger and thrust out protective branches able to stop the jade from raining down on them.

"Molimo, help me. I can't carry you. We must get under the tree." He feebly kicked and slipped as she tugged on his arm. They eventually crouched near the now-massive brown trunk, Ayondela's palace crashing in ruin all around them.

The destruction accelerated, and the protection given by the towering tree increased in proportion. In less than five minutes the cold, crisp night sky showed through the tree's leaves. Kesira and Molimo ventured out to stare at the harsh pinpoints of stars.

A knee-high mound of jade dust was all that survived from Ayondela's once-massive palace.

"I can't believe the destruction was this complete," Kesira said in wonder.

"Lenc's doing. Lenc thought to kill us all," said Zolkan from the lowest branch of the tree.

"Perhaps so." Kesira saw the tree surge once again, roots spreading like dark brown snakes through the jade dust. The intense churning action showed that the tree assimilated the jade and forced it into the dirt. In a few minutes only a patina to the soil marked where Ayondela's jade castle had been.

"The tree is going to be permanent. I can hardly believe the way it's taken root," she said. "And I don't even know exactly what I did to trigger its growth."

Molimo motioned weakly toward the gravel road spiraling back down the granite mountain. Red splotches marked his cheekbones, but his color still looked unhealthy.

"The jade did this to you?" she asked. He nodded. She lightly touched the jade tusk. Molimo backed away from her. "I'll get rid of it." Kesira grasped the tooth and started to pull it free.

The baby cried. Kesira started to calm the infant but found herself paralyzed. As the child had disrupted the substance of Ayondela's body with his cries, so now did he force her to his will. Try as she might, Kesira couldn't remove the tooth from her sash.

"Down the mountain," she said in a choked voice. Molimo nodded and stumbled ahead of her, seeming to understand that the child forced her to keep the jade tusk. A soft shower of feathers and a loud flapping told her that Zolkan had taken wing.

Kesira started down the winding road, weary in both soul and body. Lenc had used her to eliminate his competition—the other jade demons. He now had only to consolidate his power and rule however long the jade permitted him to survive—which might be centuries. Those long years would mean abject slavery for all humankind, unless she found some way of fighting Lenc.

Kesira Minette looked over her shoulder at the sturdy tree reaching for the cloudless heavens. Somehow, in that symbol, she found hope. Lenc would be destroyed. How, she didn't know, but he would be.